# A Time
## to Speak

## Riley Scott

BELLA
BOOKS
2017

Bella Books, Inc.
P.O. Box 10543
Tallahassee, FL 32302

Printed in the United States of America on acid-free paper.

First Bella Books Edition 2017

Editor: Lauren Humphries-Brooks
Cover Designer: Micheala Lynn

ISBN: 978-1-59493-556-5

## Other Bella Books by Riley Scott

*Backstage Pass*
*Conservative Affairs*
*Small Town Secrets*

# Acknowledgements

For all of us, 2016 was a very difficult year, and that is putting it quite mildly. Many of the tragic events, the perpetuation of intolerance and hatred, and the impossible-to-swallow pills of 2016 inspired me to continue writing and to do so with more fervor than ever before. As a result, this story was born.

It could not have come to fruition, however, without the love and support of my friends, readers, and the incredible team at Bella Books, whose continual encouragement and inspiration reminded me to keep writing. I would like to express my gratitude to the entire team of authors and the staff, as well as to Erica Abbott whose words of wisdom continue to flow and whose advice has helped me grow as a writer. Thank you as well to Lauren Humphries-Brooks for editing and helping to make my story stronger.

Additionally I am grateful to my best friend and new fiancée, as she is the one who has to put up with me on a day-to-day basis and off whom I bounce story ideas. To my sweet Heather, thank you for listening to my ramblings and for helping me choose the good ideas. Thank you for lightening up even the most difficult days, for laughing with me often, for making dinner on the nights when I hole up in my 'writing cave,' for inspiring me to create (and endlessly encouraging me when I do), for bringing new adventures into my life, and especially for saying "yes" to doing life with me.

## About the Author

In addition to having published poetry and short stories, Riley Scott has worked as a grant and press writer and a marketing professional. She holds a degree in journalism. A chunk of life spent in the Bible Belt has given her a close-up look at the struggles facing the LGBT community in Small Town, America, and she strives to bring these to light through her writing. Riley's love for fiction began at a young age, and she has been penning stories for over a decade. Of the things she holds dear to her heart, the dearest is her fiancée (who, if you'll note, is listed ahead of green chile), green chile, coffee, humor, dogs, and lively literature. Living in Florida with the love of her life and three beloved dogs, she is well on her way to becoming the crazy dog lady.

## Dedication

For everyone struggling to find and use their voice, may you be empowered and emboldened to add love to the world and fight for good. And of course, for the one who reminds me of the beauty of the world even in times of darkness, my fiancée.

# CHAPTER ONE

AC/DC blared through her speakers as Chloe Stanton raced home after work. Her old Ford truck let out a bellow as she stomped on the gas, thankful no one was in sight. This was what she loved about Knell, Texas—it was quiet, peaceful and, in this neck of the woods, looked a bit like an undiscovered gem, with its wide open fields and houses set so far back from the main road that they weren't even visible on her drive.

Her windows rolled down, the sweet Texas air blowing in, she let the worries of the day fade into the passing distance. A day of hard physical labor sure paid off, even if it was exhausting.

She thought of how today had become so dangerous in a second, when the latest hire of her dad's ranch, Ryan Walden, had made the rookie mistake of spooking a large herd, causing them to run amok, through and over the fences. The angry words they had spat back and forth at each other filled her memory.

She had threatened to fire him on the spot, despite the fact that it was her father's operation. Anyone who couldn't take feedback and coaching didn't have a place on this ranch.

*"You can't fire me. I quit!"* He had shouted at her, throwing his hat in her direction. *"I'll make sure you and this entire operation pay for this shit!"*

She shook her head, rubbing her temples as she tried to let it all fade. They'd need a new ranch hand, but they'd deal with being shorthanded. It was stressful being in charge, but the day was done.

As she rounded the bend, headed toward her humble abode, she looked down at her dirt-streaked jeans and the tank top that was now torn after her day of jumping fences. She smiled, remembering her father's praises and the pat on the back he had given her for getting the job done. She turned up the music, singing along to "Back in Black" as she pulled into the driveway.

She smiled as she spotted the sleek, red sports car, carefully hidden to anyone not looking for it, along the side of the house covered by trees. She parked in her driveway and bounded up the steps, badly needing a shower but looking forward to greeting her guest even more.

"I see you finally used the key I gave you," she hollered as she threw open the door.

She heard a sweet laugh as Amelia peeked her head around the doorway to the kitchen. "I thought you could use a little dinner and maybe a little rub down after a long day of work," Amelia said, her Texas drawl smooth as honey.

"Ms. Brandt," Chloe said, her smile turning devious. "You are quite the surprise, aren't you?"

"I aim to please." Amelia shrugged and sauntered closer.

Chloe's heart raced as she took in the beautifully long and straight brown hair tumbling down over Amelia's shoulders, her beaming smile, and her bright eyes. With her tanned skin and tall frame, Amelia could have passed for a model—yet here she was in Knell, Texas, the daughter of a strictly Baptist family, regularly fucking the local lesbian.

"And please you do," Chloe said. "Please and mesmerize in equal measure."

"What do you say we do with our evening?" Amelia asked, finally closing the distance between them and planting a slow, tender kiss on Chloe's lips.

Despite her need to wash off the day, Chloe's skin tingled, her senses muddled with the sweet floral scent of Amelia's perfume—the scent she had come to associate with mind-blowing sex and, of course, confusion over where they stood.

She couldn't form words. Instead, she pulled Amelia in closer, deepening the kiss. "I'd say this is just what I need."

"Good," Amelia said and flashed Chloe the smirk that melted her heart. "After dinner, this is all I plan to do."

"It's not *all*, right?" Chloe asked, raising an eyebrow.

"Of course not." Amelia shimmied her shoulders. "I have other plans too, but we'll get to those later. I know you probably want a shower. By the time you're done, dinner will be ready. And so will I."

The wink she offered sent Chloe's imagination into a tailspin. Wherever this was headed, Chloe was onboard. No one she had ever met had the power to undo her so completely, in such an innocent and unassuming manner. Wordlessly, she nodded and went to take a shower, completely willing to follow any timeline Amelia set before her, as long as it meant she had the chance to kiss those sweet lips again later.

As the water cascaded over her body, her mind ran wild. She had tried to fight it, to stave off her curious heart. But four months into their little arrangement, she was failing, and more every day. She was falling in love, despite her best intentions. Outside the shower, she buried her head in her hands. There was no way this could work out. She had been stupid to let it get this far.

She took a hard look in the mirror. She was a Stanton. Stantons didn't back down from challenges. Amelia might actually be the death of her—or she might just be the challenge most worth taking. Chloe let out a laugh, still staring at her reflection. She was going to do this, just like she did everything in life—full throttle.

An opportunity had presented itself. One of her childhood best friends, Katy, had relocated to Austin years earlier. She was Chloe's favorite party buddy, and Chloe was going down to visit her again next month. Always one to be supportive no matter who Chloe wanted to date, hook up with, or bring home from a bar, Katy had told Chloe to invite whomever she wanted on the trip. Chloe wanted to invite Amelia. As the thought cemented in her mind, she let out a shudder. Shaking her head, she glanced down at her trembling hands. She gripped the bathroom counter and let out a deep breath. *Full throttle or nothing*, she reminded herself. She gritted her teeth and nodded to herself in the mirror as confidence filled her veins. Straightening her shoulders, she smiled. She could—and *would*—do this.

Dressing quickly, no longer worrying about what the outcome might be, she bounded down the hallway, taking in the scents of the evening. Amelia's perfume mingled in the air, meeting the mouthwatering scent of home cooked barbecue. Smells she loved. Smells she wanted to get used to.

She rounded the corner of the dining room and paused, marveling at the sight in front of her. "Thank you, baby," she said. She threw her arms around Amelia, who blushed in return.

"You like it?"

"Of course I do." She kissed Amelia gently. "I love all the things you do." She noted that Amelia stiffened slightly at the use of the word "love," even when used benignly. But she didn't let that stop her. "In fact, while I was showering, I did some thinking about how much you spoil me and how much I appreciate you."

"Yeah?" Amelia asked. In place of the sweet blush that had adorned her face seconds before was a slightly guarded smile.

"Yeah, but we'll talk about it during dinner. I'm starving."

Amelia nodded too quickly, causing Chloe to bite her lip to keep from sighing. At even the slightest mention of feelings, Amelia turned into a deer in the headlights, ready to run at the drop of a hat.

A situation this delicate required a gentle touch, something Chloe hadn't quite perfected. But Amelia was worth the effort it would take to perfect it. She smiled sweetly and pulled out a chair for Amelia, gesturing for her to take a seat. "Let me take care of you a little and do the very least of serving you."

Amelia's face softened into a genuine smile. "Thank you." She took her seat, and Chloe tried to ignore the way her hands were shaking as she dished out two servings of the barbecued brisket. It wasn't like she was offering a marriage proposal. There was no reason to be so nervous—no reason, aside from the fact that she was changing the rules mid-game. That was almost always frowned upon, but how could Amelia expect her to spend every night lost in this blur of passion and comfort and not feel anything?

"What's up?" Amelia asked, giving her the side-eye.

"Nothing," Chloe said, waving her hand through the air. "It was just a bit of a rough day. It was one of those that kind of sticks with you even after you've left the job. But tell me about your day. How was it?"

"Quiet and slow, just like most summer days," Amelia said with a shrug. "While you all are out there working with yearlings and the farmers are harvesting their fields, my little shop is pretty much forgotten. It's our slow time, while it's your busy time. We thrive in the early mornings and winters like, you know, when you and all your hard working buddies come in for a cup of coffee to warm up."

"You do make my winters a little warmer with that coffee you whip up," Chloe said, winking. "But slow days can be good."

"They can." Amelia looked away from the table.

It was painful small talk. They both knew how each other's days had likely been. Amelia, the owner of a small coffee shop in town, dealt with the summertime gossip of old women and kids running in and out of her shop, while Chloe had the busiest time of the year. It wasn't something that should serve as their dinnertime conversation.

Unsure of what, if anything, to say, Chloe stuffed a forkful of brisket into her mouth. The tenderness of the meat and its shock of flavors—spicy and sweet—tingled her senses, bringing her back into the moment. "This is really amazing," she said and wiped her mouth as she swallowed.

"Is that one of the things you appreciate about me?" Amelia asked, no doubt bringing the conversation full circle.

Chloe nodded, her hands shaking again, this time forcefully enough to fling the brisket from her fork onto the floor. "Shit!" she exclaimed and reached for a napkin.

"Just leave it for a second," Amelia urged. "Talk to me. Clearly there's something going on up there, and if it's uncomfortable, I'd rather you just spill it and get it out in the open so we can deal with it."

Wiping her hands on her jeans, Chloe nodded and took a deep breath. "I just wanted to talk to you about all the things I appreciate about you and let you know that you matter to me."

Amelia's eyes narrowed and she sat straighter in her chair. She gave a curt nod, encouraging Chloe to proceed with caution.

"I know what this is," Chloe continued. "You made that clear, and we have an agreement. You visit when you can. We don't go out in public. And this is never to be spoken of in front of anyone. That said, I'm not asking to change that *too* much."

"You're not going to change that at all," Amelia said, putting her hand up in the air.

"Hear me out please," she said quietly but firmly and placed her palms on the table for support. "I'm just saying that I'd like to do things with you. I'd like to go out dancing, have a drink, and just embrace some of the normal, but fun, day-to-day things we could do together."

"You know what they would call me." Amelia recoiled as if she had been slapped.

"Of course I do," Chloe said, a sad smile playing on her lips. She pursed her lips and let out the breath she had been holding. "They'd call you the same things they've been calling me for the last decade—ever since I let it slip that I liked girls when I was fifteen. They'd call you the names and they might even make you the odd man out in certain circles. There'd be some sideways looks as you walked down the street, and people in the barbershop would talk about you behind your back. You wouldn't be their golden girl, their little princess waiting on her prince. You'd be someone different, but at the end of the day, they'd embrace you like they've done with me. Sure, there are still plenty of whispers and the occasional insult or name. But around here, you make your own name for yourself. You're strong enough to do that, just like I've been strong enough to do that."

"That's not the life I want for myself. Aside from all that, you said you wanted normal. Normal isn't an option for someone who lives the way you do. What you do isn't normal."

Chloe jerked her head back. The words stung. "Well, isn't what I do the same thing you've been doing the last several months?"

"Yeah, and maybe that's why I need to get out of here. You see, for me, it's something I'm doing. For you, it's who you are. And I refuse to be that. I'm not going to be like you, alone and lost and looking for my next lay."

"What are you going to do then? Marry the next guy who comes your way and live a lie? You and I both know what you like, what makes you come alive. We both know who you are. And you're twenty-four. It's about damn time you start accepting that you're not going to be just like the rest of them. It's about time you realize the difference in being a gem among the common stones. It's time to take a stand. Stand out and be fucking proud of who you are."

"No." Amelia's icy glare told Chloe she was pushing too hard. "There's no way I'm going to stand on some street corner and picket. I'm not going to attend a rainbow Pride parade, and I'm sure as hell not going to hold your hand in public to make a point."

"Wow," Chloe said, leaning back in her chair as if she had been struck. "It's amazing that holding my hand was the most damning of all the things you listed."

"I'm not going to be your little gay protégé."

"Stop." Chloe held up her hands. "That wasn't even the point of all of this. I wasn't trying to go down that path. That's just where we ended up. Can I start over?"

Amelia crossed her arms across her chest, looking every bit like a petulant child being forced to listen a lecture. "Go ahead," she said after a moment, tapping her foot as though her time was being wasted.

"I was going to see if you'd like to come with me to Austin next month," she said, her tone every bit as defeated as she felt. "I'm going to see a friend of mine for the weekend, and she said I could invite a friend. You remember Katy Denton?"

"A friend? Will she know me as a *friend*, or have you told Katy about us?"

"I've kept your deal," Chloe said, rolling her eyes. "I wouldn't out you like that. Also there is no label other than *friend*, so I don't think you have to worry. And Katy doesn't care. She got the hell out of Knell and hasn't been back to visit since. She, unlike some people, accepts me for who I am and doesn't give a damn who I sleep with. She's my best friend in the world, and I suppose she can know whatever you'd like her to, since you clearly make all of the rules around here. I just thought it might give us a chance to have a little bit of time to ourselves, explore something other than the walls of my house, dance together, grab a drink in a bar, something, something more than this. I'm not asking you to parade around *here* and be out and proud. I'm asking you to take a trip with me to start out with and see if you feel comfortable with it. From there, we can assess whether or not you're comfortable going to the diner and grabbing a burger with me. You don't have to sort out whether you're comfortable with the whispers and talking in this town just yet. As far as that goes, we don't even have to do anything crazy there, just as long as we're doing something together, something more than hiding out in my house."

"You'll never get more than this from me. I'm not you. I'm not the poster child for making a town accept who I am. I don't need to engage in the 'fight for equality,' as you've called it. I don't care if they don't like who I am, because there's no reason for them to know. I can live my life quietly and peacefully without their judgmental stares."

"You just can't handle any criticism, can you?" Chloe asked, her frustration mounting with every hate-filled word slipping out of the lips she had wanted to kiss only moments before.

"I don't know what the hell that's supposed to mean." Amelia stood. The movement was not lost on Chloe. She needed to have the upper hand, to look down upon Chloe. Her hands trembled as she spoke, but her eyes never wavered with their piercing stare.

"It means that you've been everyone's little princess for so long that you don't know how to be the down and out one,"

Chloe said. "It means that everything has been handed to you— from your daddy's money to your name to your reputation. I know you've worked hard for your shop and you've made sure to keep it going no matter what. But I also know that you can't handle it when there's any sign of confrontation. I'm tired of seeing you brush things aside like they're someone else's problems. They're your problems, too. You're gay. Whether you ever want to admit that to anyone but me is your choice. But at some point you have to stop running scared or you'll waste your life away."

"I'm wasting my life away here with you," Amelia shot back. "I've wasted the past few months, and I'm not going to do this. I'm not going to make anything public. I'm not going to jeopardize what I have. How dare you assume that the life I've built is all because of who my family is? I'm not doing this anymore. I'm done here. Enjoy your *different* life, and your fucking supper."

Amelia stormed out the front door and slammed it behind her. Chloe sat in a stupor. She blinked and looked around the room in disbelief. Shaking her head, she brought her fingers up to massage her temples. She had just wanted to invite Amelia to go to Austin. She hadn't wanted this, and even though she knew it was going to be short-lived, she hadn't been ready for goodbye just yet. She stared at the apron Amelia had left hanging on one of the chairs and thought about chasing her down to make sure she had it. Instead, she figured she'd leave it with the slew of things others left behind when they decided they couldn't do this anymore, when they decided they wanted to be "normal."

The piece of brisket she had flung still lay on the tile, but Chloe didn't care enough to clean it up just yet. Her breathing was shallow as she let the weight of it all come crashing down on her. Standing, still in a stupor, she picked up her tea glass and carried it to the kitchen. As she reached to set it on the counter, it slipped from her hands. Helpless, she watched it fall and shatter.

She thought of how crime stories always said whether or not there appeared to be a struggle. Today her house screamed of a struggle, and it wasn't wrong. There had certainly been a struggle—and it was ongoing. A struggle between her head and her heart.

Chloe couldn't tell which was worse, the way her heart hurt, the blow to her pride, or the sheer anger she felt. Her hands shook as she looked around the kitchen. The broken glass symbolized all she felt inside.

It always ended this way. Small towns created small minds, and she just happened to continually fall in love with those scared, small minds.

She let out a scream, even though there was no one near enough to hear. Sliding down the wall, she collapsed into a defeated pile, giving way to the onslaught of emotions she felt.

She wanted to cry, to let it all out. She had seen the movies and read the books. It seems like that was the way breakups were supposed to go. To her dismay as she scrunched up her face, only a single tear slid down her cheek. Slapping the tile underneath her, she gritted her teeth and steeled her emotions. Pissed off was an emotion she could deal with, but this was too much. Even if she could have mustered up the tears she had been taught to hide, there was no need to cry over someone who couldn't even speak up for her—who wouldn't even give a damn if she disappeared and skipped town.

Sighing, she kicked the floor, letting the rest of her outburst subside. She rose, reminding herself that she would bounce back from this stronger than before. She always did. Crazy women in this town had made sure she knew how to bounce back. Regardless of the current situation, it was time for a beer.

She grabbed her keys and made a beeline for the door. Cranking her music loud enough that she wouldn't have to hear the noise of her own thoughts, she barreled down the road, determined to make this a better night.

# CHAPTER TWO

Pulling into McCool's, Chloe parked her truck and briefly checked her reflection before getting out. She wasn't here to impress. She was only here to grab a cold beer and listen to Louie the bartender's outrageous stories in hopes of finding reasons to smile.

Neon lights littered the walls. She breathed in the scents of beer and liquor, mingled with too much perfume and cologne, a little straw, and a few patrons who probably hadn't showered off the day's work. The scent welcomed her, as did Louie's wave from the bar. She walked up to her regular barstool.

"How are you doing today, sweetheart?" Louie asked, his belly bouncing as he laughed and gave her his half-toothless grin. The sheen on his cheeks and forehead told her what she already knew. The bar's AC was subpar for the sizeable crowd that had gathered.

"Eh, next question," she said with a shrug.

"All right, then," he said. "What do you want?"

"Surprise me," she said, feeling more at home and at peace in the warmth of his smile. "As long as it's cold."

"A cold one comin' right up," he said and poured beer from the tap.

She smiled and thanked him, grateful that he had other customers to wait on. She wasn't sure she was up for a full conversation tonight, at least not with someone who knew her as well as he did and could read behind the bullshit to know something was wrong.

"Isn't this a shocker?" The voice came from right behind her, so she turned slightly in her chair. "A dyke in a flannel shirt drinking a beer."

"To what do I owe the pleasure of *your* company?" Chloe shot back, turning to face Trent Westwick.

He smiled at her, but it looked more like a predator assessing its prey. His perfectly groomed and styled blond hair spilled across his wide forehead. His square jaw was set as he raised an eyebrow at her. She glanced up at those, set right over his cool blue eyes, and noted they too were groomed and too well kept for most around this town.

"You just happened to be over here being a town disgrace, and rumor has it, it's up to my family to clean up around here," he continued.

"Tell that to your pastel polo shirt," she said, shaking her head.

"How about you ditch your lezzy ways for just one night, and I'll show you what it's really like to enjoy a good time?"

"I'm afraid I'll have to pass." She tightened the grip on her beer.

"You don't know what you're missing out on," he said, leaning in close enough for her to smell the sharp sting of whiskey on his breath. "You just haven't had the right dick yet," he hissed. "And *mine* is the cure-all drug for your disgusting disease."

"Nothing quite as disgusting as that offer or that insinuation that I have an ailment," she said, slamming her beer down on the counter and swinging around in her chair. "I'll have you know that your small-minded douchebaggery won't change a damn thing about who I am."

"I've seen it before," he challenged, staggering as he got in her face.

"Yeah, I know," she said and shrugged. There was always a back-story with this level of exaggerated homophobia. "We all know why you hate the gays so damn much. We've all heard about your mama and how 'wrecked' you were as a kid," she added, using air quotes. "But leave me be. I've had a rough enough day, and I don't need you around ruining it."

He backed up slightly, his eyes narrowing as he took in the weight of her words. "That bitch has nothing to do with this. This is all about you and the fact that you're a fuckin' joke." He slurred over his drawl, his face reddening with every word. "Aside from all that, you're alone, aren't you? Maybe if you wanted to do something the right way, you'd have found a decent man by now."

She cocked her head to the side, letting out a short laugh. Everyone thought she had "friends" in the neighboring towns—or that she went and visited them in Austin on one of her many trips. They weren't wrong. But they all failed to realize she had been with her share right here in the village limits. Even with a limited population like 12,000, there had been plenty of women who wanted to give in to their curiosities.

For a moment, she thought about regaling him with the fact that she had been with sisters, friends, daughters—and even one wife, although she wasn't proud of the fact—of many patrons in the bar tonight. Whether they wanted an experiment or they were taking their one chance at living the life they longed for with the security that she would protect their secrets, they flocked to her. They were her companions, lovers, friends, and sometimes more. Rarely more. But they all still mattered to her. She wouldn't expose them. She never had and she wouldn't start now—especially to a snake like Westwick.

"It's a damn shame and a waste of a perfectly fuckable woman," Trent spat the words at her.

"That's enough," Louie said, reaching across to take the glass of whiskey out of Trent's hand. "Knock it off, kid."

"You want a health code violation up in here?" Trent asked, reaching for his whiskey and slipping, only to catch himself on the stool adjacent Chloe's. "I can make that happen."

"I know you can." Louie shrugged. "But your threats are empty here. I don't care, and neither does anyone else who wants to get a drink in this place. Hell, you wouldn't want it closed down either, or you'd have to drive twenty minutes to get this stumbling drunk somewhere else. Leave Chloe alone. She's one of us."

"Fuck you." Trent narrowed his eyes at Louie. "And fuck this place." He reached beside Chloe, grabbing the two open beer bottles left by a couple on the dance floor, took a swig out of one of them, and staggered back to the booth where his buddies waited.

Louie sighed and shook his head, replacing the beers with fresh ones. "I'll kick 'em out myself if I have to. You really are one of us." He leaned in closer, reaching across to grab her hand. "I mean that."

The words warmed Chloe's heart. No matter how rough and tumble she might be, how jagged around the edges, it still did her heart good to know she had allies in this place. "Thanks, Louie."

"Least I could do," he said. "Now that he's cut off, I'm sure he won't stick around. But you, your beers are on the house tonight. Even if he is the mayor's kid, no one should have to deal with that kind of behavior."

She nodded and let out another deep breath. "They sure do know how to grow 'em spoiled and entitled around here."

"That they do, but you and me, we'll always be the humble ones. We know what it is to have and to have not."

She nodded and raised her glass in a mock cheers to her favorite bartender and one of her closest friends. Over the years, coming to see Louie had been more than grabbing a beer. It had also been about camaraderie with one who understood her way of life. Being children of modest cattle ranchers had meant that they had to fight tooth and nail for everything they had in their lives—unlike some people. Trent Westwick, for instance.

Watching out of the corner of her eye, she saw Trent back at his table of equally preppy friends. They stuck out like a sore thumb in this part of the world. In a place where everyone's best was something that hadn't gotten dirt on it for the day, they made every point to show off the brand names and slick logos that they had bought from a store in a bigger city—or when they were off studying at a fancy university, something people like her and Louie knew nothing about.

The class system was definitely still alive and well in Knell, Texas. She took a swig of her beer, wishing it would do something to help any of the problems she felt.

She saw as Trent pointed back to the bar. Using his hands, he spoke exaggeratedly, and she knew that whatever he was telling them, it was more than likely a stretched truth. He pointed in her direction, glaring with icy daggers for eyes. She heard the words "fucking queer" but nothing else. Shaking her head, she redirected her attention to something more positive. And when they finally all walked out without paying their tabs, she took a deep breath.

"Sorry about the lost business," she said, giving Louie a sad grin.

"Oh it's all right, ma'am," he said, his smile growing. "I'm happy to be rid of the trash for one night, and don't worry. I'll get my money back. If they ever want a cold beer again, they're going to have to answer for that tab—and I'm thinking their next drinks will be double the cost, just to make sure they walk the line a little more."

She nodded and offered him a smile. "You're the best."

He winked at her and returned to wiping down the bar.

Growing up in this town, anyone different was an outcast. It had always been that way. Amelia's words echoed in her mind, and she wanted to scream. With hatred like that splashed about at someone just trying to grab a beer after a rough day, it was no wonder Amelia—and all of the girls before her—cowered in the closet, kept there by fear and shame.

"I think I'm going to call it a night, Lou," she said, letting out a sigh. What was supposed to have brought her normalcy and comfort had only served to ruin her night more. She waved at him, put enough cash to include a generous tip under her glass, and slipped back out into the night.

It was warm and humid, muggy even with the predicted rainstorm approaching, but she felt a chill as she walked. Somehow, the night was cold and unwelcoming. She shivered, wrapping her arms tight around her body and quickening her pace.

In the safety of her truck, she glanced at her reflection in the rearview mirror and forced herself to breathe normally. Running her hands through her hair, she noted the lines around her eyes. *Hard livin'*. She heard her dad's words play through her head. The worries she had accumulated, along with the stress of keeping the guys in line at work and the stress of keeping the secrets of every one of her lovers, had left her ragged.

Still, she admired what was left of her mother in her—the bright smile, the hazel eyes, the long eyelashes. She turned her mouth up into a smile and turned on the truck. It would do her no good to dwell on her problems or the crow's feet forming from too much stress and too much sun.

Shaking her head, she put the truck in gear. Her hands still trembled as she drove, but she turned up the music with renewed intensity.

Tomorrow would bring another day, complete with new challenges. It always did.

As she pulled into her driveway, she wanted to look around the corner for the red sports car, but averted her eyes. No good would come from not seeing it where she wanted it to be. Steeling herself, she got out of her truck and straightened her shoulders, proudly walking up to her house.

Even in a day filled with so much strife, she still had this.

She took just a moment to look at it. This was hers in all its glory. The beautiful home and land she had purchased from the fruits of her labor. She might not have someone willing to stand up and affirm their love for her, but at least she was a damn good worker who was making it in the world.

A nice bubble bath and one more beer would do the trick. Then she'd be good as new for tomorrow's events. She threw open the door and thought again that it might be time to get a dog so she had some steady companionship around here.

She moved to turn on the light, but stopped her hand midair. Something was off. Nothing looked out of place. But the lighting was dim in her living room. Her heart hammered as it had in the parking lot. Her pistol was in her bedroom. But this was Knell. There was nothing to fear.

She shut the door and flipped on the light. Turning around, she jumped as she heard footsteps to the left in the kitchen.

"Amelia," she called out, hope soaring with the possibility.

"Guess again," a deep voice called out. Her blood went cold. Shivers flew across her body. She raced toward her bedroom to grab her pistol.

# CHAPTER THREE

Her alarm wouldn't go off for another hour and it was still dark out, but she couldn't sleep. Amelia sighed and stretched her arms over her head.

She hadn't needed any additional help waking up today. After tossing and turning all night and having tortured dreams in the few moments of sleep in between, her eyes had been wide open for hours.

Every time she had tried to close them, she had seen Chloe's face. That sweet face with the eyes that burned with passion, whether it was passion to get a job done or passion to hold Amelia tight. She had reflected on the way Chloe's eyes darkened right before her impending orgasm and how they lightened in the tender moments of an embrace that always followed.

More than the visuals though, she had heard Chloe's words clinking around in her brain all night, rattling her head like an old-school pinball machine. Chloe had been right. Eventually, when she was able to swallow her pride, she might just let Chloe know. As it was, Amelia wasn't sure she could undo the damage that had been done—or if she even wanted to.

Amelia rubbed her temples, hoping to ease the headache caused by lack of sleep, as well as the cloudiness of confusion. She was pretty certain Chloe wasn't the one for her, but she was special and someone who had deserved more than harshness. More than that though, Chloe was a different case. With years of experience in how to navigate the world as an openly gay person in their small community, Chloe was always going to expect too much, too soon from Amelia.

Amelia's heart pounded. Her head hurt. She wanted to crawl under the covers and cry. But it was too hot for that, and it was close enough to the time she should be getting out of bed. With a sigh, she forced her feet to the ground. It would be better to face the day head on than to sulk in the shadows of her shortcomings.

Stretching her neck from side to side, she heard her phone buzz and glanced to the side table.

*I love you, Amy*, her dad had written. *Be safe today PLEASE.*

She smiled at his nickname for her, wishing for the millionth time she had more people address her that way. But she didn't understand his text, or why it had come in so early. She shook her head and re-read the words. Deciding that he had probably heard something strange on the news again, she typed out a quick reply letting him know she loved him and she was always safe. When he didn't respond immediately, she put her phone in her purse and busied herself getting ready for the day.

When it was finally time to go to work, she was grateful. No longer wanting to be home alone with her thoughts, she headed to open the shop. Driving through town, she eyed her daily scenery with skepticism. In a town this size, there was never much traffic. But to say that it was a ghost town this morning would have been an understatement, especially in a place full of early risers. Roads typically dotted with a car here and there were empty. Houses where people had often gathered for coffee on the front porch appeared abandoned.

She heard the beep of someone locking their car door and perked up even more. No one locked their cars in Knell. She craned her neck to see what was happening and made eye contact with Jane, the owner of the local art shop. Instead of a normal wave and a nod, Jane's eyes widened and she scurried into her shop, as though she had been violated. This wasn't normal. Pulling over to the side of the road, she stopped her car. Whatever was going on around here, it was eerie. Fumbling through the cluttered mess of receipts, gum wrappers and more, she finally fished her phone out of her purse.

Seven text messages and two phone calls. Her heart raced as she opened up the text messages: *Just wanted to make sure you had heard...*

As she read the first one, her blood ran cold. Dropping the phone in her lap, her head fell onto the steering wheel. She brought her trembling hands up to cover her mouth, but it did little to muffle the scream that escaped her lips.

Even to her ears, the sound came across as foreign. It was nothing more than a shriek, nothing short of sheer trauma and shock. The tears she had held at bay all night came gushing out with force. Her body shook with violent sobs as she rocked back and forth in the driver's seat of her car. Around her, a small crowd had gathered. She looked up and saw the faces of a family she knew—the Nelson family. Claude and Tammy Nelson stood outside her door, coaxing her to open it, but she couldn't comply if she wanted to. Looking past them, her vision went blurry. She laid down across her front seat, willing them to leave her alone, willing the world to return to the kinder, simpler place she had known just hours before.

Unsure of how long she had been in her car, she righted herself, only to find her tribe of concerned citizens still waiting patiently outside of her car. She turned the key and rolled down the window, wondering how she would explain her outburst. No one even knew the depths of what she was feeling.

"Are you okay, ma'am?" Claude asked, leaning down to look into her window. "Do you need to come in for a glass of water and maybe rest a bit?"

"No. Thank you so much, Claude. I didn't mean to worry you and Tammy. I'm sorry. I just had a bit of a panic attack I suppose." She tried her best to make an intelligible statement, given the fact that they had just witnessed the most epic meltdown of her life, and that she still felt as though she might faint at any moment.

"Don't apologize," Tammy said, stepping up to the window as well. "Now, I don't want you behind the wheel and I'm pretty sure your folks would agree with me."

Amelia wanted to protest, to remind them that she was a grown woman. But what she had displayed made that feel like an untrue statement. She was hurting. She was wounded. She should probably take them up on their offer.

Nodding, she opened her car door and tried to stand. Her knees were weak and she was grateful when Claude reached out a steadying hand. She let him lead her up the steps into their home, as the others who had gathered dissipated and went back to their morning routines.

After accepting a glass of water from Tammy, she forced herself to breathe as normally as possible, even though it seemed as if the world had collapsed beneath her feet.

"A little shaken up by last night's events, I take it?" Tammy asked, after giving Amelia a moment to collect herself.

"I just found out," she said, wanting to keep the conversation as minimal as possible.

"I think it shook us all up. That Stanton girl was certainly one of a kind, and she was different—but she was one of us. She was a Knell girl and she was never mean to a soul. I think this whole place is a little upside down today. Nothing quite like this has ever happened here before."

She continued talking, but Amelia couldn't process anything else. Chloe was different. It was something they all noted. But that didn't mean she deserved to be killed. Chloe Stanton, the woman with whom she had shared so many moments—intimate, fun, adventurous, passionate moments—was dead.

"Do they know who did it?" she blurted out.

Tammy backed up slightly, a clear indicator Amelia had just interrupted. But she didn't care. She needed to know. If they knew who did this, Amelia wanted them to pay.

"I think they're keeping all that pretty tight-lipped for now. I mean it only happened last night."

"Where did it happen?" She was numb as she tried to assess the details.

"In her living room."

Amelia gasped. It was like she had been punched in the gut. In her living room—the same room where Amelia had stood yesterday, the same room where they had devoured each other's bodies time and again, the same room from which she had angrily stomped.

Thankful that she knew the layout of the Nelsons' home, she stood and bolted toward the bathroom, her body wrenching as soon as she threw the door open. It was too much to take. She vomited violently, wishing she didn't have an audience. Still, in true Texan form, Tammy came in behind her and gave her a cool washcloth for her head.

"Thank you so much for your hospitality," Amelia said, emerging moments later and shutting the bathroom door behind her. "I'm sorry I'm such a mess. I've got to go now. I have to open up the shop. And I'm pretty sure I'm running too far behind to catch up for the day." She was rambling, but she couldn't stop. It was the only thing saving her from the pain inside.

"I don't think you should have to worry too much about the shop today, sweetheart," Tammy said, shaking her head. "The whole town is in a tizzy. Why don't you just head home?"

"I'll figure it out," Amelia said, using her wobbly legs to carry her out of the house. "Thank you, again."

Back in the safety of her car, she wanted to break down again. But she couldn't do that here. No one even knew she and Chloe had been friends. As soon as the thought entered her head, it made her sick again. No one knew.

It was that simple. She was gone. And no one had ever known just how much she meant to Amelia—not even Chloe herself. Bile crept up the back of her throat again but she forced it down.

She was going to the shop—not to open, but to go prepare coffee. If nothing else, she would make sure the investigators, the family, and everyone involved had coffee. She had shied away from showing how much she cared for too long. Now it was too late but she was going to honor Chloe's big-hearted approach to life by caring—caring out loud.

At the shop, she busied herself. She tried not to let her regret carry her away, but she was losing the fight. Regardless of Amelia's doubts about the stability of their relationship—or rather, agreement—Chloe had deserved the affection she was due. She had deserved to know just how much she had meant to Amelia.

While the morning's coffee was brewing, Amelia secured the "Closed" sign on the shop door and took a seat briefly in one of the lounge chairs in the shop's sitting area. She looked around the shop. Its industrial design brought her no comfort today. For years, this was the space in which she and Chloe would flirt back and forth innocently. It was where Amelia had first worked up the courage to ask Chloe if they could meet up after work. It was where Chloe had met her long after she had closed up shop one evening, with fresh picked daisies from a nearby field in hand, for their first out-of-work encounter. Amelia ran her fingers over the tan leather of the chair she sat in, remembering how she had sat in this exact spot while explaining her scenario and need for secrecy to Chloe. Outlining guidelines was important to her, and Chloe had followed her instructions to a T. At each request, she turned, slowed down, stopped, or pressed forward. And as Chloe had said last night, Amelia had made all the rules. More than that, she had abused them. For that, she felt ashamed.

Just when Amelia thought she had cried every tear she had left in her body, another onslaught came. This one more tender, slower than the one before. She closed her eyes and let herself remember, believing it to be the only way in which she might actually find some sort of closure.

She still wanted to know how, where, and who. But for now, she could remember and honor Chloe that way. Staring up at the ceiling, she let it all wash back over her. With the lights out, and the shop lit only by candles, they had shared their first, timid kiss, followed by lust-filled kisses that wouldn't stop for months—that didn't stop until last night.

Burying her head in her hands, Amelia thought of the tender ways Chloe would greet her, the special events she would plan for their impromptu date nights, the way she never—until last night—had asked for more than a hand to hold, a companion. She had made sure Amelia always felt special and taken care of.

This was all wrong. It wasn't supposed to be like this. She was supposed to come to her senses, tell Chloe she was sorry and if nothing else, they were supposed to have been friends. Now she had nothing but a fresh brewed batch of coffee to divvy up and take to a hurting family.

She packaged the items with care, taking a slew of pastries from yesterday's batch with her. Today there would be no fresh pastries or coffee service. There would be no place for the old women to gather and gossip. She figured she couldn't have handled their conversation anyway. If she had to hear anyone else say that Chloe was *different* but nice, she might scream. If she had to hear the details thrown about like some sort of petty banter, she knew she wouldn't make it through it without telling her patrons to leave her shop.

Nonetheless, she was sure there were people who had been drawn from their beds far too early who might need a little boost to get through their day and, if coffee was the only solace she could offer, she would offer it.

Wrapping the pastries in individual bags, she glanced at the clock and realized she had let two hours slip by since entering. She sighed and put the goods into to-go bags, knowing she had been stalling. Too many times she had driven over, parked her car in the stealthy spot she had selected, and visited Chloe's house. Today would be different though, and she wasn't sure she was ready or equipped to handle that sort of emotional trauma.

Ready or not, it was time. Gathering her things into the backseat of her Mustang, she gripped the doorframe, looking back at the shop for one fleeting moment when things would be the same. Without giving in to another moment of grief, she reminded herself that there were others who were far closer to Chloe who were no doubt in pain. She threw her car into gear and headed down the highway. Just as Chloe would have done, she flipped to the classic rock station in town and practically flew down the highway.

When she rounded the last bend, she held her breath. Nothing could have prepared her to see what had once been such a peaceful and quaint little driveway littered with emergency vehicles, the town sheriff, the coroner's van, and a vehicle she recognized as belonging to Bill Stanton, as well as several other cars. Her breathing increased. She shouldn't be here. This was a private matter at this time. Even so, she had a mission and she was going to do it, whether or not she spoke to anyone. She got out of her vehicle and loaded the carry-out trays on her arms. Knowing the side entrance, she walked quickly around to the side of the patio and dropped off the beverages and bags of pastries. Hopefully they'd find them while they were still hot. She thought about ringing the doorbell but had no way of knowing what was actually going on inside.

If the coroner's van was still parked in the driveway, did that mean Chloe was still inside? Chills rippled through her body and she thought she might vomit again. Bracing herself, she reached up and grabbed the railing—a railing she had sat on while Chloe strummed on her guitar and crooned an old country love song one evening just a few weeks ago.

Nothing was ever going to be the same again.

"Thank you," she heard the gruff old cowboy's voice behind her, causing her to jump at least a foot in the air.

She turned around and was face-to-face with Bill, Chloe's dad. The two had the same nose, same build even—broad shoulders with strong arms and a narrow waist, with bodies that showcased their daily physical labor. She looked into his eyes and saw the similar fire. As if she could physically feel her heart break in two as the lump in her throat grew, she closed her eyes. When she reopened them, it was already too late. Bill was moving in for a bear hug. "We really appreciate you being out here."

"I couldn't stay away," she managed, gulping. "I just wanted to make sure everyone involved had some coffee or some food if they needed it. I know it's not much, but it was something I could do right now." As she always did, she was babbling on without a way to stop. This was not the time or place. "Anyway, I'm so sorry for your loss."

He nodded and clamped his lips together. After a second, he let out a long and slow exhaling breath. "It's not anything anyone ever expects to deal with," he said, "especially not around here, and especially not with their own." Reaching up, he grabbed the railing she had been holding onto and gave her another long glance. "But we'll weather this storm just like the last."

He made it sound as though this was just something that happened. But from Chloe's stories, she knew that he was just a tough older cowboy who didn't let many see deep into the pain he felt. She could see traces of the tears he had cried and could see the anger flashing somewhere deep below the surface.

"If y'all need anything, let me know," she offered. Her words sounded hollow, but she wanted him to know they had meaning. "Your daughter was a good friend of mine and I'd like to do anything I can to help make sure her memory shines on this place."

"Thank you and thank you for being a good friend to my girl," he said nodding, that glint of a father's knowing in his eyes. She had no way of knowing what—if anything—she had just confessed to Bill, but she wanted him to take her up on the offer if he needed anything.

Giving in to her good southern raising, she leaned in and gave him another hug. "You take care and remember I'm here if y'all need anything."

He nodded and she turned to go. Out of the corner of her eye, she saw into the kitchen and glimpsed broken glass on the floor. Her heart raced. She couldn't be here any longer, at least not while they were still cleaning things up. She'd drive back by later, but now it was still too fresh.

She hit her car at a run and locked herself inside as though the monsters that now existed in her world could be kept at bay with the simple click of a lock.

There were still no answers, but this was not her time to be Nancy Drew. She needed to remember, to mourn in solitude, as did those who loved Chloe the most.

# CHAPTER FOUR

Shuffling papers, clicking keys, occasional sighs, and the hum of fluorescent lights served as the soundtrack for Dominique Velez's day. It was at least peaceful, if not a bit eerie, given the circumstances that had caused them all to work late tonight. There had been no bickering from her staff and no questions at all. This was important and they all knew that.

At Texans for Equality, they stood together and they stood for those who had no voice. If that meant extra hours—especially on a night like tonight, following a devastating crime on one of their own—that's what it meant.

As the news had poured in throughout the day, she had grown sicker to her stomach, to the point to where she realized that by seven o'clock in the evening, she had eaten nothing all day long.

*Hate crime.* The words seemed to leap off the page and resonate within her. She shuddered, imagining someone brutally murdered simply for being who they were. But that's exactly what had happened in the sleepy little Bible Belt town of Knell.

It was over an hour away, but it felt like it had happened in her backyard—to someone just like her.

It was bigger than that though. It was the life of Chloe Stanton stamped out like she didn't even matter. It was the horrific, small-minded culture that shaped murderers who think it's okay to discriminate and commit violence just because someone is different.

Locals quoted in the news story said it was being sensationalized, since they all viewed Chloe as one of them. The local news called it a brutal murder. National news sources, however, were alleging something more sinister, a murder based on sexual orientation. She re-read the stories, noting there were possible suspects in questioning, but she felt it in her heart she already knew the way this had gone down. She wanted to cry as she read the words, but she couldn't stop reading them. Over and over, she read Chloe's story. But that wasn't enough.

She was going to take action. If Knell needed a lesson in equality, she was going to teach it. Furthermore, if there were LGBT kids in those schools who needed counseling, she was the right one for the job.

"I'm packing a bag and going," she said, as her assistant walked by her office. "I'm heading out first thing in the morning. I'll stay for a couple of days, just until I see if there's anything we can do to lessen this burden."

"You're the boss," Jason said nodding in agreement. He stopped for a minute and pulled up a seat by her desk.

"What is it?" she asked, looking up from her notes.

He tapped his foot and shook his head, scratching his chin and looking up at the ceiling as he searched for the words. "I just thought…stupidly thought we were past this, I guess," he said, leveling his gaze. "I mean, I know hatred always exists, but I thought we were working on bigger and better things, instead of trudging back through things that should have stopped decades ago."

Dominique's head throbbed. She glanced down at the floor and let out a deep breath. "You're echoing what I've been thinking all day," she assured him. "But the thing is we're not past it. The world is still as fucked up as it's always been, and as things go, it seems to be getting worse around here, rather than better."

He grimaced, and she reached out to pat him on the shoulder. "Do you remember what we talked about after the marriage ruling?" Tightlipped, he nodded. "Good." She took another deep breath. "It's still the same. Yes, we have marriage, and we are so excited to have jumped that hurdle, but that's not all we are working for. Our fight isn't just for equality under the law. Our fight stretches far beyond that to ensuring society sees us as equals. There are still people who think we're second-class citizens, that we're sick and perverted, that we can be *cured*, that we are somehow less human and less deserving of our lives than they are. For decades, our fellow LGBTQ community members have fought the most difficult fights, but it is our job to continue the fight into today's society, to make sure that things are better for future generations. They did it for us, and it's our turn."

"I know," he said, holding up his hands. "I know what we're working for and why. I know that. I just feel discouraged."

"I'm sorry." She shook her head. "I didn't mean to go off on a tangent. I know you know that as well as I do. I know they're the ones who need to hear that, not you. It's just difficult right now, and my head is pretty jumbled. I feel discouraged too. We lost one of our own. That town lost one of their own. And the only thing we can do now is remind them how and why this happens to make sure it doesn't happen again. In the meantime, you go home and get some rest. The team will need you strong here while I'm gone, so go take care of yourself first."

He nodded, spinning the chair around and standing up. "Good luck," he said before walking back to his desk.

They both knew she was going to need more than luck.

After finishing a few last-minute tasks and setting an out-of-office reply on her email, Dominique gathered her things. Some days her job took its toll on her sanity. Today was one of those days.

Her head and her heart hurt in equal measure. She wanted nothing more than to slip into a bubble bath, turn on some slow jazz music, and drink a glass of wine, letting the pain and confusion of the day slip off into oblivion. But that would not do today. That wouldn't get anything accomplished. Today and the days that would follow would be days of educating, helping, counseling, and taking a stand—for Chloe Stanton and for everyone just like her. She had a bag to pack and places to be.

\* \* \*

Rolling down the windows, Dominique breathed in the morning air and took in the scent of the wild bluebonnets that dotted the surrounding landscapes. It was certainly more peaceful out here on this simple two-lane road leading into the middle of nowhere. At least that's the illusion it gave. But Dominique had seen enough of small towns in Texas to know that peace often only existed for those who were the same and who followed the guidelines and expectations laid out before them.

Most were expected to be married to their high school sweetheart in heteronormative bliss by the age of twenty-one, popping out babies left and right and settling in the same town their mama and daddy did before them.

Despite the strange mix of emotions creating a jittery persona within her, she drove on, trying to smell the flowers along the way just as much as she was trying to figure out why someone like Chloe Stanton would want to make this small-minded town her home. Surely she had options to go somewhere safer.

But therein lay the problem. Everywhere should be safer.

Anger welling within her, she forced herself to breathe. As much as she tried not to harbor preconceived hatred for this place, she couldn't.

Up in the distance, she caught sight of an excessively large sign: "Welcome to Knell, Texas, home of the friendliest folks you'll ever meet. Pop. 12,003."

"Twelve thousand and two," she corrected with a sad shake of her head. "And certainly not all friendly folks."

Driving further into town, she took note of everything she saw. An old country store, a gas station, a total of three stoplights and several front porches filled with people clad in simple, country attire. This place truly could have passed for a Wild West movie set. She glanced down at her skinny jeans and silky red tank top and cast her eyes across the dash of her Prius. Raising an eyebrow, she looked at her dark skin in the rearview mirror. She chuckled, despite the serious nature of her visit. White, hetero, and country were the norms around here. She was anything but all three. There was little doubt she was going to stick out like a sore thumb in Knell. But maybe that's what they needed—a little more diversity.

Breathing a sigh of relief, she wheeled her car into the first coffee shop she saw—probably the only coffee shop in town, judging by what she had already seen of the area. She would have to make her presence known to the locals, let the city officials know she was available, and also post video blogs to get the message out to supporters. She knew she would need coffee to navigate this mess.

The wooden sign adorned with brightly colored flowers and the name carved into the wood brought back a sense of nostalgia for times past. Maybe she could interact with locals a bit at Amy's Place and get a feel for the people.

She swung the door open and was instantly greeted by a polite woman around her age behind the counter. She stared, noting the woman's almost cat-like, light green eyes. Dominique studied her, the bags underneath her eyes. Still *those eyes*. She had to bet they sparkled when the woman was happy, and maybe even held hints of gold at the center. What a sight that would be, instead of tired and sad—*exhausted and devastated*, she corrected herself, noting the hollow stare. "Good morning and welcome," the woman said, offering her a smile even though her lips were too tightly pulled back.

"Thank you." She nodded as she stepped inside.

She was greeted by concerned and curious eyes from the table of three elderly women in the corner. She smiled at them and waved, stepping up and ignoring their whispers as she approached the tall brunette behind the counter.

"What can I do for you?" she asked.

Dominique looked down at her nametag. *Amelia.* "Are you Amy?" Dominique asked, needing more than coffee to fuel her day's start.

"That's me, and this is my place," she said, letting out a laugh that sounded a little too sharp. Dominique couldn't help but wonder if it was the fact that she was an outsider or the fact that this woman was affected by what had happened around here. Regardless, her smile was plainly a façade.

"It's a beautiful place," Dominique said.

"Where are you from?" Amelia asked, finally taking a breath and appearing slightly more at ease.

"I'm from Austin. Just came down here to lend my services and my voice to what happened, and see if I could help anyone out."

Amelia nodded but the lines in her forehead deepened in obvious concern. "Services?"

"Counseling, insight, whatever people may need."

"You're a counselor?"

"In a former life. Now I'm an Executive Director for a non-profit," she waved her hand in the air, using her edited response, not wanting to tip this kind woman off just yet. "But I still have my background and still interact with communities who have gone through a horrific situation like the one that played out here."

Amelia balled her hands into fists, and the rate of her breathing increased. She glanced down at the floor for a moment, gulped, and looked back up at Dominique. "In that case, thank you for being here. I know a lot of people are having a rough time." Amelia cleared her throat. "What can I get you in the way of coffee?"

Dominique listened to her sweet Texas drawl and wanted to hug the woman. She had labored over the phrase "a lot of people." Dominique could read between those lines, just as she could see past the fake smile she was being offered. Amelia was hurting as well. Her green eyes were bloodshot and swollen. Even in her emotional trauma, she was strikingly beautiful, and Dominique felt drawn to comfort her. The weight of Amelia's silence hung in the air between them, almost palpable. She wanted to break down those walls and let Amelia express what she was truly feeling. She wanted to know the depths behind those eyes, to hear genuine words spoken without fear or doubt.

Amelia leaned forward, silently reminding Dominique that she still hadn't ordered.

"I'm sorry," Dominique said, clearing her throat with hopes of refocusing her thoughts. "It's been a long day for me, too." She glanced up at the menu for the first time and rattled off the first thing she saw written on the chalkboard. In a daze, wondering what kept Amelia so closed off, she swiped her card and waited while Amelia whipped up whatever she had ordered.

As she accepted her coffee, she lowered her voice. "If you know of anyone who might need to talk or might need some help, I'm going to leave a few of these cards here on the table. It's all confidential."

Amelia nodded, her eyes widening as it looked like she might speak. Instead she glanced at the floor and nodded again before waving at Dominique.

As Dominique made her way back out to the car, she shook her head. If this is what the entire town was going to be like, she had her work cut out for her. If people couldn't even admit that one of their own being murdered affected them emotionally, it was going to be difficult to bring education and equality to a place like this.

# CHAPTER FIVE

A slap on his desk drew Wes Mitchell out of his stupor. He jerked his head up and shut his notebook, blinking to adjust his eyes.

"How can I help you?" Luke, his deputy, stood over his desk with a tired expression. At only twenty-seven, the kid looked much older than that today. His face appeared weathered and ragged, but that seemed to be the look that everyone was wearing around here.

"I don't know what to do, Sheriff," Luke admitted. He cast his eyes downward and shifted his weight, his discomfort visible, same as it had been for everyone since the gruesome details of the town's first murder in thirty years came to light. He paced in front of the desk, his face reddening until he let out a deep breath. "I just don't know what to do."

"You're doing fine," Wes said. "I promise, none of us know what to do right now, but you're hanging in there and you're handling things and upholding the law just like you're supposed to."

"But what about the mayor?" he asked. Wes glanced at the kid's hands, noticing the way Luke was stuffing them in his pockets and then pulling them out again. He was jittery and his hands gave him away.

"He's just the mayor," Wes said, exhaling forcefully. This entire thing had hit him like a ton of bricks. He hoped Luke couldn't tell just how unsure he was. He was supposed to be the leader—especially in situations like this. But he couldn't even fathom how they had gotten themselves into this mess, much less how anyone was supposed to get out of it. "He's a man. He's not God. He can't undo the situation any more than any of us can. He can't turn back the clock and un-kill the poor girl. And he sure as hell can't erase what we've already uncovered. You and I were both there. We saw it together. He can't change the words his boy said, his truck tire marks at the scene of the crime, that he had promised to teach 'that fucking queer a lesson,' or anything else that we already know." He made sure to use air quotes to directly quote Trent's alleged statement but shuddered at its harshness nonetheless. "Right now, all signs point to the Golden Boy of Knell—Trent Westwick. That little twerp has assumed he could get away with anything his entire life. I'm not sayin' he's guilty. None of us can say that just yet. We're still waiting on some of the forensics to come back. We have to have all of that. I'm just sayin' that he's acting a little too defensive for someone who's innocent. That combined with his past antics and history of getting away with murder...er..." he stammered and cleared his throat. "Bad choice of words. Anyhow, we will let the facts of the case come forward throughout this investigation. We'll follow the letter of the law, and we'll make sure there's justice for this town. It's the only way any of us can rebuild."

Luke stood still, simply nodding his head while his lips stayed so tightly shut that little white lines were forming around the edges. Before he answered, he glanced down the hallway toward the holding cells.

"I know," Wes said, keeping his tone as light as possible. "It's not a situation any of us ever expected to be in. This is Knell after all. Most of our job consists of stopping speeding cars, giving partying high schoolers a warning, and just the general keeping of the peace. I know I'm supposed to tell you all the answers. That was easy when it was textbook stuff and training. This is different, kid. I'm right there with you. But we'll get through it."

"Ryan still not speaking?" Luke asked, letting out a sigh.

"He's given us all he can," Wes said, his shoulders slumping. He toyed with the pen jar on his desk, looking for any type of distraction. "We know all about his argument with Chloe on the day of the murder. We've heard from all witnesses, and all came up clean. According to him, he left that day, skipped town, and was sharing some seedy company at the time the deed was done."

He scribbled notes on a sticky pad by his desk. They would have to revisit his statements and make sure they were airtight, just to do their due diligence.

"The mayor's demanding we look at every angle," Luke said, wiping his brow. His eyes darted from side to side around the room and his foot tapped at double pace.

"You're all hyped up on caffeine." Wes sighed. "We *are* looking into every avenue. We've questioned half the damn town already. And if anything pops up that's solid, you know as well as I do, we'll let that bastard out of his cell. For now, stop subbing coffee for sleep and go home for a bit."

The rattling of bars down the hall, followed by a slew of curses and threats to cut the funding to the building made Wes want to scream. In typical Trent fashion, he was using his daddy's name and every threat in the book in his favor.

"Quiet down back there," Wes yelled. "These cells are monitored and you don't want all those shenanigans to show up in court."

To his surprise the statement seemed to quiet Trent down for a minute. He craned his neck, listening for any retort. When none came, he leaned back in his desk chair, cradling his neck in the crooks of his arms.

"Play it by ear, Luke. That's the best advice I've got."

"I'm fuckin' innocent!" Trent's wailing started up again and Wes sat up in his chair.

He wanted to drive his fist through the wood on the table in front of him. The kid had been shouting the same damn thing all night. So had his never-fail family. They'd been there to seal up an alibi that he had been having dinner with them—something a little too far-fetched to be believable since he'd been seen at the bar all night.

Nonetheless, they swore by it. His stepmom has even gone so far as to talk about how she was able to smell the booze on his breath, but he stopped by for meatloaf anyway. Trent continued to scream and rattle the bars on his cell. Wes let out a heavy sigh.

"Look, Luke," he said. "It's going to be a long night around here. Please take a break and go downtown. You can go get some dinner, stop by your house and take a short nap and come back in later. There's no sense in both of us being here."

"No sir," Luke protested. "I'm fine. I promise. I'll stick it out with you."

"No need. I insist. I'll take a break after you do. Only one of us needs to be here." Luke frowned as Wes practically pushed him out of the door. Truth was, he had no idea whether or not they both needed to be there. This was the first time they'd had someone in lock up for anything other than driving home from the bar after a couple. Regardless, he figured it wouldn't hurt to have his deputy a little more rested, a little more levelheaded. As it was now, the kid looked strung out—no doubt from the most emotional night on the job any of them had ever had.

Once Luke was out of the office, he opened up his notebook again. Like the rest of them, he wanted to be damn sure they had the right guy. Not only would it bode badly for the town if they kept the mayor's kid under lock and key if he was innocent, but it would also create a realm of sheer terror if people found out the real killer had been amongst them for the day and a half after his first kill was discovered.

His entire body convulsed as he looked again at the crime scene photos. No matter how many times he viewed the photo of Chloe Stanton's slain body, it would never cease to sicken him. Lying facedown on the floor, she was found in a pool of her own blood, stabbed multiple times, with a fractured jaw. She was a tough one, though. He looked at the picture, noting the streaks of blood where she had dragged herself along the floor, apparently after the killer had left her house. There she had dialed 911 on her own and died with dispatch still on the line.

Closing his eyes tightly, his fingers shook around the edges of the photograph he still held. Instead of seeing Chloe like that, he wanted to remember the happy-go-lucky girl who had befriended his daughter in kindergarten, the spitfire she was in high school, the woman he pulled over for speeding once a week.

A single tear slid down his cheek as he contemplated all of their encounters. It had only been three days since he had pulled her over after he clocked her going eighty in a fifty-five. They had laughed and joked, she told him about the week's work on the ranch and promised to slow down, even though they both knew it was a pretty little lie. That girl had a way about her, though. Her down home charm, her humility, and her willingness to help anyone out made her stand out even in an area known for its compassion, friendliness, and outgoing nature. She was a gem, and whoever did this to her deserved the harshest punishment available.

He had often echoed and believed the sentiments others expressed about her lifestyle being difficult to accept. Growing up in this area, it wasn't something people just accepted. Nonetheless, he had never faulted himself for loving her as a person and silently disapproving. But as he stared back at the picture of her in her weakest moments, he felt the wheels in his head begin to turn, questioning everything he ever believed.

He couldn't just go alongside believing that she was different, that something was "off" about her, and then be enraged when something like this happened. He could see the parallels between the culture they had created and the path that was paved for something like this to happen. If someone is constantly viewed as less than, as a category all their own, it makes them vulnerable.

"We could have done more," he whispered, this time allowing more tears to fall. He balled his fists and dried his eyes. He couldn't cry here. He hadn't cried in over a decade, and here he was breaking down when he was supposed to be the tough guy. But they came anyway.

He just couldn't understand. He couldn't piece it all together. What had she done? What was her crime? Why did someone so full of life have to die?

Setting the file aside, he stood, willing his lungs to fill and his breathing to return to normal. Looking down the dark, narrow hallway, he silently promised himself he would do everything in his power to ensure Trent Westwick rotted in a cell for this.

* * *

Blood orange, streaked with yellows, pinks, and blue filled the evening horizon, and the smell of cattle lingered in the heavy, humid air. This was home, but it no longer felt like it. Bill Stanton removed his hat and looked up at the sunset. He glanced down at the spot beside him and pictured his little messy-haired wild child bouncing up and down next to him.

"It's so pretty, Daddy," she'd coo in her sweet little twang. "Lift me up so I can see too." He'd grab her around the waist and hoist her up onto his shoulders, completely wrapped around her little finger and willing to do anything she asked.

He sighed and reminded himself those days were long gone now, as were the days where she'd join him in this spot after work as an adult. Sunsets were always her favorite. And even by six years old, she had learned the importance of this evening ritual with her father. They'd sit out here, watch the sunset, and talk about life. It had always been that way, especially after her mother died when Chloe was just eight years old. Left with only each other, they'd sit for hours on end, talking about life. He credited those rituals for the ease and openness they had always shared. When she had admitted that she liked girls, he already knew as much. And it never changed the way he looked at her. He wished he could have said the same for everyone in this town who wanted to change her. Sure, there had been times he had wished an easier life for her. But he wouldn't have changed who she was, and that fact changed nothing about the purity of her heart.

There were too many questions and far too much hurt in his heart to do anything else for the day. His old body ached from being on his feet all day. Though they had told him to go home, he hadn't been able to until now. He had walked the layout of Chloe's house at least a hundred times, searching for something concrete to lock the Westwick boy up for good. Aside from tire tracks that could have easily come from his lifted Duramax and a man-sized hole broken into the French doors at the back of Chloe's house, there was nothing other than evidence pointing to a large person who drove a truck. He had searched for something that might give him some sort of closure. It wasn't working. Nothing had helped.

He pulled out his phone and thought about giving Ryan another tongue lashing, but the boy had stopped taking his calls. It was worthless anyway, and he'd just be projecting his problems at someone else. He might have been a crappy ranch hand, but the worst he had done was lose his temper at the workplace on an ill-fated day. He knew that as much as that kid could run his mouth, he wasn't capable of this.

Was he? Nothing was certain anymore. This world was a place he no longer recognized. He stuffed his phone back in his pocket, pacing a few steps before sitting down on the tailgate of his truck.

His mind raced, showcasing a sea of faces. Were any of them capable of something like this? Answers wouldn't come.

He glanced upward and watched the sunset for his girl.

In due time, he planned to stop by Amy's Place. That girl had more to say than she had let on today. And after years of meeting Chloe's "good friends," he knew more about her than she probably realized. Regardless, he wanted to talk to her and find out what she might know. More than that, he wanted another glimpse into the insight of one who knew his daughter well.

As the last bits of sun faded into darkness, he sat in their sacred place, hung his head, and gave in to the tears that had been welling up all day.

# CHAPTER SIX

Surrounded by pillows and cushions, it felt like the couch had engulfed her. But Amelia didn't care. This was her only safe haven. It was the one place untouched by Chloe. Even here, thoughts refused to cease, regret refused to be pushed below the surface, and nothing seemed as it once was. Everything was different. Everything was a memory. Everything reminded her that it could have just as easily been her.

Maybe Chloe had been right to live her life so loudly without fear. But it hadn't gotten her very far. Her closet lacked the comfort that she had previously found in it, though. It was a scary, dark place of fear, one of infinite cowardice. Had she been able to live as boldly as Chloe, maybe Chloe wouldn't have died alone. Maybe she wouldn't have died at all. If there was even just one more in Knell, maybe that would have reduced the stigma.

She couldn't say for sure, but she also couldn't dispute it. Rising from her spot, she paced around the living room, stopping to tap her foot anxiously. There was no peace because there was no closure. That was true, but it was far deeper than that. There was no peace for *her* specifically, because it had been days and Chloe's service was tomorrow, and Amelia had been stubborn in her refusal to admit to anyone aside from Chloe's dad that the pair were even friends.

Giving in to the need to listen to a song that might come close to expressing her feelings, she flipped through her iTunes until she found one she wanted to hear. Connecting to her Bluetooth speaker, she let the sounds of Leonard Cohen's "Hallelujah" fill the air. With each haunting lyric, she felt the cracks in her heart deepen, until tears fell freely. As the song came to a close, she grabbed a tissue and tried to clean up her crying mess. She braced her hands on her knees and forced her breathing back to normal before she stood. She looked up at the painting on the far wall, a girl staring at her reflection near a riverbank. It was one she had cherished for years, but now she stared at it anew. She, just like the girl, was searching for answers and knew they may never come.

Had it been love? Was this heartache she felt because it was love? Or was it merely because she was grieving and felt a lifetime's worth of guilt?

Walking over to the mirror on the wall, she looked at her reflection. Her eyes were the same green they always had been, but she didn't recognize the girl staring back at her. She looked older, more jaded, and far less put together than she ever had. This shred of a human wasn't who she was raised to be.

Rising from the depths of her soul, she felt the scream boil up in her before it belted out, ripping across her throat and out into the open as she reached up and punched through the mirror, no longer wanting to look at herself.

Blood dripped down her arm and shards of glass now lay strewn about her living room, but she didn't care. She had far bigger worries than a stain on the carpet. Walking to the center of her living room, she looked around her house. She had nowhere to go, no one to talk to, no way to make this hurt less. Out of the corner of the eye, she caught sight of the business card laying on her end table. Still covered in blood, she walked over to it and picked it up.

"Texans for Equality," she read aloud for probably the eightieth time that day and let out a long breath. It could be worth a shot, but calling that number might mean outing herself. She flicked the card back and forth between her fingers, contemplating the idea.

"No," she said, tossing it onto the table and gritting her teeth, only to have a vivid memory of her refusals to Chloe flash into her mind.

Gripping the side of the table for stability, she grabbed the card again and dialed the number before she could talk herself out of it again. Her breathing was ragged and sweat dripped down her palms, causing her to drop her cell phone from her hand. Taking another breath, she picked it back up and placed it next to her ear.

It rang and she thought she might vomit. She wasn't ready for this—for any of this. It rang again and she heard Dominique's voice fill the line.

"Hello?"

She dropped the phone again, this time running to the kitchen as though she had seen a ghost.

"This is fucking stupid," she said aloud to herself, making her feel even crazier. Forcing one foot in front of the other, she made her way back into the living room and scooped up the phone, only to find the line dead.

With a sigh, she plopped onto the couch in defeat. There was no way she could call again, just as there was no doubt Dominique would think she was as batty as anyone around here did after witnessing her behavior the past three days. Regardless of whether or not she had a vessel into which she could pour her woes—be it Dominique or someone else—she was going to have to get it together. She had no other choice. Life had to go on, no matter how badly this all hurt right now.

Perhaps she just needed to find something normal— anything normal to do. Dinner.

Normal people had dinner. She hadn't in three days. In fact, she couldn't remember eating anything since the brisket she had cooked for Chloe, and she didn't really even eat that after their argument. She mentally flipped through a menu of possibilities, based on the staples she knew were still stocked in her kitchen cabinets. With each option, her stomach flipped.

Her phone buzzed on her lap and she jumped. It shouldn't scare her as much as it did. After all, it had been ringing off the hook most of the week, with her dad mainly just checking to make sure she was okay. It was as if he had some kind of parental insight she couldn't define. She had promised him she was fine and that she didn't want to talk. Other than that, her phone had been silent. Not a single call, although her only *friend* in the world was dead.

She stared at the phone, an Austin number flashing across the screen. She reached up to swipe *ignore*, but her fingers worked against her, swiping to answer the call.

"Hello," she said, her words tumbling out at rapid fire pace. "Is this Dominique? I met you at the coffee shop. This is Amelia—Amy—from Amy's Place."

"Hi Amelia...or do you prefer Amy?"

"Um..." She paused. No one had actually ever asked her that question. Whether she needed to turn over a new leaf or needed some sort of separation from her identity, she answered boldly. "You can call me Amy."

"Well it's nice to hear from you, Amy." Dominique's tone was so even and peaceful. Amelia felt her breathing return to a semi-normal pace. "I was hoping you'd call. What can I do for you?"

What *could* she do? Amelia could list a million things, but none of them were truly plausible. "What if you just tell me what it is you *can* do? That way I can figure it out. I don't actually know what to say or what it is that I need."

"I can listen," Dominique said. "We can talk about things. I can meet up with you and we can sit together in person if you'd like. I can help you sort out what you might be feeling. If you have a different approach and want to look at things based in the work my organization does, we can look at those options. It all depends on what it is you prefer."

"Okay." Amelia let out a sigh. "I honestly don't know what to talk about. I guess I somehow stupidly hoped you had some kind of magic cure."

"Unfortunately in grief, there is no magic. There is no cure. There are simply things you can do to make sure you're on a healthy path of healing."

"What kind of things?" Amelia paced around the living room, finally opting to sit on the back of the couch and dangle her feet over the edge.

"Talking, for starters."

"I don't know what to talk about." She bit her tongue to keep from babbling. Truth was, she knew exactly what she *didn't* want to talk about. But she also didn't know how to say that. She'd only ever told Chloe.

"Well, let's start with this," Dominique said. "Let's meet up tonight. It's only six o'clock. Let's meet up. I'll buy you dinner, and we can talk."

"No," Amelia said. Her voice had been abrasive, so she took a deep breath and continued. "Sorry. I don't really want to meet up in public."

"I completely understand. Sometimes being in a public place adds undue pressure to the situation. Where would you like to meet up?"

Once again, without even realizing it, Dominique had managed to calm Amelia in an instant. "My house," she heard herself saying, before she truly processed what she was agreeing to.

"Text me the address and I'll head over," Dominique said. She never missed a beat, and Amelia had to wonder what kind of woman just agreed to come over to a stranger's house. Before she could judge too harshly, she remembered she was the one who had asked for this encounter, in her personal space.

She looked around and her jaw dropped. If this woman wasn't going to think she was a complete slob, she had work to do. And she had to do it quickly. Scrambling, she leapt off the couch and began shoving things into the hall closet, under the couch, and wherever she could stash them away in a hurry.

* * *

The burgundy curtains swayed in the air conditioner, making Dominique question everything she knew. This hotel was one step away from being the roach inn, and she was out of her element. She—an out lesbian—had just agreed to go to a stranger's house in a small town in which someone had just recently been killed for being *an out lesbian*! In addition to that, she was the only Hispanic person she had seen in the entire town. She was too many kinds of different for a place this white, hetero—a place this much like Mayberry.

Pacing in her room, she forced herself to breathe. She thought about calling to cancel, but decided she was safe with Amy. The woman had exhibited legitimate stress through both their encounters—first in the coffee shop, and later on the phone. There was something more going on and, whatever it was, Dominique was the one she had called for help.

Bracing herself against the side of the bed, she looked in the mirror. Her appearance still screamed "outsider" but she didn't have anything else. Looking at her skinny jeans and halter-top, she looked like anything but a counselor and anything but like someone who should be out at night in Knell, Texas. Wardrobe had not been a consideration she had factored into this trip.

She sighed. This was what Amy was going to get. She stopped for a minute, sitting on the bed and focusing her thoughts. She pulled out her cell phone and dialed her best friend Cheyenne's number. After three rings, she heard Cheyenne's upbeat voice fill the line.

"Hey, stranger," Cheyenne said, and Dominique could almost see her smile lighting up the room.

"Hey, Chey." Dominique let out a deep breath.

"Are you okay?" There was a pause and Cheyenne cleared her throat. "I meant to call yesterday. I'm so sorry. I saw everything in the news and knew you must have been really busy. And before I knew it, time slipped away from me. I'm so sorry for not calling."

"No, don't be, please," Dominique said. "I just needed to say 'hi' and have something familiar."

"Are you *there?*" Cheyenne's deep breath filled the silence between them for a second. "Please be safe."

"I will," Dominique assured her. "I'm not in harm's way. I just needed a bit of a pep talk."

"You've got this," Cheyenne said, laughing. Dominique shook her head. She knew her friend too well to think she was actually finding humor in the situation. She laughed when nervous. Nonetheless, Dominique let her finish. "You're the single most talented person I know when it comes to helping people through a difficult situation, and making your voice heard. Hell, you make your voice heard even when it's over easy things like which football team is better." Dominique laughed, thinking about their constant battle between the Cowboys and the Texans, both who often had equally hard seasons, but who Cheyenne and Dominique argued over like a couple of children. "Not only that, but you're the best person I know. You're the one who is there for a late night gab session, a bottle of wine, to open my pickle jars with ease while I stand helplessly by after struggling to open it myself, to help me search for my missing dog, to get me into crazy adventures I'd never consider without you. You're a spitfire, honey, and you've got this."

"Thank you," Dominique said. "I knew I called the right person."

"Was there another option?" Cheyenne teased. "Who is she?"

They laughed together. Over the next several minutes, Dominique filled Cheyenne in on the case at hand and what she was doing in the small town. By the time she hung up the phone, she felt rejuvenated. Speaking out for justice, fighting for equality, helping those hurt in the aftermath of horror was what she did, and she was going to do it to the best of her ability.

Taking a steadying breath and smiling at her reflection in the mirror, she grabbed her room key and headed across town.

On the drive over, she thought again of how beautiful Amy was and shook her head. That's not why she was here.

Nevertheless she figured it wouldn't do too much harm to admire a beautiful girl in town during such a dreadful time. She would remain professional and do her job, not letting hormonal impulses get the best of her. But she would give credit where credit was due, and Amy certainly deserved credit for those eyes and those long, gorgeous dark locks of hair.

Glancing down at her GPS, she took the final right turn as directed and pulled up outside of a tiny, blue house with an immaculate yard. It appeared that, in addition to making coffee, Amy had quite the green thumb as well. She pulled into the driveway and white knuckled the steering wheel for a second. This should be nothing out of the ordinary. She did this often in LGBT crisis situations. She loosened her grip to look at her sweaty palms, chalking this anxiety up to the simplicity of Amy being her first taker in Knell.

She glanced in the rearview mirror, the light from the cab of the vehicle somehow making her eyes look even darker than they were. Staring at her reflection, she exhaled and quickly cast her eyes away. What did it matter how she looked? None of that mattered as long as she was here to do her job.

Before she could give herself another futile pep talk or second guess taking this call, she got out of the vehicle and shut the door behind her, striding up to the house with false confidence. She reached up to knock on the door, but it opened before her hand struck the wood.

"Hi," Amy said, gulping and offering a weak smile.

"Hi, Amy," Dominique replied. "I'm glad you agreed to meet with me."

"Me, too," Amy said too quickly. She shoved her right hand behind her back but not before Dominique saw the large bandage wrapped around it with fresh blood soaking through. "I think it might help. At least I hope it does."

"I do, too." Dominique waited, still standing out on the front porch. She looked past Amy into the living room, taking note of its homey country chic décor. She caught sight of a bloodstain on the carpet and cringed inwardly, careful to keep her face neutral. As if that wasn't symbolic of this whole situation.

"Oh, sorry," Amy said, stepping to the side and throwing the door open. "Please come in."

"Thanks," Dominique said. "Where would you like to chat?"

Amy's eyes darted around the room. "Anywhere." Pointing to the couch, she shrugged and looked to Dominique for approval.

Dominique nodded and took a seat. Amy paced in front of her, wearing down the carpet. Cueing on the tools of the trade she had learned in her counseling days, Dominique waited for Amy to fill the silence.

In the meantime, she took in Amy's scattered demeanor. She paced only to stop and stare at Dominique and then took off pacing again. She pulled her left hand out of the pocket of her jeans in a gesture that signified she was about to speak, and then stuffed it right back in and turned to face the wall, careful to keep her right hand out of sight. Finally, she sighed and took a seat next to Dominique, unveiling the bandaged hand and shaking her head as she set it on her lap.

"I don't know why I invited you here," she said. "I just wanted a safe place to talk and nowhere else around town feels safe. Everywhere there are curious eyes and ears, just as there are memories around every bend. I can't take it and I don't know where else to go or who else to talk to. I certainly never dreamed I would be sitting on my own couch talking to a stranger about my problems..." She took a deep breath. "But here I am," she added in a whisper.

She looked off to the distance and Dominique leaned closer. "It's okay to have a lot of feelings, even feelings you don't quite understand yet," she said gently. "Situations that are tragic and shocking like this often have a huge emotional fallout. I'm just grateful you're trying to feel what you need to in order to heal."

"I don't want to feel it anymore." Amy shook her head vigorously. "I'm tired of fucking feeling."

Dominique nodded, urging her to go on. But when she looked off again, Dominique filled the silence. "How did you know Chloe?"

"It's a small town," Amy said, her words clipped and precise—too precise. "Everyone knows everyone. It's bound to hurt when we lose someone who's one of us in a town like this."

Dominique leaned back, relaxing onto the pillows around the couch arm in an effort to look as unthreatening as possible.

Fidgeting in her seat, Amy bit her lip and sighed. "I knew her well. She was a friend of mine. I was at her house often and we hung out. And now I don't know how to look at a world that doesn't have her in it. She was a big part of my life." Dominique watched as Amy furrowed her brow and tears slid down her cheeks. "We laughed together, we talked, we shared music tastes, and I tried out new recipes on her." She gulped and tapped her foot quickly. "She was a friend, you know?" Her voice rose an octave, and she offered a plastic smile. Dominique nodded but waited in silence.

"She was someone I could count on, and I had grown really accustomed to the time we spent together, even if it wasn't all that exciting to someone else. She was my person, the one I texted when I had good or bad news, the one who helped me relax after a bad day." She paused and took a deep breath, glancing down at the floor. "She was my first." The sentence was barely audible but Dominique felt its weight.

She reached across the couch and put a steadying hand on Amy's shoulder, as Amy broke into a sob. "I've never told anyone else that before," she said. "Please don't say anything to anyone."

"This is a safe space," Dominique reassured her. "Everything you say stays with me." Her heart broke for the woman, as she watched her eyes flit back and forth across the room, clearly in fear of coming out—even to a perfect stranger.

"I cared deeply for her. She was the biggest part of my life for the past few months and even in the flirtatious months before we even crossed that bridge. She was the part that remained the same every day. And now she's gone. Worse yet, I didn't even have the courage to be near her in any way, shape, or form when other people were around, so there's no way I could have protected her. I didn't even know it had happened until after the entire town knew. I was the last to find out, even though I was the one she was...*dating*." Amy paused and frowned. "That sounds like such a foreign way to explain what we were doing. I don't even know what it was." She looked at the ground, then reached for a tissue and slipped her feet up under her knees. "I'm sorry for talking so much. It's something I do when I'm uncomfortable." She looked up at the ceiling and sighed. "Actually, it's something I do when I'm nervous, when I'm feeling awkward, all the time. I ramble a lot." She buried her face in her hands and shook her head.

"It's okay," Dominique said, patting her on the shoulder. "You don't need to apologize for anything. You're finding healing in your own way, on your own time. Talking only helps us to realize what's going on inside."

Amy looked up at her, nodded, and gulped. "The thing is, in addition to all I'm feeling, I'm very unsettled. Throughout my life, I've known I wasn't like everyone else. I've also been taught repeatedly that being gay isn't acceptable. It's wrong and dirty and sinful and what have you. I never even considered acting on the truths I've known about myself until I got too close. I've always been drawn to Chloe, like a moth to a flame. She was this creature of sheer beauty, flitting through life at her own pace, in her own way. I kept my distance as much as this town allows, running with my own circle and starting my business. For years, I was careful and admired her from afar. She must have known somehow, because she started frequenting the shop daily. That led to her stopping by with booze to spike my coffee drinks so we could enjoy a nightcap together, and that led to the rest. Now I know just how much I cared for her. I know everything I felt for her. I know she opened my eyes. And I know she wasn't afraid to be who she was…" She cast her eyes downward and her breathing quickened. "But look where she ended up. It's not safe to be who I am, but I feel like I have to do something now. Like I have to say something, to stand up in Chloe's honor, to live boldly like she always did."

Dominique wanted to speak, but she was at a loss for words. The silence grew between them as she nodded. Normally she would encourage someone to come out, to open the eyes of the world and to live a life of authenticity. In these circumstances, she was just as confused as Amy. Was it safe?

She swallowed and locked eyes with Amy. "You've poured out your heart tonight, so I'll do the same for you," she said, taking a deep breath. "I don't have the answers for you. I could tell you the same thing I tell everyone when they're ready to come out, but that advice would fall short here. Besides, I'm not here to tell you what to think or do. I'm just here to listen, offer counsel, and be a friend. It sounds like life is pretty lonely in Knell for our people, so if you'd like, I'd be happy to be your friend. What I will tell you is this…" She placed her hand on Amy's knee for additional support. "Tragedy often brings us to a point of action. It makes us feel as though we must act with urgency. What I advise you most in this time is to think things through. Live boldly and authentically however you can. Do keep in mind the dangers your community has presented, but honor Chloe's memory and the memory of many who have died for loving who they love by being you. Do that however you can, whenever you can. It may mean letting a small circle in on your identity and growing it with time. It may mean reaching out to Chloe's family and letting them know who you were to her. The fact of the matter remains that the more of us who speak up means the LGBT community is more real, more personal to a wider group of people. Good things come from coming out, but this community has also shown that bad things happen. Bad things happen around the world to people just like me. People just like you. It's horrific, and there is no way to make it hurt less. So do what you can in your own time. It may come in different forms. You'll know what you need to do and, in the meantime, I'll be around."

"When are you going back to Austin?" Amy's lip quivered and her eyes filled up with tears again. "I'm sorry," she said, holding up her hand. In the light, Dominique again saw her bandaged hand.

"What happened here?" Dominique asked, taking Amy's hand in her own and examining it.

"It's embarrassing." Amy pulled her hand back an inch before looking deeply into Dominique's eyes and letting it rest where it was. "I smashed my mirror. Emotions have been high," she added with a shrug.

"I get it." Dominique nodded. "Happens. It's nothing to be ashamed of. We've all acted in anger, passionate heartache, confusion, and more. I'd say you have enough of that brimming beneath the surface to smash every piece of glass in this house, although I wouldn't recommend it. Do you need help cleaning it up and securing that bandage?"

Amy cocked her head to the side, obviously considering the notion. Questions danced in her eyes but finally she nodded. "Please." The request was a mere whisper—gentle and sincere. Never letting go of her hand, Dominique walked beside her as Amy gestured toward the kitchen.

There was no doubt in Dominique's mind that she couldn't assuage this pain or make this situation any better. But she knew she was doing something good here, and that's all that mattered in this moment. If she could provide some sort of comfort or solace for at least one person—and it seemed Amy was the one who might just need it the most—she was doing her job. She would continue to do it as long as she was needed.

# CHAPTER SEVEN

"Yoo-hoo!" A high-pitched, pretentious squeal came from the front of the police station and Wes sighed, having already been interrupted four times during his daily routine. Whoever had interrupted this time felt the need to continually tap the bell by the front desk, which made his heart rate increase. He wished the receptionist hadn't been out sick today. Knots of tension tightened his shoulders, and he shook his head. It was his to deal with.

He secured the file he had been reading in a locked cabinet and slipped the key inside his pocket, patting it once to ensure its safekeeping. He started away from his desk, but stopped to down the already-cold coffee in his cup, needing a bit of a boost in the moment to stay sane. It didn't matter that it was four o'clock in the afternoon. Since he had stopped sleeping at night, he required heavy amounts of caffeine to get through the day.

"Hello," he called out. "What can we do for you?"

There was no answer. He gripped the Taser on his belt loop, just in case, and turned the corner. Rolling his eyes as covertly as possible, he relinquished his grip as he saw who was waiting. Clad in an impractical and ornate white silk dress, complete with gaudy gold jewelry and six-inch stilettos, stood Sylvia Westwick. Her hair was at least the sixth color he had seen it that year—bleach blond this time. Her skin was tanned, almost to a crisp, and her nails were perfectly manicured. She screamed of money and pretention in such a humble town.

"Afternoon, Mrs. Westwick," he said, working to cover his irritation with a smile. "What can I do for you?"

"You can let me see my boy," she said, never smiling and narrowing her eyes more with each word. "You can let me in to see my son, and you can call off this nonsense investigation of yours. We all know Trent is innocent, and it's damn time you all recognized that as well."

"Ma'am, we have protocol, and Trent will be locked up for a while." He kept his tone even. He wanted to let her know that technically she wasn't the boy's blood family. She was his stepmom—of only two years. That meant she wasn't permitted to see him under these circumstances. He bit his tongue.

"He should at least have reasonable bail set. Besides, you and I both know he didn't do this. You know that other boy—Ryan what's-his-name, the dirty ranch hand who worked for Bill—is the one behind all of this." She put her hands on her hips and glared in his direction. "You can't use my son as a ploy in some elaborate game to balance the power around here."

"There are powers larger than both you and I," he said, shrugging. "But he's not even here. He's at County by now. You can go over there and try to see him."

"I want to see him now, and I demand that you release him." She stepped forward, her heels clicking and her body swaying side to side. Her head looked like it was on a roller—like one of those bobblehead dolls he had seen. This woman was crazy or drunk. Maybe she was both.

"I'm afraid you didn't understand me, ma'am," he said, shaking his head. "He isn't here. And I can't help you with that."

"You can and you will!" She screeched at him.

When he shook his head, she slapped the table in front of him. "I demand it, dammit. I demand you start showing some respect for the family in charge around here. And I demand that you recognize that the life that was lost was *far* inferior to the innocent life that is locked up. My boy has done nothing wrong, while that lesbian whore was a sinner through and through."

"Enough!" Wes surprised himself with the bellow that emerged from his chest. "I'll have none of that talk in my station, and you ought to be careful saying things like that around here in the middle of an active, ongoing investigation."

"Don't you *dare* threaten me, you bastard," she shouted, stepping forward and reaching for his Taser.

In one swift movement, he jerked his hips to the right, securing his weapons behind the counter. As if in slow motion, her heel caught in the crack of the tile. She twisted left and twisted right, contorting her body and attempting to right herself, before face planting on the tile.

"Fuck you," she shouted from the floor, completely forgoing what was left of her Southern charm and manners. "I'll make sure you pay for this."

"Your name won't get you out of this one, ma'am," he said, reaching down to help her up. She slapped his hand away, and he put his arms up in the air. As she stood, he pointed to the corner of the room. "If you'll glance up there, you'll note that whole mess was recorded on camera—everything from the words you spoke to threatening an officer by reaching for my weapon. So if I were you, I'd tread lightly. As it is, if you'll behave, I'm sure you can go see him in County."

She narrowed her eyes and dusted off her dress. Eyeing him carefully, she nodded after a moment of consideration. He thought about warning her again that every interaction they had would be recorded but decided he had given her plenty of warnings about recordings.

She spun on her heel to leave, but turned back, casting daggers at him with her eyes. "Even *if* he had killed the dyke, this wouldn't be appropriate punishment for him," she spat at him. "And there is no way his bond should be set at half a million dollars," she added before rushing out of the office.

She was gone before he could remind her that, if any family in Knell could afford that level of bond, it was probably the Westwicks. With her gone, he stared after her, dumbfounded. No doubt there were huge skeletons in the closet of that family, but certainly nothing that warranted that kind of hate.

Scratching his head, he took a seat back in his office. Had it been the hatred fostered by growing up in his father's house that bred that type of murderous anger? He took a deep breath and thought back. Trent's early childhood had no doubt taken its toll on the boy's development, but that didn't account for this.

Flipping through the files on his desk, he racked his brain. None of it made sense. The two kids had gone to school together and, much like everyone else in town, they had been mainstays in the community, constantly seeing each other around town at various events. With roots that deep, there was no explanation.

That, coupled with the fact that Trent had a near-airtight alibi for where he was that evening, despite evidence of his truck having been in her driveway, made this more of a mystery than he had ever been tasked with solving.

Regardless of the fact it was no longer under his jurisdiction, he felt like he owed it to his community—to Chloe and everyone who knew and loved her—to figure it out, at least partially.

The coroner's report had told them much of what they already knew. She had suffered multiple stab wounds and died as a result. Prior to being stabbed, she also suffered blunt force trauma to the head and abdomen. Nothing else had been revealed that would shine the light they needed to put Trent up for good. If history in this town had anything to show, it was that those in charge rarely paid for their crimes—be it shoplifting, running amok, drinking and driving, underage partying, and now murder.

It was a good ol' boys' club. Always had been. But this time had to be different. He had a gnawing in his gut telling him Trent was far from innocent, but he needed something solid.

They had just enough to keep him locked up for now. But with his daddy's money, there was no doubt he'd have the best lawyer, and they'd need an airtight case.

He gulped as he again looked at the photos on his desk. The knife was one of Chloe's—a long chef's knife with the sharpest blade he'd ever seen. Whoever had done this had gone in without a weapon and utilized what was already in place. He shook his head, remembering the sight of it lying on the floor, near her bloodied body.

Now in evidence, the knife had come back with two sets of prints on it—Chloe's and one undetermined. Trent wasn't a match. In fact, Trent's prints and DNA were nowhere to be found at the scene.

He rubbed his eyes and in the darkness, all he could see were the smaller fingerprints next to Chloe's on the knife's handle. Maybe Trent was as innocent as he said he was, or maybe he had been smart about carrying out his anger. Flipping the binder of evidence shut, Wes stood.

There were too many questions, and other detectives were working on the case. One way or another, the truth would come to light. And someone would pay for what had been done here.

For now, he needed out of this place. He grabbed his belongings, got in his car, and headed across town to McCool's.

When he opened the door of the old, darkened bar, a wave of air-conditioning swept past him. It felt as if it were a welcoming sign. Even if it wasn't, he was going to take it as such.

"Hey, Wes," Louie called out from behind the bar. Aside from an old timer at the corner of the bar, the place was dead—a rare sight on any evening.

"Hey, Lou," he replied, tipping his hat in greeting. "Where's the crowd?"

Louie shrugged, as he poured a beer for Wes. Looking over his shoulder while beer poured into the glass, he made eye contact with Wes. "It's been this way all week. I don't think it bodes well for business that this was the last place she was seen alive."

"I see," Wes nodded, taking a seat on a barstool directly across from Louie.

"Are you here to ask more questions?" Louie asked. "I've been answering them for days, and I don't have much new to add."

"No more questions tonight, I don't think," Wes said. "At least none that will give us the answers we need." He lowered his voice. "Truth is, I don't know what to think right now."

"None of us do," Louie said. He looked at the back wall and then back to Wes, nostalgia washing over his expression. "It's not the same in here without her, you know? She wasn't in here every day. But she came to see me often, and she was a ray of sunshine. All that stuff that made her so *different* really didn't matter that much. She was who she was, and it's a damn shame she's not here anymore."

Wes gulped his beer and nodded. He wished they could talk about anything else, but this was it. This was all there was to talk about these days. "She was."

"I miss her," Louie said. "And I don't care what they say about evidence. It was Trent, and we all know it. I threw the bastard out of here that night for being so damn hateful. And then it happened. When the news hit, everyone who was in the bar that night knew who did it. No doubt in my mind, that boy's guilty as sin."

"We'll get to the bottom of it, I'm sure," Wes said, wanting to echo Louie's sentiments but careful about doing so with the ongoing investigation.

Louie tight-lined his lips, taking the cue. "I know you can't talk about it and you've already got my statement. I just wanted to tell you again how I feel about the whole mess. I feel it in my gut. I know it. And soon everyone else will too."

Wes nodded and held his beer glass up in a mock cheers symbol. It was the most he could do to show his solidarity. Louie grabbed his towel and wiped down the bar, letting Wes unwind in silence for a few minutes. After topping off the older man at the other side of the bar, Louie came back. "There's a ball game on tonight. Why don't we put that on, and I'll serve you up a burger?"

"You've got a deal," Wes said, thankful for the chance to let his mind zone out on something of no importance in the scheme of life. That once was the way of life around here, and he was thankful for it to return, no matter how briefly.

His phone buzzed in his pocket. With a sigh, he fished it out, setting it on the table next to his beer.

*We think the prints are from a female,* it read.

He wanted to fling the damn phone. Of course they were. They were smaller than Chloe's. Anyone could have deduced as much, but that still didn't get them any closer to an answer—to justice. Closing his eyes, he forced a deep breath, but all he could see was that bloodstained knife. Jerking his head back up, he gulped down his beer and put money down on the table.

"Cancel the burger, Lou," he called out, as he stood. He couldn't be out in public, not like this. Maybe that's why this place was empty. No one could face what had happened.

* * *

The wind whistled from the south side of the field, blowing dust along the breeze. Bill glanced up at the skies, his thoughts a million miles from where he stood. Cattle bellowing in the field reminded him that, even if he didn't want to move an inch from this spot where it felt like he was able to glimpse a little bit of heaven, he still had work to do. Dutifully making his rounds, he threw the bales of hay and glanced down at his calloused hands.

He had never felt like more of a country song cliché than he currently did. Taking a seat on the last bale of hay, he buried his head in his hands.

The service today had been nice and it had been packed enough to fill the entire football stadium. He closed his eyes and thought back to the sea of faces, all familiar—but looking foreign in the moment. Many had loved his Chloe, and he was grateful they all showed up today. Even her old, childhood friends like Katy who had moved away had come down to celebrate her life.

But it hadn't felt like the proper goodbye. This was his proper goodbye, devoid of suits and stuffiness and filled with nothing but the earth and natural beauty he and Chloe had always shared. Tears fell as he thought of her climbing up on the hay bale next to him and realizing it would always be just a thought. Just a memory.

"Excuse me," a woman's voice drew him from his thoughts.

He cleared his throat and stood, wiping his hands on his jeans. In front of him stood a stranger with dark eyes, dark hair, and a gentle smile. "May I help you?" He cleared his throat and sniffed again to remove the remnants of the tears that had gathered but not yet fallen.

"I'm sorry to interrupt," she said, stepping forward slowly and extending her right hand. "I'm Dominique Velez."

He narrowed his eyes, trying to figure out if he'd ever seen her before and why she would come on a day like this. She wasn't wearing funeral clothes, but was dressed like she didn't really belong here, in dark jeans and impractical shoes. Regardless, he removed his hat and returned her handshake. "Bill Stanton. Nice to meet you."

"I know it's probably a bad time." She took a step back and shifted her weight from leg to leg.

He wanted to tell her she was right and that there probably wasn't a good time, but he could tell she was as uncomfortable as he felt. His manners kicked in before he could tell her to scram. "It's all right. What can I do for you?"

"That's the question I should be asking you," she said. "I'm here to help if you need anything."

He looked out into the field, raising an eyebrow. What could this woman do? What could anyone do—especially someone he'd never met? He shook his head.

"I am in town from Austin. I should have started with that. I know you don't know me, and I don't know you or your history here. But I came down here with hopes of lending a helping hand if I can. My organization works for social equality. We work to educate, counsel, and change hearts to help keep situations like what occurred here from happening."

"Situations like the one that occurred here?" he asked, the words sounding hollow and useless. "This isn't a situation. This is my daughter's death...*murder*. My daughter's murder."

"I know, sir." She took a deep breath. "I'm very sorry to hear about what happened to Chloe. I can't imagine what you are feeling."

"Don't try. It'll pull you under." She cocked her head to the side and he sighed, taking his seat on the bale of hay. "You'd be better off going back to Austin and not getting caught up in this small town mess, not getting drawn into the heartache and confusion that comes with having one you love ripped from your life—all because she wasn't what people wanted her to be. Hell, she wasn't different from them. She was better than them. She was a hard worker, which is what people 'round here pride themselves on. She was kind, polite, maybe a little wild. She was exactly who we all want to be. Just 'cause she was free and lived life on her own terms, she's suddenly gone. None of that is something you can wrap your mind around, especially if you didn't know her. I don't really think there's anything you can do for me, but I appreciate you stopping by to offer your condolences."

"I know I can't do anything to make it hurt less or to make it easier," she said, obviously reluctant to leave. "But what I'm hoping is I can be by your side if you do need anything."

"What is it you're offering?"

"I'm not offering anything other than someone to listen and if you need help with anything in the future." She paused and picked over her words, moving her eyes side to side. "The thing is, I'm going to head back to Austin soon. And my visit out here would be pointless if I didn't at least introduce myself to you. There's never a really good time to talk about these things, but I want you to know who I am in case you choose to do something we can help with in the future. A lot of parents in these situations want to speak out after they've had time to process what happened. If you want to do that or would like a larger platform from which to speak, we can offer that help."

"Again with the word 'situation.' What kind of *situation* are you referring to?"

"A hate crime."

The words cut through every shroud of composure he had worked to hold. "Every crime is a hate crime, isn't it? I mean, at least every murder." His words were barely above a whisper, and he felt like he'd been punched in the gut.

"This one was specific. You and I have both heard the details. I'm sure you're more in-the-know than anyone, but you know why she was murdered."

"No, I don't," he said, standing and shaking his head. "I have no idea who would take my sweet girl off this earth or what reason they could find for doing it. If you're looking for a puppet to decry a hate crime, I'm not it. I think there was a lot more to my girl than just being gay. And I've read every story too. I've talked to the police. I know what they're saying, and I guess it might be true that *different* might just not have fit in with Knell. But I'm not your guy. The only thing I'll talk about is how amazing my Chloe was and the fact that she didn't deserve this. She also didn't deserve to be put on a poster telling the rest of the world to stop killing people. That much should go without saying."

The woman in front of him gulped and nodded. "I'll be going. I know it's a bad time and I apologize. If you ever need anything though, we're around and we'd love to do anything we can for you and your family."

"There is no family," he said, waving at her to seal her dismissal. "Just me now. Have a good evening, ma'am. And take my advice. Don't go sticking your nose where it doesn't belong around here. Even in these circumstances, I'm the friendliest guy you'll meet here. Do my Chloe a favor and stop trying to exploit a 'situation,' as you call it."

She bit her lip, and he prayed she wouldn't dare speak again. Thankfully, she nodded and got back into her car.

Her words continued to play in his head like a broken record. *Hate crime.* She was right. He knew it. But the way he looked at it, Chloe's killer should be punished to the full extent of the law for killing someone so innocent and beautiful—not just because she had been gay. She was a person, and that's what he wanted to drive home to these people. It was the same as if any of these others had lost someone. It should hold the same merit, but clearly it didn't. All he had to show for community support was a couple of casseroles, one or two people who stopped by, and an out-of-town equality lady who had tried to ruin his day. Other than that, everyone else had kept their distance.

That drove the "hate crime" language straight into his heart and made him want to leave this place as quickly as he could. But he couldn't. He was stuck here—stuck in Knell without answers, without anyone, with a "hate crime" to deal with.

# CHAPTER EIGHT

The scent of fresh blueberries wafted through the shop as Amelia pulled the oven door open to marvel at her creation. Blueberry muffins, baked from scratch.

"Mmm," she breathed in, verbally succumbing to the simple beauty in something so small. If this was her life, she was going to have to start enjoying the bits and pieces that made sense, and muffins always made sense.

She sat her hot pad down on the counter, leaving the oven door open for one minute longer to give herself the chance to close her eyes and relish the moment. In the past three weeks, nothing had made her feel as whole as this moment—this silly, muffin-filled moment.

Snapping out of it, she sighed and opened her eyes. She cocked her head to the side and peered inside at her creations. They really were *just* muffins, even if seconds earlier they had felt like an answered prayer. Shaking her head, she pulled them from the oven and set them on the counter to cool.

She heard the ding of the door and straightened her shoulders. What a fool she would look like if someone had caught her marveling at her muffins. She stifled a giggle, the words replaying through her brain. Surely she was losing her mind. There was no other excuse for the way she was easing through the day, for the first time in the weeks that had passed seeing positives instead of just Chloe's face. The thought of Chloe sent a pang of fresh agony through her heart. She stiffened and let the moment wash over her as she had learned to do in the moments of silence she'd been taking since Chloe's passing. She dusted her hands on her apron and made her way to the front of the store.

"Good morning," she called out, before she could see who was on the other side of the counter. "Sorry, I was in the back making today's bakery items."

"Not a problem." Dominique's gentle words calmed her and she smiled—the first genuine smile aimed at someone else to grace her lips in days. Her heartbeat quickened, and her mood lightened in an instant as she rounded the corner to the front, her feet moving at twice their normal pace.

"I'm glad it's you. I didn't know you were back in town."

"I got in late last night. It's time for my monthly check in— just a routine thing we're trying out in places affected by…er… this kind of thing—so I wanted to come and check in. And I'm glad, too." Dominique's smile grew. "What were you making back there?"

"Has it really been a month?" Amelia shook her head, even though she could see the date flashing in red in her mind. "Of course it has," she said waving her hand in the air. "To answer your question, I made muffins." She glanced down at the countertop, as she remembered the weirdness of her behavior. Her cheeks flushed, embarrassed even though Dominique had no way of knowing. "Just some blueberry muffins," she added. "Sorry, I'm a bit scattered this morning." She shrugged, knocking over the display of paper coffee cups in front of her. "Just like that." She scrambled to pick them up. To her surprise, Dominique leaned over the countertop to help her. When Dominique's hand brushed her own, she giggled. *Again with the giggling!* She had to get a grip on whatever was happening in her mind before she would make good company for anyone—let alone make a good business owner.

"I'm sorry," she blurted out, wishing she could erase all of her erratic behavior since Dominique had walked into the shop.

"Stop apologizing," Dominique said, laughter ringing through the air. "It's not a big deal. I just wanted to stop in and see how you were doing, and maybe grab some coffee or something to eat. You always have tasty things here."

"You like them?" Her voice was too chipper, too excited at the thought that *Dominique* of all people liked her pastries. She cleared her throat. "I'm glad to hear that," she added before Dominique could answer. "What are you in the mood for today?"

"Could I trouble you for a little conversation and one of those muffins?"

"Yes to both," she said, wanting nothing more than to shirk all of her day's responsibilities and sit on the couch next to Dominique, filling her in on everything she was feeling, as well as listening to the adventures of Dominique's day. It had become something she looked forward to every couple of days. Lately it had been via telephone or Skype, since a non-profit's budget didn't really allow for extended stays away from home. Over the course of their conversations, she had learned so much about herself, about life, about this whole "fight for equality" thing she had always brushed under the table. Most importantly, she had learned the importance of connecting with someone—truly connecting, be it for friendship or any sort of bond. She smiled as she walked back toward the kitchen. She would have gladly taken a phone call or Skype call, but this was special. This was a treat, and she was going to take advantage of it.

"One muffin coming right up!" she said, cheerily making her way to the couch where Dominique had already taken a seat. "Tell me all about life in Austin." Amelia took a seat. "I want to hear about those things. I want to hear about the work you're doing. We can get to me and things around here later."

Dominique smiled but questions danced in her eyes. "I'm fine, I promise," Amelia said. "I just want to talk about something else for a change. All I ever do is talk about—or talk around—what happened here. I want something new for a day. Talk to me. Spill it about the 'big city' life." She added air quotes and nodded expectantly.

"Fine," Dominique said, letting out a mock sigh. "I'll fill you in on my weird life, even though we talked about it just a couple of days ago. Things in Austin are just fine. They're busy. Around the office, we are worried about things down here. It seems like they're still stalling the case but you know that. We're just worried it'll go south and the good ol' boy system will win out. That's mainly my work life."

Amelia frowned and Dominique held her hands up. "Don't worry. I'm not going to stop there. I was just letting you know you probably don't want to ask about work. You know about work. Other than that, I talked to you two days ago. Not much has changed, although I did have some sushi that was out-of-this-world amazing last night."

"With a girl?" Amelia squeaked the question, unsure why the inquiry made her stomach flip flop.

"Yes." Dominique nodded, taking a bite of the muffin. "This is delicious, by the way." Amelia fought to keep her expression neutral while she waited for details of the sushi date. "And no... not in *that* way," Dominique said, raising an eyebrow in Amelia's direction. "Just a girl who is my friend. We've been friends since college."

"Is there a girl in *that* way?" Amelia pulled her legs up onto the couch, crossing them beneath her, excited to have something that felt fresh. She gazed into Dominique's eyes, transfixed. She watched them flutter and felt almost as if she was a kid at a slumber party fighting sleep and engaging in gossip. As Dominique chewed the bite of muffin in her mouth, Amelia's mind went crazy. What if there was a girl? Would that mean this—whatever *this* was—would come to a halt? Would that mean Amelia didn't hold a special place in Dominique's life anymore? Did she even hold a special place now? The questions were childish at best, but she couldn't wait for Dominique to answer. She felt her foot tapping on the couch and grabbed it with her hand to make it stop.

"There isn't," Dominique finally said, wiping the corners of her mouth with a napkin. "At least, not right now. You never know what the future holds, and from my experience, lesbians don't tend to stay single for too long. At least, I never really did until recently."

"You can't just leave it at that," Amelia urged. "Tell me more."

"I had a messy break-up about a year ago. Since then, I've taken some time to focus on myself and my career. I've focused a lot of attention on what I need in life. It's been good. One of these days, I'll try my hand in the dating game again."

"What's your type?"

Dominique straightened her shoulders and held her breath for a second before laughing. "Where are all these questions coming from?"

"Curiosity…or maybe just a need to know more. I don't know." She was talking at rapid speed again and she fought to control her words. "I guess I want to know more. I don't know that much about dating women, and I think I'd like to try at some point. Maybe. Down the road. Not now. I don't know what I want. I want lesbian gossip. Before Chloe, I always felt alone. And then I wasn't alone…and then I was. Now you're here too. So I'm not alone again, and I want to ask you the questions I never had a chance to ask anyone else."

"That's understandable," Dominique said, relaxing back onto the couch and taking another bite of her muffin. "Why don't we start slow? Let's just talk about the basics. Are you a lesbian? Are you bi? I know we've talked about it and you weren't really sure. Are you saying you're a lesbian?"

"I am," Amelia said, letting out a sigh of relief. "I've never admitted that to anyone. I always just told Chloe that I liked girls too, never that it was my only option. I mean, I finally said it to myself the other day, and of course I've done things that make it fairly obvious. But I've come to terms with it. That's who I am."

"I'm proud of you." Dominique placed a hand on Amelia's shoulder. The slight touch felt like electricity, and Amelia sucked in a sharp breath.

"Thanks," she managed, even though it felt like the world was moving beneath her. "I know now, more than ever, it's important to be who I am—even if that's scary. I know that I have to figure out the rest. And I will, in time. For now, I'm admitting that to me and to you. And the rest will fall into place."

Dominique nodded. "You're making great progress, just in the time I've known you."

"You've helped a lot in that. You've made me feel comfortable. Thank you."

Dominique leaned in for a hug and Amelia caught the scent of berries in her perfume. Her body tingled as she pulled Dominique closer. She wasn't sure what it was she was feeling, but it had to be wrong. They were here for Chloe—not for anything else. She pulled away from the hug, right as the door chimed.

She jumped up as if she had been caught and scurried behind the counter. Her face fell as she saw Bill Stanton remove his hat.

"Morning, Amelia," he said, stepping up to the counter. He glanced toward the couch and she watched his face change.

As he locked eyes with Dominique, the air in the room seemed colder. Tension was palpable. Amelia furrowed her brow and he sighed. "I was hoping you and I could talk a minute. But I can come back." He worked to keep his voice low, but Dominique was already gathering her things and heading for the door.

"Good to see you again, Mr. Stanton," she said as she reached for the door handle. "I'll see you later, Amy."

Amelia shot a questioning look and Dominique held her hand up to her face like a phone, mouthing, "Call me." Amelia nodded and waved, still confused. She turned her attention back to Bill.

"Good morning, Mr. Stanton," she said, offering him a warm smile. "What can I do for you?"

"What was *she* doing here?" he asked, no longer interested in whatever had brought him in here.

"She's a friend of mine," Amelia said, her tongue tripping over the words. "She came into town to help with things after what happened, and she and I kept in touch."

"Hmm." He raised an eyebrow and pursed his lips, turning his attention to the menu behind Amelia on the wall. "It's pretty quiet in here today, isn't it?" he asked, not looking away from the menu.

"It is today," she said with a shrug. "I think everyone is at work. And most of my regulars have already been in and out. I don't expect too many interruptions."

"Good."

"Would you like a coffee? On the house."

"You don't have to do that." His words were devoid of emotion, and she wished she could break through that wall. It was the same one his daughter had often put up. "I'm a paying customer. You've done enough by the coffee and pastries you brought over to the house."

"I insist," she said. "Anything you like."

"Black and strong, please," he said, reaching for his wallet despite her earlier statement.

She shook her head and he finally made eye contact, his expression softening. "Thank you," he added putting his wallet back into his back pocket.

She nodded and poured the coffee. It was the same way Chloe had always taken it. She reminisced and felt a soft smile tug at the corners of her mouth. They were quite a bit alike, those two. Behind her, Bill took a seat on the barstool next to the counter. When she handed him the cup of coffee, he placed his hand over hers. "Is it okay if I sit here and maybe talk to you a bit?"

"Of course," she said, pulling up the stool she kept behind the counter so they were eye to eye. "I'd enjoy that. What did you have in mind?"

"Well, I want to get to what I originally came in here for in a minute. But first things first, I'm not sure I trust that woman who was in here. What was her name? Desiree?"

"Dominique," Amelia corrected gently. "How do you know her?" Dominique had never mentioned anything about Bill.

"She stopped by my house right after Chloe was murdered… well, a few days after, and it left a bad taste in my mouth. I don't know who she is or what business she has here."

"She's just trying to help, I think," Amelia said. "I know she's not from here, but I think her intentions are good."

"Okay," he said half-heartedly. "Just don't get caught up in something where they want to use Chloe as an example. I'm not about all that."

"I get it," Amelia said. "I think it's about something bigger than Chloe. It's about a systemic problem, and she just wants to offer support and educate others to make sure this doesn't happen somewhere else."

He narrowed his eyes. "It never should have happened here." He fidgeted, lightly pounding his fist against the counter.

"I agree." She took the moment of silence to look him over and take in his appearance. His face was weathered, even more so than just a few weeks ago. The lines around his eyes had deepened, as had the circles beneath them. She wanted to hug him but instead reached across and held his hand. "I cared about your daughter, too. I know you know me as the coffee girl down the street and the kid who got straight As all the way through school. Even if Chloe was a couple of years older than I was, I'm sure you weren't able to escape the small town talk where everyone's kids know everyone else. And that's who I was to them. That's how most people around here know me, but I was close to your daughter. I miss her terribly, too. I know nothing can make this better and it all seems pretty scary. There are people here we don't even know. We've seen our share of investigators, lawyers, and even some support people like Dominique. Just because they're not all familiar doesn't mean they're bad. And just so you know, since I know her, I'll make sure everything done about this by her organization honors the way Chloe lived and how she would want to be portrayed."

"Thank you," he said, his voice thick with emotion. "I just don't want them painting her as some kind of civil rights activist when all she was doing was living her life."

"In a sense, isn't that the most bold type of activist?" she asked, thinking back to how Chloe had lived life so out-loud and proud without ever really having to say anything. She just was. "She never shoved it in anyone's face, but she never hid. She never tried to be anything other than what she was and she wouldn't take anyone's disapproval to heart. She lived her life as a proud gay woman and showed everyone how damn happy she was."

"I guess you might be onto something there," he said as a sad smile formed on his lips. "Anyway, enough about that. Why don't you tell me about the side of my daughter you knew? Who was she to you?"

Amelia bit her lip and lowered her gaze. It was now or never. There was no sense lying to a man who already knew who his daughter was, particularly right after she had just praised Chloe for living so proudly. "I was…I…" she sighed. Words were inadequate and there was no real description for what she had been. She glanced into his eyes, hoping he'd save her from having to find the words, but he waited patiently. "I was dating her," she said when no better term came to mind.

"That's what I thought," he said. "That means you knew her well. You knew who my girl was, and you can help to honor her memory. That's what I wanted to make sure. I also just wanted to talk to someone else around here who might actually talk about it, about her, instead of just shying away from it like it's too painful to talk about."

"What do you mean?" she asked, giving him an opportunity to share what he was feeling, even though she knew exactly what he meant. If it hadn't been for Dominique, she wouldn't have been able to verbally process anything either. Everyone around here just talked about how they couldn't believe it, how Trent couldn't have done it, and how Knell would never be the same.

No one seemed to delve deeper, to talk about the mark Chloe left on this place, or to even mention her name. It made mourning her even lonelier.

"You know what I mean," he said as if reading her mind. "I want to talk about that stubborn passion for life, the way she'd grit her teeth and jump headfirst into any challenge, the way she'd make anyone mad as hell with that temper and that refusal to take 'no' for an answer, the way her smile would light up a room and diffuse a tense situation. I want to talk about that, to remember it. I want her to be remembered for everything—not just for being the only gay person in this small little town." He trailed off, looking out the window. "You know, this place has always been my home. Lately it feels like hell. It feels like I'm an outsider and I don't know how to get back in."

"I know the feeling," she said, patting his hand gently. "Let's talk about her. Let's remember." She recalled their last night together and bit her lip. She still couldn't share that with anyone. "When she first started coming into my shop every day, it was a breath of fresh air. She was always humming some different tune. She was like the cool kid everyone wants to be but will never be. She had this air of confidence about her. Looking back, I know it was well deserved. She deserved to feel like the coolest person on the planet, because she was. Always listening to rock music, dressing like one of the guys and working harder than all of them. She was strong but not just physically. She was mentally strong and fierce in determination—whether it was fixing a leaky sink or finally mastering baking an apple pie. Whatever it was she was going to do, she was going to be the best. I miss seeing someone so alive and driven."

"Me, too," he said. A half smile lifted the left corner of his mouth. "She made an apple pie?" His eyes sparkled with amusement. "She once told me she could burn water, and I believed it. I ate some of her early creations."

"She did," Amelia said, settling on her stool. She smiled and recounted the memory for Bill. "I told her it was my favorite in passing, and she and her big heart got in the way of her just buying it or letting me make one. I had a rough week a while back. Some stuff was going on financially and the stress of running a business had gotten to me. I was stressed and she called, insisting that I come see her. I gave in and drove over, only to find a freshly baked apple pie on her dining room table. Later, after I raved and raved about how delicious it was—and it was—she admitted it was the third one she had tried to make that day. She had told me 'those damn recipe books just don't tell you all you need to know.' Even so, she mastered it. I never found anything she couldn't master."

"That was my Chloe." A single tear slid down his cheek. "Sorry," he said, hiding his face.

"Don't apologize for that," she said, leaning forward. "I've cried many tears myself, and it's okay to miss her. In fact, I'd be worried if you hadn't shown that kind of emotion. She was the most genuine, most beautiful soul I'd ever met. And it's okay if tears come with memories."

He nodded and cleared his throat. He tipped his coffee cup up to his mouth and drank the last of it. "I've got to get going, but I'm going to stop back in here from time to time, if you're okay with that. I think this did my old heart some good."

"You're welcome anytime," she said, standing when he did. She walked around the corner and wrapped him in a hug.

"Thank you…for the coffee, the chat, and for telling me the truth. I just want someone who will remember her the way I do." He turned to go but stopped before he reached the door.

"What is it?" she asked, as he looked over his shoulder.

He shook his head and walked back toward her, taking time to look closely at her right hand, which she had placed on the counter. Knitting her brow, she glanced down at her hand as well while he stared in silence.

"Small hands," he said quietly, after a moment of observation.

"Yes, sir," she said. "Any reason that's important?" His behavior was odd, but she didn't feel uncomfortable.

"I'm sorry," he said, taking a step back. "It's just that they can't find the prints of the Westwick kid or anyone else anywhere. Ah damn! That's supposed to be stuff I don't know. They just told me because I'm friends with Wes, but no one is really supposed to know the details. Don't say anything, okay?"

She nodded and stepped closer, needing to know more. "I won't say anything."

He eyed her cautiously and sighed, leaning against the counter. "All right. If Chloe trusted you, I guess I do too. Thing is, Ryan's name is cleared for the most part. We can't put him anywhere near the scene of the crime. In my heart of hearts, I also know he's not capable of this. But everything in my gut points to Westwick." He shook his head, disgust seeping through his features. "His damn prints aren't anywhere in the house though. His truck tires are a match for the ones in her driveway, and they match the time stamp when he would have been there to commit the murder. But there were only two sets of prints on that knife. Chloe's, and one set with smaller prints. Thought maybe you might know something about it."

His tone wasn't accusatory. She breathed a sigh of relief. "Thanks for not thinking it was me who did this," she said, letting out a sad laugh. "I think that would have been my first guess had something like this happened and I thought it could have been someone's prints on the knife." She glanced at the ground, recalling the last time she had used that knife. "They probably were mine." She gulped. "I made her dinner that evening...before she went out. I did my share of checking on things in the case. Benefits of a small town full of gossip. I got chills when I saw the knife, the same one I used to slice her brisket that evening."

Bill winced. Turning away, he nodded. "I won't say anything," he said, waving as he headed back for the door. "I know you don't want all that out in the open yet, so it's just good peace of mind for her papa. Now I can target all of what I feel at the Westwick boy and know there's not someone else out there."

She nodded and waved as he walked out the door. Dominique's face flashed in her mind, next to Chloe's. It felt as though they were ships about to collide, even if one was no longer in the water. She knew what she was feeling for Dominique. Her feelings were forbidden, but they were growing daily.

But it wasn't right. How could she even entertain the thought of wanting to flirt with someone when Chloe was supposed to hold that spot? And given what was unearthed over coffee with Bill, it was apparent those memories weren't going to just fade away.

She walked over to the window, noting how everyone had gone on about their lives, just as Bill had said. No one was coming into the shop for a while, so she flipped the sign to "Closed" and locked the door. Sitting back down on the couch, she laid her head back as hot tears stung her eyes.

She knew only one thing: her heart had never been this confused or in this much pain.

# CHAPTER NINE

Fireflies flitted through the air, mixing with the stars near the riverbank. Dominique breathed in deeply, pleased to find that it smelled of nature—not city. The small campfire they had lit filled the air with a scent reminiscent of childhood and vacations. It danced in the background, creating a magical glow to an already perfect setting. Of course, there was the slight hint of cow manure mingled into the mix of smells, but it was a welcome change, a chance to unwind.

"What are you thinking about?" Amy's sweet voice interrupted her thoughts but in no way changed her level of serenity.

"I was just thinking how nice it is out here. And even though the circumstances suck, I like getting to come down here and visit." Amy smiled and moved closer to stand beside her. Though they were still half a foot apart, Dominique's body went wild. She was playing with fire, but she wasn't the only pyromaniac out there tonight. "And to see you," she added quietly.

"I get it," Amy said, turning to face Dominique. "I hate the reason you have to come visit. But I love when you do. Sometimes I feel guilty because I enjoy your visits so much, and I don't want you to leave. I know you have important work and that this is part of that work. Even so, I'm really thankful you get to come see me. Being here in person with you sure beats seeing you on a Skype screen—not that I don't like that, but this is better." She winked and turned her face upward to the sky. Dominique was grateful she had turned away, because that wink was almost enough to undo her.

"It is pretty tonight," Amelia said, tracing her fingers through the sky as if to connect the stars.

"It sure is," Dominique said, not looking up at the sky. She was staring at the one who had her attention—the quirky, rambling, hot mess of nerves with a bold heart, Southern charm, and just enough mystery to drive her crazy. Amy's soft-looking lips were curved upward into a smile and the moonlight spilled over her, glinting off her green eyes and showcasing the flecks of gold Dominique had known were in there somewhere. She longed to wrap her fingers in those locks of thick, dark hair. But she steeled herself. She was still here for work, and Amy was still someone who was hurting from a significant loss.

This was wrong. She bit her tongue, hoping to feel pain instead of lust, and let out a sigh when the move failed to still the tightening of her stomach.

"Why do you like it out here so much?" Amy's question danced in the breeze.

"I like the peaceful nature and change of pace. I also like the company." Her voice came across low and husky, and she wished she could take the words back into her mouth.

"I do, too," Amy said, the right corner of her lips turning up into a half grin. "I really do. I appreciate you spending so much time with me."

"In true Texan fashion, this is where I say 'it's my pleasure, ma'am,' but it really is." She felt every bit as cheesy as that line. But she couldn't help herself.

Amy winked again, and Dominique tensed. Everything in her body felt as though it was melting, yet tight as a knot, all at once. "Yeah?" Amy asked. "So I'm not as crazy as you must have thought I was that first night?"

"I never thought you were crazy. I thought you were shaken up, which you were. You're not crazy at all. You're a good person. An amazing person."

Amy leaned in for a hug, and Dominique's skin tingled from being so closely pressed up against Amy's entire frame. When Amy pulled back slightly and gazed into her eyes, Dominique's breathing quickened. Amy leaned forward and gingerly placed a soft kiss on Dominique's cheek. She pulled back again, but she wasn't smiling. Much like she knew her own had to be, Amy's eyes were smoldering. Dominique could feel Amy's heartbeat quicken with every passing second. Amy took one hand and placed it over Dominique's heart, never breaking eye contact. Dominique wondered if Amy could feel the way her heart hammered in her chest, just the same as she could feel Amy's. Amy bit her lip and breathed in deeply. Then just as quickly as it had all started, it was over. Amy jerked herself back a foot away, as if catching herself in a dangerous position.

"Do you want to roast marshmallows?" Amy asked, quick—too quick—to fill the silence. "I have a bag of them in my backpack. Roasting sticks too."

"What a good wilderness explorer you are," Dominique answered, laughing to keep the mood light, even though her body was still trembling. "I'd love a marshmallow."

She gulped and tried to calm her frantic breathing. Wrong or not, the spark was there. She could feel the wetness that had formed between her legs at just a simple touch and knew she needed to back away from the dangers that lay ahead—dangers of hurting someone in such a vulnerable state, of making an even bigger mess than the one that currently existed in this sleepy little Texas town.

Still dazed, she took a seat on the log next to Amy and watched as Amy fumbled to open the bag of marshmallows, dropping it twice to the ground.

"Sorry," Amy said, smiling sheepishly as she picked up and dusted off the bag a second time. "I think maybe I caught a bit of a chill and it's making it so that I can't even grip this damn bag." She sat the bag in her lap and rubbed her hands on her jeans, even though they both knew it was an act meant to disguise the real reason Amy had freaked out.

"Need a hand?"

"Sure," Amy said, her hand shaking as she held the bag out. Dominique reached for it, careful not to brush against Amy's hand, knowing her body couldn't take much more of a jolt without intensifying the craving that had been spiraling out of control within her.

Focusing on the task at hand, she deftly opened the bag and handed it back over to Amy.

"I loosened it up for you," Amy laughed. "Just one of my many talents."

"I think you have more of them than you'd imagine."

Amy shrugged, then smiled. "Thanks," she said after a second. She put her marshmallow on her stick and placed it over the fire. Dominique couldn't help but stare. Amy's small, slender hands were soft. Dominique knew as much. But she wanted to know so much more. She longed to explore Amy's body, to give in to the tension that had been on a perpetual climb.

Amy glanced back at her, raising an eyebrow. "Am I doing it wrong?"

"No," Dominique laughed. "My bad. I think I was a little dazed. It's beautiful out here, and this night is great. I just got caught up in it."

Amy nodded and Dominique glanced over behind the log, diverting her attention to anything other than Amy for a minute. She was usually better at social cues and had known she was staring. But she felt unable to do anything else. Out of the corner of her eye, she saw her backpack.

Thankful for an excuse to get up, she walked over and grabbed it, smiling at the surprise waiting inside.

"I brought you a small gift," she said, taking her seat again, but this time leaving as much space in between them as possible.

"For me?" Amy shook her head and glanced down. Lifting her eyes, she smiled. "Thank you. You don't have to be as good to me as you are."

Dominique shrugged and pulled the bottle from inside the bag. "It's nothing huge. Just something I thought you might like." She held the bottle in one hand, waving the other over it like she had seen countless game show hosts do when presenting a prize.

Amy beamed as she accepted the gift. "Pecan whiskey?" She cocked her head to the side and gave a pleased smile, her dimple showing her joy. "How did you know?"

"I saw your collection when I was at your house. This may not be as fancy as the bottles you've got in your whiskey locker at home, but it is unique."

"Thank you," Amy said. She moved like she was going to offer a hug but then straightened her shoulders and leaned back into her original position. "Really. Thank you."

"Have you ever tried it?" Dominique took joy in the excited smile Amy was wearing, and wanted to keep it easy between them, to keep this joy intact.

"I haven't, but I'm excited to." Without warning, Amy leaned in for a side hug. "Thank you. You are amazing."

"As are you. I hope you like it."

"I can't wait to…" Amy trailed off and glanced in both directions. "I was going to say 'I can't wait to try it,' but I can't see a reason I have to wait. Let's get this sucker opened up."

Her eyes sparkled with mischief as she opened the bottle. She held the bottle up to her nose and took in a deep breath. She moaned in delight and Dominique again bit her lip, wondering if Amy had any idea what she was doing to her. "It smells so good, you won't even need to mix it." Amelia leaned her head back and took a sip. "I was right," she said, smiling as she wiped her lips with the back of her hand. "Try it."

Dominique marveled at Amy's ability to be overjoyed by the small things in life. Just one more attribute that made her so irresistible. Dominique accepted the whiskey and savored the taste. "It is good."

Warmth flooded through her, partially from the whiskey, but mostly from Amy's laughter.

Passing the bottle back and forth, sipping whiskey and watching the fire dance, conversation came easily.

"What was it like growing up here?" The question came out of left field in her mind, but Dominique scooped it up gratefully.

"Did you ever see Little House on the Prairie?"

Dominique raised an eyebrow and let out a small laugh. "Yeah?"

Amy shrugged. "It was that, but with color television and microwaves." She glanced down at the bottle of whiskey in her hand, took a swig, and glanced up at the sky. "Kind of makes me nostalgic thinking about it, you know?" Her face held no glimmer of teasing, but her words were laced with sarcasm. "Ma and Pa, chopping wood for the fire, a simpler time in a simple little town." Finally, her face broke into a smile and her laughter filled the air, ringing out crisp and clear and warming Dominique's heart.

"Come on," Dominique managed through her own laughter. "I don't buy it."

"Fine," Amy said, still laughing. "It wasn't quite that old timey. It was about like what you're experiencing with me tonight. Peaceful. Gentle. Full of memorable moments. Quiet. Full of hard work too, don't get me wrong. It was great, though. I left for a bit, thinking I'd find my home elsewhere. But this place draws you back in. Some think of it as a trap. I've always just thought of it as home. Home is the place you need to be— the place you want to be. I need to be here. I thrive here. This is my place and I wouldn't trade it for the world."

"Even now?"

"Especially now." She closed her eyes and took a deep breath. "Horrible things happen everywhere. I once thought they didn't happen here but they do. Clearly. It still doesn't change the fact that this is my home. And if I can find a way to make it an even better place, that's exactly what I'm going to do. I'm going to leave my home a brighter place."

Dominique nodded. "Understandable and admirable."

"I don't need to be admired." As she spoke, she turned to face Dominique. "Don't get me wrong. I love being admired as much as the rest, but I don't need it."

Her smile grew. "Devilish" was the only word that came to mind as Dominique watched her eyebrows rise. Amy scooted closer on the bench. "Do you like to be admired as well?" Her tone had dropped, holding the huskiness of hunger.

Dominique gulped, trying to find the words. It felt as though her tongue had swollen up to twice its normal size. She swallowed hard and nodded.

"Good," Amy said. "Because I admire many, many things about you." Amy bit her lip, then shook her head. Standing, she walked back and forth in front of the log, her confidence from only seconds earlier vanishing. "What I mean," she said, laughing nervously, "is that I think you're really great at your job, and you've been such an amazing help to me—and to others, I'm sure…" She trailed off and looked into the distance, downing another sip of whiskey before spinning on her heel and looking Dominique in the eye.

"Thank you," Dominique said, saving her from her nervous rambling. "I appreciate your kind words. And I enjoy the time I spend with you as well." The words felt forced, but she pushed them out anyway, both of them clearly masking the things they wanted to say.

She stood, closing the distance between them, and reached for the bottle of whiskey when Amy offered it. As their fingers brushed, Dominique's breath caught in her throat. She moved to pull the bottle closer to her, but Amy didn't relinquish her grip. When Dominique made eye contact, Amy looked confused and uncertain. Dominique smiled, hoping to ease the tension.

"I'm sorry." Amy dropped her grip on the bottle, letting it fall into Dominique's hand. "I…I don't know where my head is tonight. Maybe I'm just distracted." She let out a series of half-laugh, half-sigh sounds and threw her hands in the air. "Here I go again, being the crazy one." She shrugged and looked off into the distance.

Dominique laughed and placed a reassuring hand on Amy's shoulder. "You're not crazy, and you don't have to apologize."

"I'm rambling. I don't know why. I just am." Her words tumbled out quickly, and she turned around again to face Dominique.

"It's okay." Dominique's words were steady, even though her heart hadn't stopped pounding like a marching band within her chest.

Amy bit her lip and moved closer. "I..." She sighed and shook her head.

"I know," Dominique said quietly. "I know."

For a moment, Amy stared at her dumbfounded. Cocking her head to the side, she raised an eyebrow. "You too?"

The question was simple, but Dominique had thought the answer was obvious. "Of course." She trembled as she watched Amy's eyes darken—with knowing or with lust, she wasn't certain.

This time, when Amy bit her lip, Dominique reached up, running her hand up Amy's arm. In a flash, the sweet, innocent, rambling woman beside her had turned into a seductress, and Dominique couldn't find the words to halt the freight train. And worse yet, she couldn't decide if she wanted to. Amy followed suit, letting her fingers roam and explore, if only as brazenly as to touch Dominique's arm. As Amy's fingertips sizzled with electric fire on her skin, Dominique let out a ragged breath and held her hand up in protest, using all of the strength she had.

Amy stopped in her tracks. "I'm sorry." She cast her eyes down to the ground. "Did I cross a line?"

"I touched you first." Dominique looked up to the sky for answers.

"I wanted you to."

Dominique gulped, the last of her willpower hanging on by a thread. "Is it the whiskey?"

Amy let out a low, throaty laugh. "Not at all." She bit her lip, looking unsure once again, and Dominique sighed.

"You didn't do anything wrong." Dominique assured her. She lifted her hand to touch Amy but dropped it by her side. Amy laughed nervously. "Do you want me to touch you again?"

"I do," Amy said with a nod. "At least if that's what you want."

"It is."

"Come here," Amy beckoned, walking back to the log. Taking a seat, she appeared to be holding her breath while Dominique took a seat. But once they were both seated and she turned to face Dominique, her eyes shimmered with lust. "If this is what you want, and it's what I want, don't stop this time."

Dominique reached for Amy's hand, but Amy clearly had other plans. Amy placed her hand gently on Dominique's leg and pulled her closer. With a smile, Dominique threw her arm around Amy's shoulders. Amy's contented sigh filled the air, and Dominique nestled into the embrace.

"Tell me more," Dominique said. "What drove you to open up the bakery?"

Amy looked up, her nose crinkling as she thought about her response. "I'm good at it." She took another swig from the bottle. "Truth is, I was always pretty handy in the kitchen, and I like to make people happy. I like the smile they get when they reach for a muffin or bagel. I like watching kids' eyes grow as they see the pastries behind the glass. I know it's offering the world a simplistic kind of joy, but I really get a lot out of being the one to provide that joy. Whether it's a 'just broke up with someone,' eating-your-feelings kind of satisfaction or a truly decadent splurge, people seem happier when they leave. That, and the coffee shop kind of went in line with it, because coffee makes people into functional humans."

Dominique laughed. She liked that—the ease with which Amy made her laugh. "That's right. I know when I'm without coffee, I'm basically just a fussy toddler who needs a time out."

"We all are." Amy took a deep breath, her smile softening, as she traced the outline of Dominique's face with her fingertips. Dominique bit her lip and breathed in. A simple touch right now was enough to jumble her every thought. "What about you? Why do you do what you do?"

"Same reasons...but different." Dominique laughed. "Guess that doesn't make much sense, so I'll explain. I'm not sure there's a pinpoint moment that shaped my fate as an equality advocate, other than growing up feeling different. I had so much *different* placed on me as a kid. My parents came here from Mexico, and we were already the different ones in town. On top of that, we were broke. Incredibly broke. So, we were the poor, Hispanic family. I was already an outcast kid. When I got in touch with my feelings and realized I was gay in addition to everything else, I saw the depths of hatred. I was picked on, bullied, made to feel less than. But I wasn't alone. So many others were in the same boat. Someone had to speak for us and, since I was already so different, I figured it might as well be me."

"The hero we've been waiting for…" Amy chimed in. To Dominique's surprise, Amy's eyes held genuine admiration, not a mocking stare.

"I'm no hero," Dominique said with a laugh. "I just needed people to be better, to be decent. We all have good in us, and I want more people to show that. Truth be told, I am pretty sure I got into this field because I was pissed off at the disparities in the world. I'm not the first, by a long shot. This has been going on for decades, and I'm just lucky to be a part of it at this point in history."

"I get the pissed off thing." Amy looked off into the distance and set the bottle on the ground. "I really do."

"You have every right to be as pissed off as any of us." Instinctively Dominique reached down and laced her fingers through Amy's. "Every right," she repeated.

"What do I do about it?" Amy tightened her fingers around Dominique's.

"I think you're on the right track."

Forming her lips into a tight line, Amy nodded and let out a sigh. "Tell me more about you."

"What do you want to know?"

Amy raised an eyebrow and stroked her chin playfully. Without warning, she bolted upright in her seat. "I've got an idea. Why don't we make this a true girls' night out at the campsite and play a little truth or dare?"

Warning signals flashed in Dominique's mind, but she inexplicably nodded. "Sounds like a plan." She gave a thumbs-up signal and mentally chided herself. Who was she right now?

She didn't give thumbs-up signs. That was the equivalent of shooting your crush the finger guns, complete with a clicking throat sound.

Amy just smiled and slid back on the log to sit cross-legged. "You go first. Truth or dare?"

"Truth."

Amy looked up at the stars, crinkling her nose as she searched for the perfect option. "Hmm," she said after a moment and then leveled her gaze. "Time to dig deep. If you were stranded, what are three things you would want to have with you?"

"I'm assuming I don't have a cell phone?"

"Nope. No cell phone."

"In that case, chapstick, food, and someone who makes me laugh."

"Damn," Amy said, shaking her head. "I was hoping I'd get to come."

"How do you know you're not the one who makes me laugh?" Dominique winked as the words dripped off her tongue. If only Amy had the slightest idea how often she lifted Dominique's spirits, that wouldn't have even been a question.

"Good," Amy said. "I guess that makes it my turn, and I pick truth as well."

"What is the stupidest thing you've done that someone dared you to do?"

Amy let out a groan and looked upward. "Let me preface this with the fact that I was young and stupid and if you're asking to see how many stupid things you can make me do on a dare, I'll warn you that I've grown up a bit." She put her hands up in mock caution. Just as quickly, she shook her head. "Who the hell am I kidding? I'm still too competitive to let a dare stand. Anyway." She let out a sigh but didn't cast her eyes downward. Instead, she made full eye contact and raised an eyebrow. "When I was sixteen, we had a huge snowstorm. We're talking drifts a few feet deep. It was a freak thing, but we were playing truth or dare, and a friend of mine dared me to take off all my clothes, except my snow boots, and run around in the snow for ten minutes. I did it. I also dove into a snow bank to cover myself up so I didn't get caught when her parents came outside to check on us."

"Ouch," Dominique winced.

"Yeah. I got some frostbite in some places and some cold burns in others, but I won the game." Dominique couldn't control her laughter. She watched as Amy shrugged and laughed along with her. "Your turn."

Dominique bit her lip, considering her options. "After that bold of a dare was even mentioned, I think I'll stick with truth."

"Come on, spice it up with a dare," Amy teased. "There's not even snow on the ground." She laughed for a second and then her demeanor changed. Her devilish smile returned, and her dimple twitched. "What do you find attractive in a woman?"

"I like a woman with a sense of humor, who can make me laugh, even if she's not trying to be overtly funny. I like someone who gets deep on life issues, but also has a playful side. And I'm a sucker for sweet women, women who make a difference through their kindness. Being genuine and honest is also a huge turn-on."

"What about physically?" Amy narrowed her eyes.

"You're only supposed to get one question, but I'll let it slide this time. Pretty eyes are my weakness—and those can be any color. Green, blue, brown. As long as they're the type of eyes that glimmer in the light, that show me the sparkle of the woman. I also prefer women with longer hair and of course..." She looked off into the distance. "Of course, boobs."

Amy giggled. "Who doesn't love boobs? I think that's why I'm gay."

"Really? It's all about the boobs?"

"Not all," she said. With a shrug, she added, "I mean, maybe that's not the entirety of the reason...but it is close."

Dominique laughed and shook her head. "Your turn."

"Truth," she said, her eyes dancing as though a gauntlet had been thrown down between them.

"What are you afraid of?"

"A lot of things scare me. Losing those I love, being unsuccessful, and lizards. I hate lizards. They're snakes with legs and they creep me out."

They both laughed, and Amy motioned for Dominique to take her turn. "What the hell? I'll mix it up. Dare."

Amy straightened her back and wrung her hands together deviously. "I dare you to..." She paused, placing a finger to her lips in concentration. "Kiss me."

The breath Dominique had been holding slid out hissing like a snake. She bit her lip, her heart hammering in her chest. She opened her mouth to speak, but Amy moved closer, placing her finger over Dominique's mouth. "Look, if you're going to keep getting this close to me, flirting and biting your sexy bottom lip, you're either going to have to tell me you're never going to kiss me and let me get the notion out of my head, or you're going to need to kiss me and let this raging fire within me finally explode."

No longer able to resist, Dominique caved when Amy brought her full lips closer. In the split second before their lips met, Dominique's breath caught in her throat, the full intensity of her feelings escaping in a small sigh, as she pressed her lips to Amy's.

Simple. Sweet. At least, it was at first. Quickly the moment changed. Amy pulled back, lust evident in her darkening eyes. The right corner of her lip rose in a devious smile, and she dove back in. Deepening the kiss, Amy tangled her fingers through Dominique's hair. Dominique shivered.

*Should we be doing this?* Dominique's thoughts ran rampant. She should stop but...she couldn't. Or wouldn't. Either way, it didn't make a difference. There was no stopping the train. She ran her fingers across Amy's face, never breaking the kiss, trailing her fingertips lower and making a path down Amy's neck and back. She pulled Amy's body closer, wanting nothing more than to get lost in every inch.

"Damn," Amy said after a moment, her lips still dangerously close to Dominique's. "That was everything I thought it would be and so much more."

"Yeah." Dominique couldn't form all of the words she needed in the moment, so she just nodded.

Amy shimmied her shoulders seductively. "How about another dare?"

Dominique gripped the log beneath her and found her breath. "I want to. I *really* want to, but I think it would be best if we took this slow—at least for now."

"I can do slow," Amy said. Her shoulders slumped slightly, and just as quickly she righted them. "Actually, I appreciate slow. Thank you." Before Dominique could respond, Amy's lips were on hers again. "This is slow. We'll only do this," Amy said between kisses. "Only this."

Caught somewhere between wanting to give in and standing firm, Dominique agreed. "Only this."

\* \* \*

Surrounded by plush pillows, Amelia sighed contentedly and snuggled herself deeper into the comfort. The previous night's events swirled through her head, set to music, playing forth like a music video of her favorite sensual songs. She grabbed the pillow beside her and pulled it close, wishing she had the opportunity of waking next to Dominique, seeing if those big, brown eyes shimmered in the early morning light the way they did after dark.

Moving her body against the pillow, she positioned her head to smell her shirt, where scents of Dominique's perfume still lingered.

Amelia wanted her badly, longed for her. She let out a moan and continued to grind. Drifting back to the way it had felt to kiss Dominique, she gave in to her imagination and let the feeling cascade across her lips again.

Going slow was agonizing. She wanted, *needed*, more. Reaching for her bedside table, she quickly threw open the first drawer and pulled out her vibrator. If this was going to take so long, she was taking matters into her own hands. Her body trembled with need and, despite the wetness increasing between her legs, she rubbed lube up and down the shaft. What she needed wasn't going to be slow and steady enough to justify not using extra lubricant.

She bit her lip as she brought the toy closer and closed her eyes. With her free hand, she softly caressed her upper body, imagining Dominique's gentle touches. Sliding the vibrator inside herself, she arched her back and let out a loud moan.

As she moved it in and out of her, she cried out Dominique's name, and as she came with a crashing wave, she pictured those brown eyes looking into her own.

Waves of pleasure shot through her body, but she lay still, soaking up every last tingling sensation. If a fantasy was this good, she couldn't wait for the real thing.

She heard Dominique's voice in her head reminding her to be patient, and she let out a sigh. She would be patient, but she wasn't sure if she could tame her imagination after what she had just experienced.

# CHAPTER TEN

The fluorescent lights made whirring sounds above his head and everything was calm—at least for a moment. Clayton Turner downed the last bit of coffee and crunched the Styrofoam cup in his fist. He grimaced, noticing the grinds in his teeth. Cheap coffee, the same type they always had. Glancing down, he tucked in his polo and adjusted his badge.

*FBI.* He ran his fingers over the letters, still wondering how he had made it this far. It had all been a pipe dream, and now he was actually doing it. His first case had been a breeze, but this second one was turning out to be *the case*. Clayton pitched his coffee cup into the wastebasket and rubbed his hands together nervously. Since he'd only been called in for the minor league stuff—the repeated interrogations and fact-building—he wanted to do his best so he could get a chance to stay on the case.

It had been quite the process, interviewing everyone around town and piecing the puzzle together. But he was ready for something bigger. There was an answer, and he knew it waited in that room.

He thought back to the email he had received this morning, reminding everyone on the case to continue looking for answers. It had made him just as angry then as it did now. They had the answers. They had evidence. They had motive. Trent Westwick deserved to be behind bars, but he knew as well as the rest of them did that Mayor Westwick was going to run them all ragged looking for any other answer. He balled his left hand into a fist and brought it crashing down on the wall in front of him. Only a couple of passersby even bothered to look up. He shook his head in disgust. His outburst wasn't new with the frustration they were all experiencing.

The rules of the good ol' boys' club weren't going to fly today. Today he was going to demand answers and get this case closed.

He narrowed his eyes at the tall man sitting in the interrogation room. Trent's jaw was wide and jutted out, but his face had grown thinner. His shoulders slumped, and his blond hair was wild and unkempt.

Jail had not been kind to the kid, but with his name and his alibi, Clayton knew Trent could have handled this in a smarter fashion. He might just get away with it if he learned to stop changing his story.

"Going back in there today, Clay?" Stella Washington, a senior agent asked, nodding at him as she walked through the hallway.

"Yes, ma'am," he said with a broad smile. "I have a hunch. I'm going to get him to tell me something that matters. It's about damn time too."

"Good luck, kid," she called back as she rounded the corner. He caught sight of her shaking her head before she disappeared into the adjacent hallway. Taking a deep breath, he straightened his shoulders.

Practically strutting in stubbornness, he cleared his throat and opened the door to the tiny, barren room. "They said you were ready to talk to us," Clayton said, taking his seat across from Trent.

"They sent you again?" Trent rolled his eyes and turned to stare at the wall.

"What is it you have to say today?" Clayton ignored Trent's question and pressed onward. "And why did you opt to have this discussion without your lawyer?" Trent narrowed his eyes. "You know, that's not too smart, kid. But I'm happy to talk to you, so lay it on me. Why are we here?"

"I just wanted to be out of my cell." Trent shrugged. "I don't belong in here anyway."

"You have a pretty solid case against you, so I wouldn't be throwing out too much lip. I'm sure they've already told you as much. Let's just talk about that night."

"They don't have anything," Trent said, moving his shoulders back as much as possible with his wrists cuffed to the table. "They can't, because I was never there."

"Who do you suppose was, then?" Clayton raised an eyebrow and leaned forward, intensifying eye contact. "Who do you think was there that would have done this, aside from you?"

"I have my guesses. There are some in this place who might be crazy enough to blow a gasket and do something stupid. But it's not my case to crack. That's on you, bud."

Clayton stiffened. "Why don't you lay some of those guesses on me."

"If I do, are you going to get me out of here?"

"Not quite how it works, but I guess you've got nothing to lose. If you don't want to talk, you can go back to your cell. You can call me again when you do want to talk, but I'm getting really tired of coming all the way down here just to have you jerk us around. You know things. Hell, you were there when it all happened, so you know even more than our team. But knock off the cocky attitude, because we know quite a damn bit more than you'd like us to."

He watched as Trent shifted his weight to his left side and hardened his jaw. They were able to finally place him at the scene of the crime, with evidence showing his truck tires were the ones at the house that night. Other than that, they still didn't have much, but he wasn't going to let on.

He picked up a pencil and pad from the edge of the table and leaned it toward his chest. With nothing at all to do but wait, he started sketching.

"What are you writing down over there?"

Clayton didn't acknowledge the question and continued scribbling, now with a purpose. He had observed enough to learn Trent's triggers for talking.

"Look, it was probably an angry girlfriend or something. I don't know how gay things work, but I'm sure if you've got two crazy women in one relationship, things are bound to get out of hand and heated. I'm sure it was probably something like that. It wasn't me."

Clayton nodded, pacifying Trent. "Well, it's a small town. Everyone knows everyone. You've said so yourself. Who was she dating?"

"Beats the hell out of me," Trent said, shaking his head. His lips turned down in disgust. "I don't know anyone as fucked in the head as Chloe was around here. We all kind of stick to the straight and narrow. None of her types were around here, I don't think."

"Hmm…" Clayton waited, watching Trent's eyes flit back and forth across the room before settling back into his lap. Someone needed to teach this guy how to have a poker face. He didn't think there was much weight in whatever Trent was covering up, but he clearly knew something. "You don't think she might have quietly been seeing someone around here? Sounds like this might not be the friendliest place for someone to be honest about dating Chloe, especially given the way Chloe was so *brutally murdered*." He let his words sit for a minute, reminding Trent of what he had done.

"I don't know. Talk to the women around town. Maybe one of them will break down and tell you something."

Clayton nodded and went back to scribbling on the pad in his hand. He ticked off seconds, wondering how long he'd have to wait for an answer.

"I've helped you all I can."

Forty-seven seconds exactly. Clayton laughed. Trent was so predictable and stupid.

"You're not helping me," Clayton said, putting the pad on the table face down just in case he needed the façade of note-taking later. "Thing is, I thought you were going to at least try to take the blame off yourself today, but you've done nothing with this meeting other than to show me that you're still the same bratty, spoiled son of the mayor who thinks he's invincible." He smiled, careful to keep his voice level, but stern. "Let me tell you something. If you keep wasting our time like this, it's going to continue to look like you think you're above the law. And if you really believe you're innocent—by the way, cut the crap, we all know what you've done here—but if you really believe it, you're going to have to start trying a little harder to clear your name. Yes, you're innocent until proven guilty, but we know you were the one she got into a heated argument with right before she was killed. We have some other information saying you were at her house that night. So stop saying you're helping me. If you want to help someone, you might as well start trying to help yourself."

"I don't need help. I wasn't there. Why don't you try talking to Amelia Brandt? I have a suspicion that whore knows a thing or two." Trent's words dripped with hatred.

"You've told us in previous interviews that you weren't all that close to Chloe. How is it that, in such a tight-lipped town where no one seems to know a thing about her love life, you have a hunch?"

"I don't know anything else, and I am done talking to you," Trent hissed, slapping the table and turning away from Clayton.

"Fine. I'll figure it out on my own." He stood and pushed in his chair, turning back only to tip his hat in mock politeness. "Good day."

Smiling broadly, he stuck out his chest and walked through the office, a man on a mission. Once he heard the door of the station shut behind him, he let out a deep breath and leaned against the wall. Looking up at the sky, he smiled. He had held it together and he had been granted at least a grain of information.

Clayton rubbed his thumb against his temple and let out a sigh. This was probably a wild goose chase, knowing how that

Westwick kid liked to do business, but he figured it was worth a shot.

He pulled out his phone and punched information into Google, before hopping into his car and setting out for Amy's Place.

* * *

Amelia stretched her neck from side to side, wishing she had time or money to spend on a professional massage. Or that there was even a place to get one here in Knell. She sighed and reached over to wipe down the machines.

She hummed a tune she couldn't place, even though it had been stuck in her head all day, and marinated on the accomplishments of the past week. She still hurt. But she'd learned to smile and laugh again. She had told at least two people about her relationship with Chloe, and she was determined to tell someone else, even though everyone posed a risk. Her business could lose support. She could lose her family.

Chloe's face flashed into her mind and she knew there was no reason to stay silent. She had too much to lose if she did.

*Tell someone. Anyone.* She closed her eyes, willing herself the strength to stop hiding.

She heard the beep of her front door and forced a smile. Stepping to the side, her finger trailed along the machinery.

As she brushed against the hot coffeepot, she jerked her hand back and winced, biting her lip to keep from cursing.

The man walking up to the counter was broad chested and broad shouldered, his short hair neatly kept. She watched as he pulled the aviator sunglasses from his face and flashed her a smile. Glancing down, she saw his emblazoned polo. *FBI.* Three simple letters.

"Good afternoon," she said cheerily. Too cheerily. She had to stop being in her own world so much or people were going to think she'd gone mad. Gay and mad. It would be a combination people around here couldn't deal with in the slightest.

"Afternoon, ma'am," he drawled. "I'm Clayton Turner. I'm with the FBI, and I'm in town to do a little business. Can I get a cup of coffee and maybe ask you a few questions?"

"Absolutely," she squeaked. Her heart raced as she poured the coffee. She was careful not to burn her hand again. Her hands shook as she set the mug down for a minute. So many things could have gone wrong. Maybe her conversation with Bill had drawn scrutiny. He said he wouldn't tell anyone, but maybe he had.

Her worst fears flashed in her mind. She was wearing an orange jumpsuit, being pinned with a murder she didn't commit. If her family and friends wouldn't accept gay and mad, they certainly wouldn't accept gay and convicted of murder.

Her prints were on the knife. Her blood went cold. She shivered. She glanced over her shoulder. Calm and collected, he was sitting on a stool watching her every move. She smiled and grabbed his coffee, turning away briefly to take one last deep breath.

"Here you go," she said, setting it in front of him. "What else can I do for you?"

"You look a little upset," he noted, raising a brow. "Are you okay?"

"I am. Okay, that is. I'm okay. Thank you. It's been a long day. Several long days, actually."

"I can relate," he said, motioning her over with his hand. "Come take a seat."

"I really shouldn't." She shook her head. "I do have to man the counter in case anyone comes in."

He shrugged but then motioned again. "If anyone comes in, you'll have time to help them out. You look like you could use a break."

She pressed her lips together. Nothing pissed her off quite like a man coming in, telling her she looked upset and tired, and then insinuating that her work wasn't important. Nonetheless she wasn't here to make waves with the FBI when her prints were on a murder weapon.

Taking the seat beside him, she swiveled the stool to face him. "What brings you to Knell?" She asked, even though it was glaringly obvious what had brought more law enforcement into the town.

"I'm one of the investigators on the Stanton murder case. I'm just here to ask you a couple of questions. Someone close to the case told me you had ties to Ms. Stanton, so I wanted to see if there was anything you could tell me about her."

"We were all close." She didn't want to come out to him. Not here. Not now. "We're both from here. We'd known each other since elementary. It's a small school, so we all knew each other."

She reached across the counter and grabbed her bottle of water. He watched her every move, making her feel like a bug under a microscope. Slowly she unscrewed the cap and took a swig, making sure to divert eye contact at least for a second.

"Okay." He nodded and then brought his coffee cup up to his lips, downing the entire cup in just a gulp. "How did you know her?" This guy was intense.

"Would you like more coffee?" He nodded but continued his direct gaze. She scurried to fill his cup, thankful to have a moment to stop the frenzied images in her mind of just how well she knew Chloe. She thought of Chloe's hair, spilling over her pillow as she moaned in ecstasy. Amelia closed her eyes, warding off the onslaught of memories, and filled his cup before dutifully returning to her seat. Everything about this encounter felt like she was a little girl following orders.

"So back to our conversation. How did you know her?"

"We were friends. I knew her from the time I started school. She was a couple years older than I was, but I knew her. We all played together. Softball, basketball, volleyball, street dodgeball games, you name it. We were friends…" She cleared her throat. She couldn't keep saying "friends" without it sounding fishy. "In later years, she would stop in for coffee, sometimes in the morning, sometimes in the afternoons. Some days she would come in twice. We became friends. Good friends."

"Did you ever hang out outside the coffee shop?"

The question felt like a slap across the face. She was lying. He knew it. And soon everyone else would too. "Yes."

Again he tipped his coffee cup back and downed it in a single gulp. "Where did you hang out?" he asked without missing a beat.

"Her house." The admission was so simple, benign even. But it felt like she was opening up Pandora's box.

"And what did you do while you were hanging out."

*Sex. Lots of sex.* Having never been one to hold up well under pressure when dealing with authority, she had to bite her lip to keep the answer from coming out. "We cooked dinners, watched movies, stargazed out at the ranch. There's not a ton to do here, so it's really all about the people you surround yourself with. We enjoyed each other's company."

"I see." He nodded. "I just ask because..." For the first time, he trailed off, catching glimpse of the decorations around the store. She gripped the side of the stool, silently begging him to continue. In the background, she could hear the ticking of the old clock that had been in her family for generations. It intensified the chaos welling up inside of her. Sweat was forming on her brow and her mouth was dry. She reached for her water again, gulping it down with urgency. "I ask because it was mentioned to me you might know something about her love life."

"Her love life?" she croaked. "Who told you that?"

He leveled his gaze at her and pushed the coffee cup away from him. "Trent Westwick said I should ask you if I was looking to find out who, if anyone, she was seeing."

"Me? He said to ask me? Why?" Her questions came out as a blur and she felt faint. Her stool wobbled beneath her, but she caught her balance on the counter.

"That question obviously makes you uncomfortable. You don't have to be uncomfortable. It's just a tiny piece that can help us solidify this case. Was she dating anyone?"

Amelia stared at the walls of her shop in disbelief. Her hands trembled as she pulled her weight back to the center of the stool. This place had always been her safe haven. Now it felt like hell. Tears blurred her vision. She wanted to run away screaming, but that would do her no good here. Unable to fight the inevitable, she simply nodded.

"Okay. Good." Clayton encouraged her by nodding slowly. "Who was she dating?"

"Me." Her voice was barely a whisper, but that one word took every ounce of courage she had. "She was dating me."

He cocked his head to the side and she looked away, not wanting to deal with him looking her up and down. She had stared in the mirror thinking the same thing when she was younger. She didn't *look* gay, but she was.

"Hmm," he said, clearing his throat. "Well, I didn't see that one coming. But that means we have some questions for you as well. How long had you two been dating?"

"A few months."

He pulled out a pad and a pencil and her heart raced even faster. "When was the last time you saw her?"

"I made her dinner the night she died," she said. There was no longer anything to hide. It was all going to come out at once. "I saw her that evening. I left her house around seven o'clock. I went back to my house and I never saw her alive again."

"You weren't one to stay the night?"

She fought the urge to show her disgust. "I feel like that's a little inappropriate, but no. We did our own thing at night. I went home. I like sleeping at my house."

"And she never stayed at your house? You wouldn't have known she was gone is what you're saying?"

"No. She never stayed at my place. This wasn't something I was ready to go public with. It's still not. At least not *that* public. I wanted to keep it a secret. I wasn't ready to be the only other outcast in this tiny town, especially not when I own a business. I rely on people liking me. I couldn't have them know I was dating Chloe." Her words were coming out too quickly. She stopped and took a deep breath. "I didn't usually stay over, and she never stayed at my place. It was either here at the coffee shop or at her house."

"So how did Trent know you were the one I needed to talk to?"

"I have no idea." She looked down at her lap, scanning for answers. "No one was supposed to know. The only thing I can think is that he might have seen something that belonged to me while he was in her house. Or he might have overheard. I don't think Chloe would have told him. She hated Trent."

"Mmhmm. Well, you're saying you weren't there after seven that night?"

"That night I didn't stay. I went home. And I never heard from her again." The admission hit her in the gut, like it did every time.

"Was that unusual for the two of you not to talk for the rest of the evening?"

She saw the freight train coming at her and she was powerless to stop it. Straightening her shoulders, she looked him in the eye. "Sometimes we'd talk all night. Sometimes we didn't talk after I left. There was no set course. That night we didn't."

His brow shot up in curiosity. "Were you angry at her?"

This had taken a turn in a hurry. "Look. Have you ever dated someone?" She waited for his nod and took a deep breath. "You know there are disagreements. We didn't leave on the best of terms. We had a brief argument and I left. That's what I do when we argue. I leave. She stays. We don't talk until the next day when we've cooled off."

He took down notes. Her stomach churned. "Were you alone at your house?"

"Yes," she said, closing her eyes. She'd seen enough crime dramas to know what was happening. He had motive and no alibi against her.

"I guess that bastard didn't send me on a wild goose chase after all," he said. He shook his head and pursed his lips, looking every bit like he might utter, "I'm not mad. Just disappointed."

"Why are you questioning me anyway?"

"I was just trying to solidify a case against Westwick. But it looks like you know more than you've told anyone to this point. I'm not going to cuff you, but I would like you to come down to the station with me. You're not a suspect. But you're a person who knows deeper points of a case we've been trying to solve."

"Can I lock up?" she asked, her voice shaking.

"Yes, ma'am." He stood. "I'll wait by the front door."

She nodded and reached for his coffee cup. As it slipped from her fingers, she didn't even move to stop it from shattering or look to see the shattered fragments on the ground.

"Small hands," he noted.

She nodded, unable to form words and followed him out the door, flipping the shop's sign to "Closed."

# CHAPTER ELEVEN

The flickering of cheap overhead lights and the sounds of a stapler occasionally punching into stacks of paper would have made her head spin, if it weren't already. Around her, Amelia could hear the shuffling of papers and feet and so many muted voices. The few people in the station moved past her as if she wasn't even there, and she hadn't seen Clayton since he dropped her off and told her someone would be out to see her. She wasn't sure how long she had to wait or if she was even going to get to go home tonight.

Was she a person of interest? A suspect? What was she, and why was she here?

They had been kind. That much she appreciated. A woman who had to have been a receptionist had given her something to drink. She recognized the woman, but in her daze couldn't place her. Wes had come out once to check on Amelia and assured her someone would talk to her soon. She liked Wes and wished it could have been him that she talked to about this mess. She knew Wes. She didn't know these other people.

Not too long ago, it had just been Wes and a couple others in this place. They'd come in the coffee shop, and Wes had always talked about being short-staffed. She looked around, taking in the influx of officers in the small space. No doubt this was spurred on by Chloe's death, but it didn't make her feel more comfortable. Every person here looked tired and more than a little on edge. She looked around the waiting room and noted the complete lack of anything she could deem uplifting. It was bland. The laminate lifting off the edges of the aged tables, the yellow paint peeling off the walls, and the water damaged ceiling tiles that had turned from white to brown made her cringe.

There was nothing beside her on the table, aside from her Styrofoam cup in which they had provided her water from the cooler. Not a magazine to be seen. Now she had nothing to do but sit and wait. For what? For whom?

She didn't know. But she felt like she was going crazy.

Potential newspaper headlines circled in her thoughts. *Lesbian Lover Thought to Have Committed Crime of Passion.* Or worse yet, *Lesbian Love Gone Bad.* She sighed. It was a lesbian horror story. There was no need to sensationalize what was already horrific, but she knew the possibilities were endless.

While she knew she was being dramatic, it didn't change the fact that her prints were likely the ones found on a murder weapon used to kill the woman with whom she had secretly been carrying on an affair. She knew how easy of a sell that could be. Coupled with the fact that she had no alibi, it would be a homerun for any prosecutor. They'd say she was angry. Whether it was a relationship fight or perhaps Chloe had wanted to go public and she hadn't, they would be able to spin whatever story they wanted.

This town had already done away with one lesbian. Why not throw the other one behind bars?

She shifted her attention to what was happening at the station and watched a dopey kid with a buzz-cut almost run into a door because he was so frantically shuffling the papers in his hands. He looked stressed out, and he couldn't have been more than twenty. In the corner of the room near the door, she heard a commotion. Sheila Dennings, a woman who worked at the grocery store, was trying to kick the police officer bringing her into the station. She was clearly drunk and was screeching incoherently, but it was obvious she was upset.

Amelia closed her eyes and let out a deep breath. People-watching had always been one of her favorite ways to learn about the world. She couldn't do it here, though. In a police station, people-watching for the sake of entertainment was like trying to calm down by watching *Psycho*.

"Ms. Brandt." The sound of her name jolted her upright in her seat. It was time.

She rose to her feet and thought about straightening her white button-down shirt but found the effort futile. It was wrinkled beyond repair. That was fitting. She felt wrinkled and beyond repair. There was no need to try to be acceptable.

She stepped up to the receptionist who had called her name. "Detective Stark will see you now. First office on the right." The woman halfheartedly pointed in the general direction of the office without looking up from her files.

She wasn't being monitored or being led to the office, which Amelia took as a good sign. But she couldn't be sure. For all she knew, walking into that office could be the beginning of the end. Dutifully, she followed orders and focused on putting one foot in front of the other, even though her feet suddenly felt like they were made of lead. Her hands trembled and her breath caught in her throat. Shaking like a leaf, she rounded the corner into the office with *Stark* written in sharpie on a piece of printer paper and hung above the door. Quite a downgrade from what he was used to, she guessed.

Her mouth opened and she knew she was supposed to announce her presence, but her throat went dry. No sound came out, so she stepped inside.

"Ms. Amelia Brandt?" he asked, looking up at the sound of her footsteps. He extended his hand, motioning for her to take the seat in front of him.

She cleared her throat and tried to casually wipe her sweaty palms onto her pants as she took a seat.

"I'm Detective Stark," he said, once again extending his hand, this time for a handshake.

"Amelia Brandt." Her voice sounded foreign, as if she were listening to someone else speak.

"I'm sure you know why we asked you to come in today," he said. She looked at him and wondered if it was the stress of the job that had created the sharp lines around his eyes and mouth. His gray hair was thick and wavy and, despite his weathered look, he had kind, gentle blue eyes. She imagined he would have made a good Santa Claus in another life, albeit a slimmer version.

He cleared his throat, and she realized he was still waiting for her to answer.

"Yes, sir," she said. "I spoke with Clayton Turner before he brought me here."

"Clayton told me you might have some information on the Stanton case, and I just want to gather that information from you in your own words." His voice was matter-of-fact, but his eyes still looked kind. He lifted the left corner of his mouth into a small, sad smile. "Can you do that for me?"

"I can." She took a deep breath. "Do I need a lawyer or anything?"

He shook his head. "No, ma'am. You can have one if you'd like. But we just need to gather some information from you. Think of it as research."

That didn't make her feel any more at ease. Research could be damning. "Okay," she agreed. "All I told Clayton is that I dated Chloe. We were together. I saw her the evening this all happened, but I left her place in the early evening and went home. I made her dinner and then went home."

"You were dating her?"

She started to get angry until she realized he wasn't judging her or trying to decide if she fit the "lesbian" bill. He was simply doing his job.

"I was." Whether it was becoming more normal for her to say the words, or if it was due to her need to adhere to authority, telling him she was gay was easier than it had been before with anyone else.

"I'm sorry for your loss, ma'am," he said, nodding his head as if he was tipping his hat.

She covered her mouth with her hand, not wanting to let the emotions rip through. "Thank you," she said after a moment. "That's something I haven't heard a lot since it happened."

"Do you know of anyone who could have wanted to harm her?"

"I don't know why anyone would have wanted to." She glanced down before making eye contact again. "None of it makes sense to me. She was good as gold, sweet, funny, and hardworking. She was everything people raise us up to be here in Knell. She didn't deserve this, and I don't know why anyone would have wanted to harm her. That said, I think we all know that Trent did it. Everyone who was at the bar that night has made pretty clear the kinds of things he said, his actions, everything. Why is it even a question when Trent is in custody?"

"We just want to make sure we've got the right guy." He jotted something down in the notebook on his desk and furrowed his brow. He opened his mouth but didn't speak, and Amelia knew there were things he wasn't saying. "Trent maintains his innocence, and he's innocent until proven guilty. We're doing due diligence." He tightened his lips and exhaled, making it clear he was done speaking. He looked off into the distance. Letting out another sigh, he reached up his right hand and then let it drop back to the desk and shook his head.

"Can't discuss that part of the investigation, I take it?" she asked.

He broke eye contact and placed all his focus on the water glass to the side of his desk. He took a long sip, obviously stalling. Gingerly, he placed the glass back on the desk and turned his head back in her direction. In the silence, she replayed his words: *Innocent until proven guilty.* Something that was supposed to bring hope only seemed to reinforce the good ol' boy system of this little town. Trent was the mayor's kid. No doubt there was pressure from someone higher up to keep him from sullying the family name.

"I'm afraid I can't," Stark said, finally. "But I can tell you that anything you know that would help us would be much appreciated."

"Of course. What can I do?"

"Did she have visitors often?"

"Aside from me, her dad, and some of the guys who worked on the ranch, she didn't. She kept a pretty private life. She was a social butterfly, but she liked it on her terms. When she wanted to see people, which was frequently, she would go out mainly to McCool's. She also went on road trips to visit friends in other areas when work allowed. She had many friends, no enemies… at least until that night. But few ever came over to her place."

"Okay." He made notes in his notebook again. Amelia wished they didn't have to do that. She could see the recorder on the edge of the desk and didn't know why he had to add to the element of making her feel like a suspect if she wasn't one. "So you would say that the tire tracks in her driveway were strange if you had seen them there?"

"Absolutely," she said. "I went over that next day to take pastries to her father and those investigating, and I've never seen tracks like that on the east side of the house. No one would park there. That was her garden and everyone who knew her well knew that she'd pitch a fit if someone killed her okra or tomatoes. Most of the guys who come over with trucks would park in the circle driveway."

"And where did you park when you visited?"

As if she were watching a movie, the excitement she felt each time she parked her car in her hidden alcove came rushing back. She would check the road for any passing cars and then punch the gas, accelerating quickly back behind the west side of the house, in between two towering pine trees.

She balled her right hand into a fist, making sure her fingernails pressed into her palm to draw her out of her nostalgia. "I parked further back on the west side, in a hidden spot, covered with trees."

"Why the secrecy?"

She wished she could tell him how stupid a question it was. "Obvious reasons." A sound resembling a laugh escaped from her lips. "Chloe was out. And Chloe is dead."

"Fear?"

She nodded.

"Of something like this, or in general?"

He had never been any type of *different*, she could tell. She looked at him again. White, male, heterosexual. He was the epitome of privilege. She didn't want to look at him that way, but he was making it difficult. Only someone who had always fit the mold they were supposed to fit would ask a question like that. "Fear of everything," she said, her words coming more quickly, sizzling with passion as they slid off her tongue. "I'm a business owner. You think anyone around here wants to buy *gay* cupcakes, muffins, or pastries? You think anyone wants to keep me around at family gatherings or continue to be my friend? Chloe had friends, yes. She had plenty of friends. But Chloe was different than I am. I had to work to build my circle of people. Chloe came by it naturally. She was a force of nature. Everyone wanted to be around her. She had that charm and the type of personality that brings people closer. It's a type of charm that let the small-minded folks around here overlook the fact that she was gay. They'd almost dismiss it for the sake of loving who she was. Me, on the other hand, I'm different. I talk too much, too fast. I'm quirky. I am the downhome girl who wanted to leave and then realized this was home, even if I didn't quite fit. I made myself fit. But being gay on top of it was too much. I hear the way people around here talk about gay people. You should listen to the coffee shop chatter. Women announcing to their gossip circle that, gasp, 'my nephew just told everyone he likes boys, and now I'm not going to Christmas if he's coming.' It happens all the time. They talk about supporting hospitals choosing not to treat gay patients and about how it's just wrong for a child to have two mothers. They defend bullies. They stand firm in their hatred. I've never heard anyone mention Chloe's name. It was as if they forgot she was gay or didn't want to risk bringing her up for a point of controversy. I have lived in fear that I'd be the one they gasped and gossiped over, the one they weren't afraid to rake over the coals. I was never like Chloe, and I don't know that I could be if I tried. So yeah. I'm afraid of all of it."

His eyes were wide, but he nodded as if everything she had thrown at him was what he was expecting. He was good at this, she noted. She looked at the lines on his face again and reminded herself it came from years of practice.

"So no one ever really used the spot where the large truck tires were found?"

"No. Chloe used the driveway, too. Wait." She held up her hands to stop him from asking another question. "Didn't the tire tracks match Trent's truck? We know he was there, right?"

Instead of answering, he again sighed and looked down. Frustrated, she upped the ante, careful to keep her tone calm. "People talk. We know the details. We know too much about the case to pretend we don't all think he's guilty. You all here—as well as all of us in town—know his pretentious, large tires were at the scene. And even if you don't want to confirm that, we've already gone over the fact that I was there delivering pastries the next day and saw the tracks firsthand."

"They did." His eyes looked tired and he shrugged as if he had messed up somehow. "Tire tread and time match." Tapping his fingers on the table, he knit his brow. His eyes shifted back and forth and Amelia fought the urge to tell him to just ask his question. Clearing his throat, he leveled his gaze on her. "Any reason why he would have been over at Chloe's house?"

"None at all. She didn't associate with Trent. He didn't associate with her. It's a small enough town and they knew each other. But she didn't care for his pretension. And he didn't care for her gayness. They didn't interact."

"Until that night?"

"Until that night."

His lips formed a tight line and he nodded, scrawling things on that damn pad again. She could hear people scurry back and forth in the open area behind her, and she had to wonder what was going on in this town. People didn't get up in arms this often around here.

"Aside from Trent and his actions that night, did she have anyone who treated her that way, as an outcast?"

"I'm sure people did behind closed doors, but not that I know of."

"Hmm," he sighed. "Any ex-lovers she mentioned who might have had it out for her?"

"We didn't really talk about those things too much. We talked surface level about ex-lovers. We weren't there. We were just starting out. We didn't know each other *that way* for very long. And now we never will."

The weight of her statement hit her in the gut. It would have been nice to have been afforded the chance to get to know Chloe in the deepest of ways. She thought about all she had learned and how it would never be enough. The world would never have enough Chloe and the sunlight she brought with her when she entered a room.

She was grateful when he took another strange, focused drink of his water. It gave her time to get her heartbeat back to normal rhythm. Cueing on the method her mother used to lower her blood pressure in heightened situations, she took a deep breath in through her nose, held it, and exhaled through her mouth. Deep breath. Repeat. In the time it took him to take his labored drink, she had gone through five repetitions, just enough to settle her and bring her back to normal.

"Did you have a key to her house?"

Amelia flashed back to their fight on the fateful and only day she had ever used it. She nodded. "I did. Why is that important?"

"Just need to know these things, ma'am."

Her right eyebrow shot up as if jolted by electricity when she realized where this was headed. "There was broken glass. Whoever did this—I'll resist blaming Trent just as a formality—broke in through the back double doors. That was in the news story, too. Is that why you need to know?"

He gave her a gentle, but condescending, half smile. She was breaking the rules and speaking before being spoken to. Taking the cue, she nodded.

"I have one other thing I would like to talk to you about, if that's all right?"

She nodded, wishing she could have said "no."

"There were some fingerprints discovered around Chloe's house that don't match hers. They don't match Trent's either, and we've come up dry in our search for whom they might belong to. They're small prints. This is just a hunch, but Clayton mentioned you had small hands. Any chance those prints are yours?"

A laugh shot up but she squelched it in her throat. This was no laughing matter. "I'm sure they probably are. I was in that house just hours before this nightmare occurred. I made dinner that night, brisket, for her before she got off work. She worked long, hard days and I wanted her to have something nice. I was in that kitchen, that dining room, that living room, her bedroom for most of the day. I had gone over early to clean the place and make it feel homey. I had taken care to light candles to give it a happy scent. I had spent most of the day trying to spoil her the way she always spoiled me. Aside from that day, I was there often—several times a week. So yes. I'm sure those prints are probably mine."

"Understandable," he said, jotting notes. "Mind if we take your prints, just so we can rule out another suspect in the case?"

She tried to hide the gulp that formed in her throat. Did they want to rule out another suspect or add one? She nodded, despite her worst fears.

With that, he stood and she was led down the hallway. Within minutes, she had been printed and returned back to his office for waiting. She couldn't help but feel like she was in the principal's office as he quietly waited with her for the running of her prints against the evidence.

Running through topics in her mind, she tried to find something that would make suitable small talk. Nothing really seemed to follow murder questioning well, so she remained silent. He too kept quiet. In the silence, her stomach growled. She tried to remember when she had last eaten but came up blank. By the wailing sound in her belly, she realized it had probably been far too long.

"We have vending machines out front if you're hungry," he said quietly, pointing out into the entryway.

"Thank you. I'll be fine," she said. She cast her eyes down to her lap and had to wonder how much of that was a lie. Would she be fine?

The same dopey twenty-year-old emerged in the doorway and shuffled past her chair to place a sticky note on the desk in front of Detective Stark. He nodded and thanked the boy, ushering him out of the office.

"Well?" she asked, wanting to rip the Band-Aid off as quickly as possible.

"It's a match." His kind eyes now held a darker hue and hints of sadness, as if he had wanted the results to prove otherwise. He was probably a father and grandfather, or maybe she reminded him of someone he knew. Either way, he hadn't wanted to have to extend their questioning. She could tell by the way he looked up at the ceiling and leaned back in his chair. "I do have to ask you another question."

"Okay."

"What do you drive?"

She felt as if someone had took a hammer to hear head. "Ford Mustang."

Relief flooded his face, and he smiled. "Okay. That makes sense. We did find smaller car tire tracks that were likely yours. But they appear to have been there prior to the rainstorm that occurred that evening, which means I think we're done with questioning for the night. We are going to have additional questions in the coming days. You'll be in town?"

"I never leave," she said, relief filling her veins. Even if she wasn't entirely off the hook, at least she was for now.

She shook his hand and headed for the door. She wanted to run but figured that would look suspicious. Never in her life had she felt so much like a criminal. As she got to the front door, she saw Ryan Walden stroll through, escorted by an unfamiliar detective. He locked eyes on her and nodded a greeting. He had aged since she had seen him last, she noted, staring at the way the lines around his eyes had deepened. He shrugged and gave her a sad smile as he turned away, everything in his body language symbolizing defeat. She wanted to shower off this experience, wishing there was some way to make this dirty feeling go away. This whole town was fucked. They couldn't bear to point the finger where it needed to be pointed because it would tarnish the image of the picture perfect little area they all felt like they had helped to build. Her stomach lurched, and she quickened her pace, finding a trashcan right outside the door. Leaning over, she emptied the contents of her stomach before righting herself again and forcing herself to breathe.

Soon this would all be over, although she doubted justice would be served. If they were so hell bent on bringing her and Ryan back in for repeated questioning, they sure as hell weren't focusing their manpower where it needed to be. In the parking lot, she fished her phone out of her purse and saw texts and a missed call from Dominique.

She didn't want to ghost her, but she wasn't sure she felt like talking to anyone right now.

Checking to make sure nothing was amiss, she typed a quick reply. *Sorry I missed your call. I got tied up with some stuff tonight. I'll call you in a bit.*

She labored over whether or not to add a kiss emoji and opted to leave it off the text. She hit send and put her phone back in her purse.

She needed to talk to someone tonight, and she knew exactly where she needed to go. In her car, she headed north.

# CHAPTER TWELVE

Fresh sunflowers had proven difficult to find in the fall at almost nine o'clock. After internal deliberation, Amelia had settled for the wildflowers she was able to pick from the side of the road. It was quite fitting, after all, to bring the wildest and most beautiful soul she knew flowers known for their unpredictability.

"You would've never been tamed anyway," she said, wiping a tear from her cheek as she set them down in front of Chloe's newly erected headstone. It was beautiful—at least as beautiful as something so tragic could be. She had heard the town talk about it being put in over the weekend and knew she'd see it one day.

Today, in the wake of her mental breakdown caused by a traumatic reliving of the details of her relationship and the brutality of the murder, had been the day.

Gingerly, she ran her fingers across the engraved lettering and noticed the large, overturned feed bucket next to the stone. No doubt Bill had been out here more than a few times and had set up a place made for sitting and visiting.

Her knees were weak, and she still felt faint. Gratefully she took the seat, careful not to disturb the grave in front of her.

She shivered as she brought her elbows to her knees in an effort to hug herself. It was chilly out, but she knew this had far more to do with internal chill than the weather. Guilt mixed with heartache filled her soul, and her lips quivered as the tears fell.

"I'm sorry, Chloe," she said, wiping her tears with the sleeve of the sweatshirt she had found in her car. "I'm sorry I missed the funeral. I'm sorry I haven't visited yet." She let out a loud sob. "I'm sorry that everything ended when we were on such bad terms. I can't stand the things I said to you. It wasn't right. *I wasn't right.* You were and I was too damn stubborn to listen. I'm sorry for that, and I'm sorry you're not here. I know it's all I keep saying, but I'm just sorry."

She looked around, thankful no one else was crazy enough to be in the cemetery at night. Even so, she kept her voice down. This was between them. It always had been.

"I couldn't let anyone else see me like this. Hell, I never even wanted you to see me like this. Somehow I think you can, though. I like to think that you're with me and with your dad. He's struggling Chloe. He misses you, but I'm sure you know that. I miss you too, in case you didn't know that."

The wind picked up, creating the eerie sound of the leaves being scooped up and tossed about in a flurry. She looked behind her. She should be frightened, but she wasn't. She ran her fingers again over the etched letters and numbers. Such a short timespan between the years. "How did twenty-six years go by so quickly?" she mumbled. She closed her eyes, longing to hear Chloe spout off a smart-ass retort. There was none, and there wouldn't be one, no matter how long she waited.

She gulped and tried to get back to her reason for coming. Even in the darkness and without Chloe's physical presence, her breathing was labored. "It's stupid, Chloe. It's really stupid. I don't even know why I'm having a hard time telling you these things when you're not even here. But this is tough. I think I met someone. You'd like her...Or you might hate her. I'm not really sure. You both have...*had* strong personalities. But that's beside the point."

Fidgeting on the bucket, she let out a sigh. "I think I like her, and I think you'd be proud of me. If nothing else, I'm learning to be me. I know that's something you always wanted for me, and I'm trying. I guess that's what I want you to know. I'm trying like hell to be who I need to be for me. We'll get to that 'no secrets' place at some point. For now, though, I think I'm making progress."

Glancing around, she felt like she'd been punched in the stomach. All around lay the unfinished lives of those who thought they had more time. And right in front of her lay the only one she wanted to talk to. She wanted to bounce ideas off her, even if they weren't in a romantic setting. She covered her eyes and cried for all the conversations they'd never get to have. "I was so closed off. I needed to be tough and guarded, and I never let you in." The tears came harder to the point she knew her words weren't even coherent anymore but she had to speak them. "I should have let you see who I am. I shouldn't have been so fucking scared. But I was. You suffered the fallout of my stubbornness. And so did I." She bit her lip until she could taste blood, making the physical pain more of a pressing issue than the emotional pain.

Her hands were shaking as she stood. She couldn't take any more pain tonight. It was too much. Before she turned for the car, she glanced back at the headstone. "If you could talk, maybe we wouldn't be in such a mess over this case either. Trent is a prick still—no shocker there. He's making a mess of everything, and I'm scared he might get away with this. But I want you to know I'll fight for justice, if that's even a concept anymore."

Having spoken her piece, she shoved her hands into the pockets of her jeans and made her way to the car. As she walked through the entrance, she looked up, catching sight of a solitary black bird near the flood lamp. She watched as the bird craned in her direction and then took flight. A smile played on the corner of her lips as she thought of the solitary bird she knew, taking flight without caring what anyone else thought.

She leaned against the car, thinking of Chloe's passion. This wouldn't have been an unsolved mystery if she were around to deal with any part of it. Her stubborn determination and strict need for justice would get in the way, make her a nuisance to police and ultimately end up helping to crack the case.

Whatever it took, she was going to do her best to channel that tenacity.

* * *

Televisions were turned up far too loud in at least three of the rooms on this floor, and next door, Dominique could hear the hushed tones of a couple fighting over money. With nothing good on the basic cable channels the hotel offered, Dominique was left with nothing to do but try to drown out the sounds around her. At least the pillows were comfy, she noted, but it did little to quell her frustration.

Craning her neck from side to side for some relief, she felt the catch of her left shoulder—another pinched nerve. Either the stress of the job or the weight of her stupid decisions was beginning to take its toll on her body.

Feigning casual behavior, she told herself she was picking up her phone to read emails. But she knew the truth. After a quick scan of both her email accounts, she flipped back over to text messaging, just to see if Amy was typing a reply. It was the beauty and the curse of the iPhone to be able to tell whether or not she was being blown off completely. In frustration, she set her phone facedown on the bed in front of her. She needed to know if she had completely screwed things up. Yes it had been Amy's choice. It had been at her urging that their lips had met in the first place, but now she was flaking out. And Dominique had nothing to do but sit around and wait until everyone in this sleepy town decided it was time for morning again.

She stood and walked over to the pile of posters she had made and kicked the leg of the chair holding them in place. In all her work here thus far, she had garnered a total of three people willing to take a stand for more equality, for justice for

Chloe. Three out of thousands willing to stand up and say that what happened to one of their own shouldn't stand here—or anywhere else. And they were all high school kids.

Pressing her fingers to her temples, she gritted her teeth. This was the job, whether she liked it or not, whether everything she touched turned to dust or not.

She put on her jacket, no longer able to stand the sight of this tiny room, and headed for the door. There might not be much to do here, and she certainly wasn't going to fit in, but she had to try. No more would she lock herself away for the sake of making everyone else more comfortable.

A quick Google search brought up the only bar in town, and her blood went cold at the name: McCool's. She had read every news story on Chloe's case a hundred times. The place it all started was her only option for a drink. Her knuckles went white as she tightened her grip on the steering wheel. Maybe it was dangerous, but maybe it was her only chance at sanity.

She put the car in gear and ignored her heart's frantic pounding. She rolled down her window for a breath of fresh air while she drove and a short five minutes later heard her tires crunch across the gravel of the parking lot. The old wooden sign out front screamed of decades past, but no one seemed to care. The railing in front of the parked cars was lined with smokers lighting up and talking in excited tones. It all sounded like a blur to her, especially when coupled with the country music coming out from the speakers inside.

"Honky tonk central," she whispered to herself. She was going to stick out like a sore thumb in this place, with her brown leather jacket, white lace shirt and skinny jeans. Boots, flannel, and faded jeans were all she could see, aside from one woman in a short, cut-off denim skirt.

She couldn't look that way if she tried. It was a far cry from what she had always deemed "the Walmart cowboy look" she saw too often in Austin, with boots and jeans that had never seen a hard day's work, often in bright colors and overly fitted. That's not what these people looked like to her. Boots were scuffed, some still caked with the mud of the fields, and most looked like they had just come from a day of physical labor without too much freshening up. This wasn't just their look. It was their way of life. She sighed and looked in the mirror. Whether or not she looked the part, she was going to go inside and enjoy herself.

She applied her lip-gloss carefully. If she couldn't fit in, at least she'd feel confident.

Taking a deep breath, she grabbed the steering wheel to ground herself. She was out of her league here. Back home in Austin, she was never afraid to dine or grab a drink by herself. She was sure that was something these people couldn't understand, not being afraid in the big, bad city. But here, she was the minority—in more ways than one. And here was where she felt unsafe. Nevertheless, she grabbed her clutch and rolled up her windows.

One step inside confirmed her fears. At least four heads turned in her direction as her heels clacked against the hardwood floor. A scruffy looking man of probably thirty eyed her and winked, taking his time to look her up and down.

"Damn," he said under his breath but not quietly enough to escape her earshot. "You're not from around here."

It wasn't a question but a statement. She simply nodded and tried to move past him.

"Wait," he called out, reaching to grab her arm. She dodged his grip and skillfully moved around another barstool, making it more difficult for him to encroach on her personal space. "Where are you from?"

"Austin." She offered him a smile and turned to the bar. He was still talking but she wasn't ready to listen. This kind of thing happened everywhere, but in the places she was used to, she at least knew there were others who would join in and come to her rescue—whether they were strangers or not. Here she could already tell this was the norm. It was acceptable "boys will be boys" behavior. Luckily a chipper, blond bartender who looked too young to be behind the bar was waiting for her order. "I'll have a cosmo please."

Her smile faded and she knit her brow. "Louie," she called out to the heavyset man pouring a draft beer behind her. There was no way he could hear her over the noise of the group of guys calling out beer orders to him, and the obvious new girl had no clue. Dominique didn't want to get involved with handholding, so she waved her hand to cancel the order. "You can make it a whiskey on the rocks."

The blonde nodded and set to work. Suddenly Dominique felt exposed and glanced to her right. The scruffy man had moved over to the seat next to her. "What do you do in Austin?"

She sighed. This was the point where she would normally tell him she liked women and he could scram. But that wouldn't do her any favors here tonight. "I work for a non-profit," she said. Her hands found the only thing she could find to toy with to distract her, a bar napkin. As she listened to him describe work at a nearby oil plant, she fidgeted and pulled at the corners of the napkin mindlessly.

"What are you doing?" he finally asked, taking a second to actually look at her entire body instead of just her breasts, as he had been doing since she walked in.

"Nothing." She pushed the napkin away.

"You know what they say about behavior like that?" She shook her head. "Pent up sexual frustration is a leading cause of fidgety behaviors like playing with napkins and peeling beer labels back. At least that's what I read somewhere. It's science."

In any other situation, she would have laughed at his confidence in his "science," but she just shook her head. "Look," she said, grabbing her drink and giving the waitress cash without ever looking away from the man in front of her, "it's not going to happen, okay? Let's just drop that subject completely."

"Do you have a boyfriend?" he asked as she stood to walk away from the conversation. She continued walking, as he followed. "What is it?"

"Stop," she said, her voice deepening. "I don't want to have this conversation, and I don't want to be pestered by you all night."

He straightened his back, pulling back as though he had been slapped. Confusion danced in his eyes and she wanted to scream. Was it news for all men to realize that not everyone wanted to sleep with them?

"Everything okay here?" The heavyset man from behind the bar had made his way to the corner where she stood.

"Is it?" she asked, turning her attention back to the man still standing in front of her.

"Yes, ma'am," he said as his shoulders slumped. "Sorry," he mumbled before trudging back to his seat.

"I'm Louie," the bartender said, extending his hand for a proper greeting. "That's Johnny Ray. He's a bit of a jackass when he drinks. I'll keep an eye on him, okay? And if you notice anything I miss, flag me down. I'll cut him off and send him home." His eyes went dark and he looked at the ground. She watched as he took a deep breath and gripped the table. "And if it comes to that, I'll personally make sure you get home safely."

Putting the pieces together, her heart fell. This poor man. He must have tried to make things better after the altercation with Chloe.

She placed a hand gently on his shoulder and smiled. "Thank you. That means a great deal. I'm Dominique by the way."

"Nice to have you here. Are you here alone or meeting someone?" He cleared his throat. "I'm only asking to make sure that Johnny Ray doesn't act up again. He'll settle down some if you have company."

"Just me tonight."

He looked around the crowded bar, scanning for a decent spot. When he couldn't find one, he sighed. "I have no idea why we're this busy tonight. I guess everyone around here was looking for something to do to warm up from the cooler air outside. But I tell you what, I'll grab you a stool from the back, and you can sit up next to the bar right here." He pointed to a spot underneath the bartender window. "Does that work for you?"

She felt like she should wave it off, tell him she was fine, and mingle. But she knew the dangers of a place like this, even if it felt so homey and quaint to everyone else. "That would be great. Thank you. Really."

When he came back with the barstool, she climbed on top and finally tasted her drink. She winced. It wasn't quite what she expected and it certainly wasn't whiskey. Whatever it was, she was going to drink it and hopefully next time she would have the chance to order from Louie instead of the young girl.

It was her first real time out experiencing the nightlife of Knell, and she knew she should be using that time to work and network. She wanted to know the story behind each of these faces—well, aside from her scruffy assailant from earlier. She wanted to know what made them tick, what they liked and didn't like, who they were, how they knew Chloe, and if they were willing to expand their small mindset. But she couldn't bring herself to cross that bridge, not when intoxicated people could be so volatile. Resigned to enjoy solitude and small talk, she took another sip. *Rum. It has to be rum.*

Regardless, she drank it down halfway and eavesdropped on the conversation happening in the nearest booth. She let out a quiet laugh as she listened to them, a man and a woman in their fifties if she was guessing correctly, talking about their fears regarding their teenage daughter being involved in the wrong crowd.

"She was listening to music by someone called…I don't even want to say it, Roger," the woman's voice was high and agitated.

"Say it, Marlene," he coaxed. Dominique wished she could see them to put faces to the voices. "What was she listening to?"

"It's called…well I don't even know the full name, but I know it has 'Pussy' in the band name."

*Pussy Riot.* Dominique mentally put herself in their conversation and wanted to discuss the bigger issue of how cool the Internet was that a kid in podunk Texas could get in touch with one of the most socially revolutionary musical groups she knew.

Her thoughts were interrupted when she saw the front door swing open. Amy stood in the doorway. Dominique stared, wanting to take in the sight of her beauty, but stopped. She gasped as Amy walked closer and she saw the tear streaks down her face. She wanted to go to her, comfort her and take her out of this place, but she resisted the urge. If Amy had wanted her company, she would have texted. She held her place on her barstool but waved as Amy got closer.

To her relief, Amy smiled and walked over toward her.

"Hey," Amy said, confusion wrinkling her brow. "What are you doing here?"

"I just thought it would do me some good to get out of the hotel room so I don't go completely stir-crazy. What about you?"

"I honestly don't know." She shook her head. She raised her hands but then dropped them to her side.

"Are you okay?" Dominique slid off her barstool and gestured for Amy to take a seat.

Amy eyed the seat and finally nodded. "Thank you," she said. "And I don't know. I will be fine. Right now I'm kind of a mess."

"Want to talk about it, or do you want to have some drinks and I'll drive you home?"

"Is it okay if I take a rain check on talking it out?" Amy eyed Dominique's half full drink on the bar top.

"Yes, and you can drink that as well. I'll be around if and when you want to talk. For tonight, though, I'm happy you're here. If you want company, we can have drinks, dance, and not worry about anything."

Amy downed what was left in Dominique's glass and motioned to Louie.

"Amelia!" He called out and came over to offer her a hug. "I haven't seen you around much lately. How have you been?"

"Busy," she lied, "but good."

Dominique watched him look at her in concern. There was no doubt he read through the lies too easily, but as a skilled bartender, he treated them like truth. "Glad to hear it." He peered around the corner and caught Dominique's eye. "You gave up your seat?"

"She needed it more than I did," she said with a smile. "Just passing on the courtesy to keep the friendly nature going around this place."

"I knew I liked you." He smiled at her and nodded. "I'll get a drink for both of you on the house, something for my two favorite ladies in this place tonight."

They placed their orders and waited. Amy lifted up her right hand, beckoning Dominique to come closer.

"What is it?" she asked, stepping up to close the gap between them.

Wordlessly, Amy leaned her head against Dominique's body. Dominique gently stroked Amy's back. Remembering Amy's fear of coming out, she looked around to make sure they weren't causing a scene. It seemed everyone, including her persistent suitor from the beginning of the night, had moved onto bigger things.

"If it's all the same to you, I think I'd like to go home after this drink." Amy's voice was barely above a whisper, sounding tired and gravelly.

"Whatever you need." Dominique continued to massage Amy's tense muscles. "I'm here for whatever you need."

"I think I'll take you up on the ride home." She turned her face upward to make eye contact. Even in sadness, her green eyes were gorgeous. "Is that still an option?"

"Of course." Dominique fought the urge to kiss Amy's cheek and gripped her drink when Louie set it in front of her instead. "Like I said, whatever you need."

"I think I need to have you there. Would you mind staying with me instead of at the hotel?"

Dominique thought about the idea and hoped Amy wasn't going to try something in her emotional state. "Don't worry." Amy shook her head. "Not like that. At least, not tonight. I just want to be close to you, if that's okay."

"That's more than okay. But are *you* okay?"

Amy nodded and looked off into the distance while toying with the napkin under her drink. She bit her lip and let out a slow sigh. "I know it's not fair to keep you on the edge, wondering what's going on inside my head. So I'll give you a glimpse. I feel like I'm cheating on someone even though there's no one to cheat on and even though we really didn't have rules of exclusivity lined out anyway before she died."

The words hit their mark and Dominique straightened her back, leaning away from the embrace.

"Don't back away please." Amy reached for Dominique's hand and took it in her own. She took a deep breath and offered a sad smile. "I'm not a lost cause. I'm in a weird place, made even weirder today, so I'm sorting out some things in my head. But I know with certainty I want you here by my side." She leaned her head against Dominique's chest again, and Dominique settled into the comfort of the position. "I also know there's no harm in what we're doing. I just need to sort those things out, which I fully intend on doing. For that reason, I just want to be near you tonight. I want to feel you next to me and know we are moving forward."

Running her fingers through Amy's long hair, Dominique leaned down and planted a single kiss on the top of Amy's head. She waited in silence for a moment, making sure Amy had spoken all she needed to say. "That's good with me," she answered quietly. "We'll move forward at whatever pace is right for both of us."

Amy looked up at her, relief evident in her eyes. "Thank you."

Dominique tightened her grip on Amy's hand. Amy looked around the bar cautiously, and Dominique took the cue, releasing her hand but never moving from her place. Whatever pace they moved at, she knew she wanted to be by Amy's side.

# CHAPTER THIRTEEN

Soft, sleep-filled mumbles floated through the air, causing Dominique's eyes to open briefly. She glanced toward the soft peach curtains in Amy's room, noting it was still dark outside. She shut her eyes tightly, wanting to stay in the warmth of their embrace. Legs tangled around each other, they lay with Dominique holding tight to Amy. She breathed in deeply, relishing the scents that still lingered from Amy's perfume and the hints of floral shampoo. As gingerly as possible, she adjusted the upper half of her body to allow for even closer contact.

From her big spoon position, she had everything she could have asked for. Amy's soft body tucked against hers, she could feel the rhythmic beats of her heart. She nuzzled her head in closer, kissing Amy's neck gently. Amy wriggled her behind softly into Dominique's lap, making her body tighten. Dominique let out a deep breath to release the tension that was forming.

This was not the time or the place, even if she desperately wanted it. She glanced down, seeing Amy still peacefully sleeping, and laid her head back against the pillow.

*Sweet and tender.* That's how she would have described their night. It had been so long since she had snuggled with someone without the precursor of sex that she felt like she had forgotten the magic of being so entirely wrapped up in another person, offering the simple intimacy of comfort.

A phone buzzed on the nightstand, breaking her away from the beauty of the moment. She sighed and craned her neck, avoiding sudden movements that would shift her weight on the bed. Relieved to see it was Amy's phone, she hoped it wouldn't disturb Amy's peaceful sleep, even though as a baker, she would have to be up soon. Dominique wondered what time it was and what time her day must normally start. She scanned her memory for details, only knowing that Amy was always already awake and at work whenever Dominique sent her early morning text messages.

Amy's eyelids fluttered open, causing the corners of Dominique's mouth to droop. Throughout her slumber, she had finally looked like she didn't have to carry the weight of the world on her shoulders. Now it would be another day in the midst of this chaos. Dominique closed her eyes, reminding herself this was life. Life was bumpy, and it was never encouraged to run from one's problems. Amy had issues to deal with right now, but that didn't mean that life had to be negative.

When Dominique opened her eyes, she smiled, watching Amy glance angrily at the phone on the nightstand giving another buzz to remind her she had missed a call. She glanced over her left shoulder, making eye contact with Dominique, and her face broke into a sleepy smile.

"Good morning," she said, letting out a yawn. Her eyes widened and she brought her hand up to cover her mouth. "Morning breath," she mumbled as her cheeks blushed.

"Don't worry about that," Dominique said, her voice still low and husky from having just woken up. "Good morning," she echoed, leaning in to kiss Amy's cheek.

"Mmm," Amy moaned, this time consciously wriggling her body against Dominique's. "This feels really nice." Her voice was so sultry and melodic, Dominique's mind shot off in a million directions.

"It does," she agreed.

Amy lifted up the sheets just enough to allow her to roll over. Facing Dominique, she smiled her devilish grin and wrapped her legs around Dominique's. "In a minute," she said moving closer until only an inch remained between their lips, "I'm going to return that phone call. But before I do, I need some motivation to start my day." She winked and closed the distance between them, her soft lips parted and inviting.

As if fireworks had gone off inside her, Dominique could feel the wetness and the throbbing sensation in her most tender areas. Amy hungrily quickened the tempo, thrusting her body against Dominique's and pinning her on her back, only to climb on top for a full make out session. She ran her teeth across Dominique's bottom lip while she grinded back and forth. Dominique let out a loud moan, running her hands down Amy's back.

"If I don't stop now," Amy said, pulling back, "I don't know if we'll be able to."

Dominique's heart was pounding, and she forced herself to slow her quickened breathing. "We are only going to move forward when you know you're emotionally ready," she said, offering as much of a smile as she could muster in such an intense moment.

"I'm physically ready as hell," Amy said, winking. "So fucking ready. But I should sort some things out first." She straightened her body to sit back in her straddle position. "Just know that when it happens, it'll be amazing."

"Judging from the way you say 'good morning,' I know it will be." Dominique laughed and returned the wink.

As Amy sidled off the bed, Dominique tried to catch her breath. This woman was a firecracker. Amy picked up her phone and listened to the voice mail. Dominique watched the graceful nature of her movements, a complete shift from the wild seductress she had been only seconds before. Amy's eyes widened as she listened. Her hands shook as she pulled the phone from her ear.

"Is everything…?" Dominique's voice trailed off, knowing she already knew the answer to her question. People didn't turn ghost white if everything was okay.

Like a professional actress, Amy turned to face the bed fully with a smile painted on her lips. "Just small town drama. I think I need to go see my parents before I open up the bakery. I'll call you tonight." With that, she turned and disappeared into the bathroom.

Dominique rose from her spot on the bed and gathered her things. From the sound of things clanging around in a frenzy behind the bathroom door, she knew it was time for her to leave.

"Good luck," she called out before she walked out the door. "I'll talk to you tonight."

She had work to do today, but Amy clearly was right. She had things to figure out.

\* \* \*

Wide-eyed, Amelia stared at herself in the mirror. Wringing her hands, she reminded herself she didn't have time for this. It didn't matter if she recognized herself this morning or not. Frantically, she washed her face and applied new mascara. It didn't help. She still looked hollow.

She sighed, pulling out her hairbrush to run it through her tresses as quickly as possible. Deciding that would have to suffice, she walked back to the bedroom, thankful to find Dominique had already let herself out.

They would talk, she reassured herself. But today's agenda was something she had to conquer on her own. Standing in front of her closet, she felt the sting of tears but forced them away. This was not the time for crying. She would be strong and stand her ground. Her hands trembled as she ran them over the tops of hangers. No outfit would be good enough; nor would it make her feel any better.

She pulled a simple blue cardigan out of the closet, only to drop it and cover her face with her hands. Her breathing quickened but she couldn't get any air. Collapsing onto the floor, she pulled her knees to her chest and worked to calm herself. None of this would help her cause.

Gritting her teeth, she stood and picked up the cardigan. Pairing it with a white camisole underneath, she slipped on a pair of jeans and her Toms, refusing to glance in the mirror before she headed out the door.

She almost fell getting into her car, but her heart was racing too much for her to care. In the car, she flipped through radio stations, finding nothing to either soothe her deepest fears or to amp her up for what was to come. Finally, she settled on Bon Jovi and cranked up the dial, letting the sounds of "Livin' on a Prayer" resonate within her. She sang it loudly, deciding that's exactly what she was doing today. She would be living on a prayer and fighting like hell for some semblance of a normal life.

She white-knuckled the steering wheel. Pressing harder on the accelerator, she zipped across town as quickly as possible. She knew if she allowed even one of the festering seeds of doubt in her mind to implant, she'd turn the car around. She didn't have time for that. Not today.

Within five minutes, she pulled into the familiar driveway. The blue shutters on the front of the red brick house remained a welcoming beam, even if the sun and wind over the years had taken their toll on the wood. "Those need to be painted," she said, exhaling. Maybe she would offer to do it for them, if they still wanted to talk to her after today.

She gripped the steering wheel for one final moment of stability and opened her car door. Before she could get out, she saw her dad round the corner, dressed for the day's work. His faded coveralls and flannel shirt were the same as they always were. Everything seemed normal, albeit his gray beard was a little longer than he usually grew it. She smiled at the sight, relishing in a solitary, fleeting normal moment. The minute he saw her, he broke into a huge smile and double-timed his steps moving toward her car.

"Hey there, Amy-bug!" He called out, his deep voice booming through the morning air. "What are you doing out this way so early?"

"How early do you have to be at work today?" she asked, knowing that as the owner of his truck tire shop, he had some flexibility. Even so, much like her day, his began too early.

"I have an appointment in just a couple of hours." He locked eyes on her and a frown replaced his smile. His brow knit together. "What's wrong, honey?"

"I just needed to talk to you and Mom for a few minutes, if you have time."

"I'll make time." He wrapped his big strong arms around her and pulled her in for a bear hug. "I'll always make time for my girl. Go on inside. I'm going to make a call to Brent down at the shop to let him know that he'll need to do morning set up. Then I'll be in right behind you." He picked up his phone but turned back in her direction for a minute. "Your mama made biscuits and gravy this morning. I'm sure there's still some left. Go in and eat, get some coffee, and then we'll talk about whatever is troubling you. Just remember not to stress and that God is in control."

She walked up to the front step, replaying his words. She knew he believed in them and hoped they'd bring him some comfort once she had dropped a bomb big enough to destroy his mental focus for more than just today. She reached for the door handle but quickly pulled her hand back. Relying on the rail next to the flowerbeds out in front of the house, she stabilized herself. Yes, she was going to be ruining his day and her mother's. Hell, she was probably going to ruin their year. But there was no turning back now. Straightening her shoulders, she twisted the door handle and let herself into the house she had always thought of as her one true home.

"Mom," she attempted to call out, but her voice cracked. She rounded the corner like a woman on a mission and found her mom in front of the stove, scooping gravy out of a pot with a ladle.

"Honey?" She turned around, a mixture of shock and joy on her face. The reminder was clear without having been spoken—Amelia didn't come around enough. "I wasn't expecting you, but take a seat and I'll fix you a plate."

Amelia let out a deep breath. "I'm not really hungry. I just came over to talk."

"Nonsense." Her mother was already pulling a plate out of the cabinet and slathering a biscuit with gravy. "Have a seat." She motioned to the stools around the bar and Amelia heeded her order. "You came over during breakfast time, and I'm still not used to cooking for just your father and I, even after all these years. So there's plenty."

She plopped the plate down in front of Amelia. "I…" Amelia started to protest but stopped when her mom placed her hands on her hips.

"You look thin as a rail, honey, and I'm sure you haven't already eaten. Have you?" Her no-nonsense tone hadn't lost its edge, even without a kid in the home.

"I haven't," she admitted, taking the fork in her hand reluctantly. Her stomach churned, but the gravy did smell good. It smelled like home. Her mother busied herself around the kitchen, pouring Amelia a cup of coffee. She took a small bite and her stomach gurgled, reminding her she hadn't eaten at all in over a day. Greedily she scooped another larger bite into her mouth, thankful for her mother's home cooking.

"What brought you here today?" her mother asked, climbing up on the barstool beside Amelia. "Don't get me wrong. I'm thrilled. It's a pleasant surprise, but you look upset. What's going on? Are you okay?"

As Amelia listened to her throw fastball questions, she was thankful for her mouthful of biscuits and gravy. She realized again exactly where she got her tendency to ramble.

She swallowed and took a sip of the coffee before turning to face her mother. "I need to talk to you and Dad. I have some things that I just need to talk to both of you about."

It was the worst non-answer she had ever given in her life, but she was trying to buy herself some time. She shoved another bite of food into her mouth, licking the gravy from the fork. "This is really good."

"Even as an adult, I have to remind you not to talk with food in your mouth?" Her mother raised an eyebrow and Amelia laughed.

Thankful to have the mood lightened for a minute, she continued to devour her breakfast. A last supper of sorts, she mused. Meanwhile, her mom had almost entirely forgotten she came over with a purpose and was rambling on about the Bible study she was leading, neighborhood gossip, and more.

"Glad you got some breakfast," her dad's voice boomed through the kitchen with a gleeful sound. "It's good stuff, so eat up."

"Are you both trying to fatten me up?" She laughed when her father walked closer, patting his belly.

"It's worked well for me, and I'm just saying you could stand to have a few more pounds on your frame. You don't look like you've been eating much."

She gulped and set down her fork. Glancing down, she knew they were right. Eating was the least of her worries these days. She didn't have time, didn't feel like it, or couldn't stand the thought of food when so much of her life was up in the air.

Whistling as he moved around the kitchen, her father poured himself a cup of coffee and set it in on the counter across from Amelia. He propped his elbows up on the opposite side of the bar and leveled his gaze. "You ready to talk about whatever's got you down?"

Amelia opened her mouth, but words wouldn't form. She nodded instead, taking a sip of her coffee and then clearing her throat. "I think so," she finally managed.

She closed her eyes, ran her fingers through her hair, and took a deep breath.

"Did someone hurt you?" her mother interjected.

"Mom, please be patient." She held up her hand and scooted her chair back from the bar a few inches. "I'm going to need some room to breathe. I'm also going to need the opportunity to pick my words."

"We're both patient." Her mother jerked her head back as if she had been slapped. "Aren't we, George? We're patient people. What are you insinuating?"

"Mom, stop." She glanced at her dad, silently pleading for help. He shrugged, so she turned her attention back to her mother. "What I have to say is hard for me. It'll be hard for both of you too. Because of that, I need you to let me finish speaking before you interrupt."

Her mother snatched her coffee cup off the counter and took a sip. Raising an eyebrow in Amelia's direction, she nodded for her to proceed.

"Thank you." Another deep breath served as another failure to gain composure. "Okay, here goes."

She bit her lip and grabbed the edge of her barstool, hiding her shaking hands. "I love you both very much." For just a second, she took in their faces and smiled. "I really love you and appreciate all you've done for me. That's why it's taken so long for us to have this conversation, to be honest. I wanted to protect you from things I wasn't sure you could handle. I wanted to protect all three of us from losing what it is we have together."

Her father stiffened across the table and then leaned in closer, reaching across to put a hand on her shoulder. "Honey, don't talk like that. We can get through anything. Nothing will change who we are together—what we are."

A single tear formed in the corner of her eye and she winced.

"Sorry I forgot the rules," he said, casting his eyes downward. "I won't interrupt again."

She reached up to grab his hand on her shoulder, tightening her grip and nodding at him. His eyes widened when her cold, trembling hands touched his, but he said nothing. Tightlipped, he nodded at her. She bit her lip and glanced down. When she straightened her body, she smiled at each of them individually.

"I'm not going to belabor the point anymore. It's too hard. So know I had a lot of lead-in, but I'm ditching it and going off the cuff." She let out a sigh. "I'm gay."

Her father opened his mouth but stood still, his brow furrowed. His shoulders dropped and his eyes went to the left, then the right. She glanced to her mother, whose eyebrow was raised. It looked to Amelia like it might stick that way permanently.

She brought her hands up to the counter, preparing to say something, anything, but clasped them together in front of her instead.

"Can we speak now?" her mother asked, shifting her weight in her chair and leaning forward in Amelia's direction. Amelia nodded and her mouth went dry.

"Good." She drug out the word, her voice far more high-pitched than normal. "I think I misunderstood you and guessing from your father's reaction, he probably did too. Can you elaborate and maybe tell us what it is you were going to use as your lead-in, so this all makes a little more sense?"

They both wore the same confused expression. She nodded and reached for her coffee cup. Holding up her finger to signal she needed a second, she took a drink. Her nerves buzzed within her, so she set the cup back on the counter. Filling her already crazed body with caffeine wouldn't be in her best interest. She gripped the side of the counter. "You didn't misunderstand. What I said is true. There was going to be a more graceful lead-in, but I had to rip the Band-Aid off."

Both her mother's eyebrows had risen up so high they almost touched her hairline, and if looks could kill, Amelia was fairly certain she'd have been blasted off the earth that very second. Not able to look at her father, Amelia cast her eyes to the tile on the counter, focusing on the lines in the marble.

She cleared her throat. "I like women. I always have. It's something I suppressed for a long time because it made things easier, not just for us as a family but just for me, too. It made my life easier to assume I'd just grow old by myself and be happily single forever. But that changed recently."

"Who is she?" Her father's voice croaked, cutting straight into her heart. It was a tone she'd only heard from him a few times in her life, mostly in moments of defeat.

Without moving her neck, she let her eyes drift up to see the tears in his eyes. "Who is she?" he asked again.

"I'll answer that in a minute." She looked down again. "Right now this has to be about me, because she is no longer in the picture. I don't have someone to be the scapegoat or someone to blame for making me this way. I've always been this way. I just need to get that out and make that clear." Forcing herself upright in her chair, she looked both of them in the eye. "I know this will be hard for both of you to deal with and you might need some time to think things through. I just want you both to know that it doesn't change who I am, who I've always been. For years I've struggled with accepting it myself, and I'm finally happy. I am happy with who I am and I intend to live in that happiness, even in a town such as this."

Her mother laughed, but the sound was devoid of humor. "It does change who you are." Her voice remained flat, her gaze penetrating. "We will not stand for this. We will not accept this. And it changes everything."

"It doesn't. I'm the same me I was when you set a plate of biscuits and gravy in front of me this morning. I'm the same kid you raised and the same woman you've always been proud to call yours. I'm still me."

She looked to her father, wishing he were better at hiding his inner turmoil. His face was red and scrunched, his teeth gritted together. "Dad, it's still me."

Swallowing hard, he looked away, opting to focus on the detailing in the woodwork of the cabinets rather than respond.

She exhaled slowly, pursing her lips. "Look, I don't expect things to be easy at first. I will give you all some time to think about it. I just wanted you to know from me, not from someone else."

"Who else knows?" Her father asked, still looking off in the distance.

"Currently you both and a couple of other people, but that's probably going to change soon. It may become bigger news than I would personally care for it to become, but I wanted you to hear it from me."

"Who?" Her father repeated his question, this time leaving no room for her to dodge it.

"If you're asking who *she* was, it was Chloe Stanton."

His head seemed to roll back over the top of his neck in an exaggerated turn in her direction. Wide-eyed and mouth agape, he stared, shaking his head.

She held up her hands in defense. "Please don't give me that look, Dad. I know what you all said about her behind closed doors, but you know as well as I do that she was kind-hearted and full of life. She was a salt-of-the-earth type of person, and I know you think she was flawed. But the same qualities you fault her for are the ones that live in me. You liked her as a person with a 'love the sinner, hate the sin' type of attitude, but you didn't like her because she was gay. So am I, and I've been having a really hard time since she passed. We were together up until the day she was killed."

"You do realize they are saying she was killed because she was gay, and now you're just ready to jump on that train as well?" Her mother's voice rose with every word, until she was shouting the question at Amelia.

"I don't have a choice."

"What do you mean?" Her mother stood, angrily slapping her palms against the counter and leveling her gaze. "You don't have a choice whether you want to be gay or not, or you don't have a choice about screaming it from the mountaintops?"

"Honestly, I don't have a choice about either," Amelia said, shaking her head. "I know you have always thought being gay was a choice, a temptation people give in to. But it's not like that. I wish I had another way to explain it to you other than the fact that I've tried to fight it my entire life, and I'm incapable of fighting it. And no, I don't have a choice over who knows what and when anymore, either."

"Why's that?" Her father's words were clipped, his face pained but stern.

Amelia cupped her hands around her forehead. Her head throbbed from the rollercoaster of emotions she was riding. "I was with her the day she was killed. I was there that evening, but not that night. I don't know the full details of what happened that night, and I guess we may all be trying to solve that mystery forever. But I do know, as of last night, that my fingerprints were found on a number of items around her house. Of course I know why they were. I was there..." Their pinched expressions told her they were ready for this conversation to end, but she had to press through to the end. "I was there often." Her mother shivered and turned away in disgust. Amelia cleared her throat and continued. "I cooked her dinner that night, placing my fingerprints on the murder weapon, apparently."

Her father's face whitened. "They don't think..."

"No. They don't. At least not right now. But it is a breakthrough in their case. They know they're not looking for another suspect. I don't know how to explain it other than that I have to go back in for questioning at some point. They know now those were my prints. It's complicated. But I don't think I'm in trouble."

"Then why would they make it public? That seems truly unnecessary." Her father was pacing around the kitchen while he talked, wringing his hands together and devising a plan. She had seen that face a million times and knew he was working to solve her problem. "They don't have to make that public until there's a reason to do so. The only reason they'd need to say anything is if they thought you killed her, which you don't think they do."

"Dad, it's not that easy."

"It can be." He turned on a heel and pointed in her direction. "I'll make some calls. I'll talk to Wes. He can make sure this doesn't get into the wrong hands."

She held up both hands in his direction. "Stop, please. It's not a simple fix. I got a call from Mandy at the Telegram today. She's already caught the scent of the trail. Apparently she's been going to the detectives daily, asking for updates. She left me a voice mail telling me as much, and she already knows I was called in for questioning last night. They gave her the Cliff Notes version, and she wants the full story from me."

"No. You're not doing it." Her mother's voice was shrill. "You're not running our family name through that. We have no reason to be named in a story about a murdered gay woman. That's not who we are."

Amelia rose from her seat. She wanted to hug them or offer them some comfort, but both were stiff as boards. "I wanted to give you a heads up. I'm going to do what I have to do, and I'm going to be who I am. I just wanted you to know ahead of time, rather than reading it in a newspaper, if that's how this all shakes out. But I've got to get going. I'm going to go open up the bakery and get back to my day. I'm sorry if I've upset the balance of both of your days, but I love you both."

Neither moved from their spots, stubbornly glued to the floor. Her father's face looked as though it might explode, and she knew he had to be holding back a slew of things he wanted to say. "Call me when you're ready to talk," she added as she scurried out of the kitchen.

Only when she was in her car, halfway to the bakery, could she let out the breath she had been holding. When she did, she had to pull over to the side of the road to deal with the sob that worked its way up from her core and ripped out of her mouth, bringing with it an onslaught of tears.

Their faces, their words, their stubbornness all flashed back in her mind like a bad movie. They wouldn't yield. She had always known as much, but she still could have never been prepared for their refusal to accept the truth.

She allowed herself time to wallow in the pain of such rejection and cry it out before flipping down the overhead mirror of her car and looking at her reflection. She wiped away the streaks of mascara and used a tissue from the console to fix her makeup. Rolling her neck from side to side, she heard the creaking of her bones and felt the pain in her shoulders. Tension truly was hell on the body.

Fumbling in her purse, she pulled out her cell phone. With trembling hands, she hit the button and listened to the voice mail once more before locking her phone and putting it back in its place. She had time to decide what she wanted to do. She could opt not to comment.

Her mind went wild, wondering whether they'd construct a more heinous story without her input. Shivers went through her. She shook her arms, willing herself to get it together. She would figure it out, but first she was going to set her mind at ease making pastries and muffins and brewing some coffee for folks who would come see her—even if the news story kept them away from the shop tomorrow.

She still had today, and she would appreciate that for all it was worth.

Arriving at the bakery, her first step was to prep the ovens. Glancing at the clock, she forcefully ran her fingers through her hair. It was already six-thirty. She was going to have to move in double-time. Although she preferred to hand mix the dough, she set the automatic mixer and filled the coffeepot. She had no time for personal touches today. It was going to be a "take it or leave it" type of day.

Once she finally had everything on to mix and make, she let out a long sigh and looked around the kitchen. Everything was a mess. Dough was strewn about the counters in globs, coffee grounds littered the area underneath the large pot, and her apron was splotched with any number of things.

Ripping it off over her head, she scurried across the room and flipped the sign on the door to "Open," before hitting play on her Pandora station. Soft jazz filled the room and she shook her head. Flipping through stations, she finally settled on Sara Bareilles radio. An unrecognizable pop song came through the speakers. She decided it was better than the angry rock she wanted. At least it would make her customers feel more at ease.

She looked to the door. No one had come into the shop yet. She thought it odd, but decided it gave her a few more minutes. Racing across the floor, she grabbed a fresh apron out of the closet and put it on, checking the ovens. Twenty minutes remained on cook time. With a shake of her head, she grabbed the daily special chalkboard and used the side of her hand to wipe it clean. As craftily as possible, she tried to decorate the sign with happy symbols, flowers and curling letters for her sad message, "Pastries half-off until 7:30."

She couldn't justify selling day-old muffins and pastries for full price. She placed the sign near the display window and set out yesterday's baked goods.

No movement showed outside her front door, and her heart fell. This was supposed to be her last day of sorts—her last normal day, at least. She let out a long, deep breath and busied herself with cleaning the kitchen.

The dinging of her door brought a smile to her face. As quickly as possible, she washed her hands and rounded the corner of the kitchen to greet her customer.

"Good morning, Walter," she said, beaming with joy. This was her happy place and she'd take it as long as it was offered.

"Morning, Amelia," he said, tipping his hat in her direction. "I'm moving a little slow this morning. I'm going to need a strong cup of joe to get me going."

"I understand that. I'll have it right up." She took in his face. Its wrinkles seemed to increase with every passing time she saw him. One of the few ranchers in the area who had actually managed to retire and pass his working operations down to his sons, he was something of a town legacy. His thick glasses and grandfatherly charm, combined with the stories he liked to tell of the "good old days," always made her feel warmer inside. Today was no exception. She listened as he told her about his oldest son's baby on the way and congratulated him again.

When she came back with a hot cup of coffee in a to-go cup, he smiled at her. "Thank you, ma'am." He glanced to the sign and smiled. "Half-off today, huh?"

"Yes sir," she said, giving him a sheepish grin. "I got a late start today, so those were made last night. Fresh ones should be ready in just a few minutes. But if you'd like one of these, I can get you one."

"I'll take that blueberry muffin," he said. As she put on a glove and reached for the muffin, he followed her over to the glass. "No need to be ashamed about a little late start once in a while. Life is full of things that pop up, and sometimes you have to take care of them. Looks like you've got a pretty good grasp on that though." He laughed and looked around the shop. "In fact, it looks like you've got a pretty good grasp on most things. Remember, Amelia, roll with the punches of life, and you'll be all right."

She stared at him as she bagged his muffin, wondering how he had known exactly what she needed to hear today.

"Thank you," she said, handing over the bag and accepting his money. As she bid him a good day, she used the glass of the pastry case as a mirror. No wonder he had chimed in with encouragement. She looked as awful as she felt.

Taking a seat on the stool she kept behind the counter, she laid her head in her hands. Breaking through the clutter in her brain, she heard the opening notes to "Silent Legacy" by Melissa Etheridge playing through the shop's speakers. She let the words wash over her, reminding her she didn't have to contribute to a culture of silence and hatred. Each lyric breathed into her soul, lighting a fire that had been burned down to embers only moments before.

Giving in to her emotions, she experienced each for what it was worth. Anger for the hatred. Frustration with the intolerance and lack of understanding. Hatred for what had happened to Chloe. Sadness and disappointment aimed at her parents, at herself. Inspiration by Melissa's legacy.

As the song drew to an end, she lifted her head and breathed in deeply, exhaling freedom. She had the power to speak out. She had a voice. And it was high time she learned to use it.

Even though her hands trembled, she picked up her phone, knowing what she had to do.

# CHAPTER FOURTEEN

Filled with teenagers chattering, the room was a hotbed of life and drama. Dominique stifled laughter as two of the girls talked in excited tones about a boy who had looked their direction. She had already overheard one boy tell his friends that he couldn't wait to see the pissed-off look on his mom's face when she saw the pictures, and she figured that's why several of them were here. Regardless of their reasoning for being in the room with her after school, she was thankful they were here, even if just for a taste of teenage rebellion.

She shook her head, surveying their artwork, and wished standing up for what was right didn't have to be a rebellion. Closing her eyes, she quietly tried to exhale her negative energy. She didn't want them to get the wrong idea.

Their multi-colored posters were strewn about the floor. Her favorite, from one of the quieter students, simply read, *Love not hate. Justice for Chloe.*

"Great job, Quinn," she said, patting the girl on the shoulder. "I think you captured exactly what needed to be said."

The girl looked up, her blue eyes shiny with the remnants of tears. "Thank you," she whispered. Dominique knelt to her knees, noting the depth of the phrase. She wasn't being thanked for complimenting Quinn's artwork. She was being thanked for her work.

"If you need to talk, I am here," Dominique whispered the words, careful not to be overheard by other students.

Quinn's eyes widened and she looked around the room timidly. She shook her head, looked down at her lap and mouthed, "Later."

Dominique nodded. "Whenever you're ready."

She walked around the room again, congratulating and thanking various students for their participation. It might have only been a group of six kids, but it was a start—one this town desperately needed.

*Shape the next generation and you can help spread love.* She replayed the words of her mentor in her memory. It was much easier to teach a group of young people about love and equality than it was to try to change long-standing views in a stubborn older person's mind. She thought about the people she had tried to talk to around town. They were set in their ways, refusing to acknowledge the depth of what had happened here.

For these kids, it was different. For the two older boys in the room, it was about shock factor for their parents. For the rest of them, it seemed as though they understood. They were part of a bigger, much more diverse world.

Looking from face to face, she saw hope for the future of Knell.

"Everyone, let's gather in the corner of the room for a photo," she said, clapping her hands to get their attention. "Grab your signs and stand over there."

All stood except Quinn, whose paint covered hands shook as she reached for her poster.

"Come on Quinn," one of the boys urged while they waited for her. "Why are you always so afraid of everything? Stop being shy and get over here."

Instead of offering encouragement, his words seemed to freeze her in place, causing her to drop her poster to the floor again.

"Yeah, you're always afraid," the other boy said, his tone mocking her. "Scaredy Quinn, stand up for something. We're all waiting."

She turned and looked over her right shoulder, and the boy shook his head at her, his jaw set and challenging.

"Enough," Dominique said, stepping between the two students. "Your taunting and pressuring is the exact opposite of the goal we're trying to accomplish." He frowned at her, so she stepped closer to him. "We're all different. That's the point."

"Yeah," he said, laughing snidely. "You're gay. You're definitely different."

"And you're definitely missing the point of this entire day." She sighed and put her hands on her hips. "I haven't addressed my sexual orientation with you all. And I'm not going to right now. That's not at the heart of the matter. The issue is that this town was the site of hate-filled actions, and hate is bred through intolerance and bullying. You're bullying right now, and you may not even realize it."

His face reddened, but he stood firm, pushing out his chest. "I'm not bullying her. I'm encouraging her. There's a difference."

"There certainly is." Dominique kept her tone matter-of-fact. "And most of it is in the delivery. Let Quinn make her own decisions and applaud them. Don't push and shove, even if it's just verbally. Don't point out differences as flaws. And learn to love one another for who you are, not despite who you are. That's the point of what we're doing today. That's why we're taking a stand. We're working to help shape the next generation of this town and ensure that the type of hatred shown here in Chloe Stanton's hate crime murder is not repeated in the future."

Everyone, aside from the two older boys, nodded. She took in the determination plastered on a junior high boy's face and cleared her throat. "I am not from here. I'm not in this community full time. That's why I need you all. I need you all to be the continuation of my voice in this community, of your own voices, speaking for a better and more loving society. Can you do that for me?"

Again, all but two nodded. "You two." She pointed. "Can you do that for me? It means not only standing up for what is right, but also doing what is right and treating each other with respect."

"This is lame," the boy who had been arguing with her said. Tossing his sign to the floor, he stomped on it and strode out the door. His friend followed suit, and once she heard the door slam behind them, she let out a deep breath.

Making eye contact with each of the remaining students, she forced a smile. Four committed students were better than six with a couple of defiant, hateful ones thrown into the mix.

"It's okay." She kept her tone light and upbeat. "We're all okay in here, and we can still take our group photo. Quinn, do you want to join us?"

Behind her, Quinn was already standing. "I'm ready," she said, nodding. With newfound determination, Quinn walked over and joined the group. Dominique couldn't help but notice how her shoulders were straightened, no longer slumping the way they had been every other time she had seen the girl.

A ball formed in the pit of her stomach and she tried to ignore the nagging nausea, wondering if anyone had ever stepped up in the girl's corner before. She snapped several photos and put the camera on a timer to hop into the back of one of them.

"Thank you all," she said, offering them sincere smiles. "Remember to have your parents sign the photo release forms and bring those back in tomorrow." A couple of them hugged her on their way out the door, but Quinn remained behind, still standing in the corner of the room.

When it was quiet in the room, Quinn walked over and shut the door. "I'm ready," she said, taking a seat on one of the chairs.

Dominique took a seat in a chair and faced it toward Quinn, making sure to keep a safe, non-threatening distance. She nodded and offered Quinn a soft smile.

Quinn placed her hands folded in her lap and looked to a blank space on the wall. "I'm not like all the others." Her words were quiet and slow. "I haven't ever really fit in with the other kids. They think I'm quiet and shy. I am, but it's just because I don't want to stand out. You saw Jace and Roper." Dominique made a mental note of the boys' names, in case she had to remember them later. "That's how everyone treats me. They poke fun and treat me differently, all because I don't fit their idea of who I'm supposed to be. That's why I'm here. I was excited when you came to town and I heard that someone was trying to do things differently here. That's the problem. No one ever tries to make a difference. They just figure everything is going to be the same forever, and anyone who doesn't fit in is destined to go through a series of growing pains. Do you know what I mean?"

Quinn turned her eyes toward Dominique. They seemed to have darkened and the lines forming across her forehead begged for encouragement.

"It doesn't have to be like that." Dominique kept her words gentle. "I understand what you mean, and it must feel that way. But it doesn't have to be that way."

"My mom calls them growing pains." Quinn shrugged. "She says it's just something I have to go through and that I'll find friends who understand me better in college. She said it's always been like that, and if I want to move somewhere else where I don't have to fit in, I can do it when I graduate."

"That's true to a degree." Dominique leaned in and lowered her head, so she could make eye contact with Quinn. "Things around here *can* change. That's why I'm here. And you may not be just like everyone, but no one is. They just don't realize it. They each have things they do, think, feel, or are that aren't the norm. They just won't admit it. They're too focused on being just like everyone else. You're one of the brave ones."

Quinn sat back in her chair, scrunching her nose. "Brave?" she asked. "You think I'm brave? I'm the furthest thing from brave. I'm a quiet coward."

Dominique shook her head. "You are brave enough to stand out, whether that's in your quiet presence or in your refusal to be just like the rest of them. You're brave, and you'll make a difference here. You're already working on it. And it's not going to change here overnight. The lack of understanding of differences has been passed down for generations. Families throughout this town's history have shaped the mold they want you to fit. They expect people to fit it. They demand it. And that's not an easy fix." She placed her hand gently on the girl's shoulder. "But you are doing something to make that better for the future. You're working to make a difference in Chloe's honor, for everyone who might be a little different."

"That's the other thing." Quinn's lip quivered and she cast her eyes downward again. "I don't exactly know what makes me so strange, but I know that I've thought about things…" She trailed off, tightening the clasp of her hands. "Things that make me wonder if I'm like Chloe was and if I'm in danger. Her death really upset me, and it really made me scared." Her breathing quickened, as did the pace of her words. "I don't know for sure that I'm like *that*, but I know there's something different. I know I'm scared to even think of it."

"You don't have to figure that out overnight," Dominique said. "Just so you know, I understand that struggle. That boy— Jace or Roper, I'm not sure which one said it—he was right. I am gay. I'm a lesbian, and I know that struggle. You may be. You may not be. That's something only you know for certain. But I will tell you this. I'm here to talk if you need someone to talk to, and I'm here to make sure that, when you figure things out, you have a safe place to do it."

Tears slid down Quinn's face, and she nodded. She opened her mouth to speak, but only ragged breaths came out. She nodded again, stood, hugged Dominique, and rushed from the room.

Alone in the room, Dominique looked around at the mess of markers, paints and paper. As she took it all in, she thought about the mess of this town and shook her head. Rubbing her fingertips against her temples, she wished for Quinn's sake, for Amy's sake, and for the sake of this entire place, things were easier.

Taking deep breaths, she calmed herself and set to work cleaning the mess and saving a copy of the photo to post to

social media once she had the appropriate parental consent—
something she feared she might not get once parents knew
where their kids had been spending their afternoons.

When she finished, she gathered her things and heard her
phone ding. She checked the message and smiled when she saw
Amy's name flash across the screen: *Dinner at my place tonight at
7 if you're free?* As Dominique read the words, her smile grew.
After this morning's crazed start, she had wondered how Amy
was doing all day but had resisted reaching out. It now appeared
that whatever she was working through, maybe she'd want to
clue Dominique in.

# CHAPTER FIFTEEN

The scent of pepperoni filled the air as steam rose from the box in Amelia's hands. She looked around her house, trying to decide where dining would be more intimate. The living room offered comfort and a cozy, casual atmosphere. But the dining room could be transformed easily into an alcove of romance with a few candles.

She set the box down and shuffled through her cabinets, finding two long candles. She was being silly, she knew, but she wanted—*needed*—to make it special. Dominique was incredible and today was a day to remember. Dinner, even if it wasn't gourmet or home cooked, deserved the same type of prominence.

She glanced at the clock on the wall, grateful it was only six. She maneuvered her way around the kitchen, opening the bottle of red wine she had purchased to let it breathe, and sliding the pizza into the oven to keep it warm.

Once upstairs, she flipped through items in her closet. Her fingers brushed against the soft red fabric of her favorite dress.

Memories of the last time she had donned the sultry dress flashed in her mind.

*"You look unbelievably sexy." Chloe's voice quivered as lust built in her eyes.*

She shook her head, warding off the memory at least for tonight, and settled instead on a simple but sleek black dress, one with no memory of Chloe on it. Tonight was about Dominique and Dominique only. Pairing it with sensible heels, she set to work on her makeup.

In the mirror, she stared at her reflection, proud to see a new blaze in her green eyes. Tonight they shined with empowerment. She was proud of herself, broken in some ways but proud. From this, she would rise and she would be stronger. And in time, so would the community.

She wanted the sparkle in her eyes to pop, so she opted to use a glimmering eye shadow. She wanted the same for her plump lips, selecting a pouty pink gloss to coat them. Thinking of Dominique's dark and mysterious eyes, she smiled at her reflection, hoping her gloss wouldn't stay on too long. The thought of their lips colliding with the same passion they had earlier today made her tense. She needed to feel Dominique's body under hers, to hear those moans again. Only this time, she needed more.

With one final glance in the mirror, she fluffed her hair and winked at her reflection. She looked good, but more importantly she *felt* good. Shoulders back, and with a broad smile on her face, she was ready for a night of celebration.

Stronger than she had felt in months, she strolled down the hallway, casually taking a seat at the dinner table to wait on her date. As the minutes passed, she closed her eyes, taking a moment of reflection and meditation.

In the silence, one thought resonated within her, blossoming until it became a mantra. *Whatever may come, I am me.* She could hear footsteps outside her front door and was thankful for living in such a quiet area. She opened her eyes and rose from her place, freedom and peace emanating from her body with each step.

She flung open the door, a huge smile on her face, catching Dominique pacing with her back to the door.

"I didn't want to come in early." Dominique turned around. Her mouth fell open and her eyes widened. Raising an eyebrow, she let out a low laugh. "Damn," she said. Her mouth opened again and she let out a flustered sigh. "You look amazing." She looked down at her jeans and fitted black shirt. "I didn't know we were dressing up. I can go change."

"You look amazing," Amelia said. "Don't even think about changing. This is just something I wanted to wear tonight."

"It's…" Dominique shook her head, awe evident on her face. The corners of Amelia's lips turned up even more into a devious smile. It felt good to be appreciated. "It's incredible. Good choice," she added, dropping her head as her cheeks reddened.

"Thank you. Come inside." Amelia stepped back from the door, holding out her arm in welcome.

Dominique slipped past her inside the house, stopping in the living room and turning to face Amelia. "You are the sweetest. You didn't have to go to all this trouble." She pointed to the lit candles on the dining room table.

Amelia laughed. "Trust me. I didn't go to much trouble. You'll see. But first, there's something I've been wanting to do all day."

Dominique raised an eyebrow as Amelia walked over to her. She opened her mouth to speak, but Amelia didn't give her time to say anything. Instead, she covered Dominique's lips with her own, delighting in their taste. Dominique wrapped her hands around the back of Amelia's neck, tangling her hands in her hair.

Their bodies came together to the point Amelia couldn't tell whose was whose. She moaned, feeling Dominique's heart pounding against her own chest. When Amelia finally pulled her head back, she let out a contented sigh.

Dominique tightened her arms around Amelia's body. "Was it worth the wait?"

"Mmm," Amelia responded, her body tingling in every place she wanted Dominique to touch. "It was more than worth it."

Leading with her shoulders to give Dominique a glance at just how low-cut her dress was, she shimmied backward out of the embrace and made her way to the kitchen. "Dinner's ready," she called out in her best June Cleaver voice.

She brought out two glasses of wine first and set them on the table. Dominique's eyes lit up, and she leaned down to watch Amelia slink off to the kitchen once more.

"And now it's served," she said, laughing as she set the pizza and paper plates in the middle of the table.

"It's perfect," Dominique responded, her voice still thick with lust. "Thank you."

Amelia bit her lip. Suddenly she wasn't hungry—for pizza anyway. She closed her eyes, reminding herself that good things came to those who waited and pulled out her chair, inching it even closer to Dominique's. She longed to feel even the slightest brush of Dominique's skin against hers.

As they ate, they regaled each other with stories of their workdays. Amelia listened intently, careful not to let her big news slip out before it was time.

Halfway through her second slice, Dominique set down her pizza and shook her head. "I'm so sorry," she said, wiping the corners of her mouth with a napkin. "I got so caught up in everything that happened when I first got here that I forgot to ask about your day, or your morning. I know you were upset earlier. Is everything okay?"

"It's more than okay," Amelia answered with a smile. "We'll talk about that later. For now, tell me more about the kids."

As Dominique filled her in, she couldn't help but see the superhero Dominique was. Strong, collected, geared for changing hearts and minds. And incredibly sexy, too. Amelia's thoughts trailed off and her eyes scanned over Dominique's body. Her soft brown skin, her kind but intense eyes, and the way she smiled when she talked about the work she was doing all made her even more attractive.

"Are you done eating?" Dominique pointed to Amelia's untouched second piece of pizza.

Amelia shrugged and crumpled her napkin in her hand. "I guess I wasn't as hungry as I thought. I was a little distracted to be honest." She was rambling. She shut her mouth and stood.

Dominique cocked her head to the side and wiped her hands on her napkin. Following suit, she stood. There was no more waiting. She was ready. She grabbed Dominique's hand and bounded down the hallway.

Dominique's heart raced in her chest and her head spun in confusion. Still, she couldn't help herself. Following Amy was exactly what she wanted to do and when she rounded the corner into the bedroom, there was no need to question anything.

When Amy turned to her, breathlessly kissing her with a passion Dominique didn't know was in her, confusion stopped. Everything stopped. Amy was in full control, pushing her backward until her body lay splayed out on the bed.

Amy kissed her tenderly, then with fervor, moving her fingers down to unbutton and unzip her jeans. Dominique ran her fingers across the back of Amy's dress looking for the zipper, only to have Amy pull back slightly and shake her head.

As Amy trailed down her body, kissing first her neck, then her shoulders, she turned to putty. Everywhere those soft lips touched seemed to set ablaze. Amy expertly reached down, pulling off Dominique's jeans and tossing them aside. Amy teased Dominique's body, straddling her and grinding.

Within seconds, she removed Dominique's underwear as well, and pulled her shirt over her head. Lying completely bare underneath Amy, Dominique wanted to remove Amy's clothing, to see what was underneath, but as Amy drove her fingers deep inside Dominique, she couldn't move. She felt as if she was tied down by invisible rope, completely lost in the pleasure.

Her body trembled as she let out moan after moan, until they became nothing more than a string of satisfied cries. Panting as Amy quickened her pace, thrusting in and out, Dominique threw her head back. Throwing fuel on an already exploding fire, Amy took one nipple in her mouth, softly sucking, causing ripples of pleasure to shoot through Dominique's body.

As her orgasm subsided, she fought for air, reaching up to pull Amy's body flat on top of hers, but Amy didn't stop. She flashed Dominique her now notorious devilish smile and slowly continued her thrusts, reaching up to circle Dominique's hardened clit with her thumb.

Their lips met in wild lust, and Dominique couldn't wait any longer. As if unleashed by the power that had held her still, she reached up between Amy's legs, surprised and excited to find no panties in the way, and slid inside her. The wetness engulfed her fingers as Amy thrust her hips forward, driving Dominique deeper, riding her fingers.

Lost in a sea of moans, Dominique moved deeper inside, matching her pace. As Dominique felt the second wave of pleasure bursting from her body, Amy tightened around Dominique, coming with a scream before rolling over next to her.

Dominique rolled over on her side, breathless and in awe of the radiance beaming from Amy's tired smile.

"I have so many more things I want to do with you," Amy said, draping an arm around Dominique's shoulder.

"As do I, as soon as I catch my breath."

Amy nodded, sinking her head into the pillow. She snuggled up closer into Dominique's arms and laid her head on Dominique's chest. "Thank you," she breathed.

"No," Dominique laughed. "Thank *you*. I didn't know that's what you had planned for the evening."

"That…and other things," Amy said, tracing her fingertips across Dominique's breasts.

Dominique smiled and kissed Amy tenderly. "I can't wait to see what's in store."

"I can't either," Amy said, wiggling out of the snuggle. "But first I'm going to need some more pizza." She stood, straightened her dress, and practically glided out of the room. Returning with the pizza box and wine bottle in hand, she winked. "Are you ready for a slumber party?"

Dominique bit her lip, nodding. "I'm ready for anything, as long as you're here."

Amy's giggle filled the air. Whatever had broken loose inside her had brought forth a brand new woman, and Dominique wanted everything she had to offer.

# CHAPTER SIXTEEN

Grease and sweat filled the air by the time evening fell, and despite George Brandt's best efforts, the whirring of equipment hadn't distracted his blur of thoughts and questions throughout the day.

"Go on home, Brent," he called out over the sound of his service writer's tire change. "That one isn't even on our list." When Brent didn't immediately reply, George crossed the distance between them. "That's my project car. That's not even a priority. You can go on home for the evening."

Brent flashed him a sheepish grin. "Sorry, boss. You know I love this old thing." Brent patted the side of George's 1966 Camaro.

"I do too, but let's call it a night. I need to go home and take care of some things."

"Sure thing," Brent said, tipping his cap in George's direction and shutting down his workstation.

Truth was, George wasn't sure home was where he wanted or needed to be. He had other plans for the evening. He watched as Brent gathered his things and headed out the door. He longed for a day like that kid was experiencing, free from any real worries, going home after a hard day's work to soak up life.

He looked down at his watch. It was time to leave the shop behind him for the day. Shutting off the lights and locking the doors, he thought back to that blissful time just twelve hours earlier when he thought he knew how his day was going to go. Of course, he wasn't so naïve to think things went as planned. But even so, this had been quite the shock.

He scratched his head, not caring that he was likely smearing grease on his scalp. Where he had to be, it wouldn't matter. All that mattered was that he got a little insight on how to handle a situation like this.

As he drove his truck, he thought back to simpler times when his little Amy-bug would bounce up and down in the front seat, babbling on about school or friends, times when she'd sing along to Reba McEntire on the radio, off-key and at the top of her lungs. For old times' sake, he flipped open the console of his beat-up old Chevy truck and fished out the Reba cassette he still cherished.

He popped it into the player and let the songs take him back. "Walk On" flooded through his speakers, and he rolled the windows down and turned up the dial. For just a minute, he let himself imagine her brown hair swaying in the wind as she belted out the lyrics with spunk. She had always been a little spitfire, someone determined to make it no matter what she did. This morning, she had been right. He had always been proud of her, and he always would be. He just didn't understand her right now.

Keeping his left hand on the steering wheel, he pressed his right palm into his forehead, wishing away the tension that had mounted throughout the course of the day.

He took a left and wound his way down an old dirt road. When he pulled up into the driveway, he waited for the dust to settle before he got out of his truck. He tapped the steering wheel with his fist, summoning up the strength to do what he needed to do, despite the voices in his head that told him to suffer in silence and keep his family's business to himself.

Emboldened by the thought of helping Amelia, he got out of the truck.

"George Brandt," a leathery old voice called out across the field that sat next to the old, two-story farmhouse.

"Yes sir," George called out in return. "How ya been, old timer?"

"Who are you calling old?" Bill Stanton asked, making his way over to greet George. He reached out his hand. "It's good to see you, and last time I checked, we're both getting on up there. If I remember correctly, you've still got me by a little bit."

"Ah, I see that memory is going, too," George joked, even though his voice was strained. His throat was raw from holding in the warring emotions he had felt all day. He cleared his throat.

"What brings you up this way?"

"Well, I needed a bit of advice, and I thought maybe you'd be able to shed some light on a mucky situation for me."

Bill looked off into the distance, removed his hat, and scratched his head. "I don't know that I'm much of an expert in any advice column, but I'll give it a shot. What's going on?"

George shoved his hands into his pockets and let out a deep breath. He watched as Bill turned to look at the sunset. In the silence that followed, George tried to find the right words. He opened his mouth, then bit his tongue.

"It's not easy," he said after a moment.

"I'll tell you what," Bill said, patting him on the shoulder. "How about I go in and grab us a few beers and some chairs, and we can sit out here and watch the sun go down? Then you can tell me all 'bout it."

A lump formed in George's throat but he nodded. If nothing else, it would buy him some time to find the right words to discuss this as delicately as possible. He was, after all, talking to a man who had just lost his daughter. And to complicate the matter, his daughter had been sleeping with…he shook his head. He didn't want to think about that. Bill's daughter had been dating his daughter, and now he needed some insight on how to still be there for his girl when his world seemed to be turned upside down.

By the time Bill returned, he accepted the beer gladly. "Tough times go better with beer." Bill tapped his bottle against George's. He set up the folding lawn chairs in the direction of the sunset and took a seat. George nodded, letting out a sigh as he took the second seat. "Lay it on me," Bill added, opting not to make eye contact.

"I feel bad coming out here asking you for advice after all you've been through."

"Don't." Bill held up a hand to stop George's apology. "We're hardy folks. We get by and get through. That's how we've always been, and I'm no different. Just 'cause I've had some really hard days don't mean I can't be there for a friend in need. I said 'lay it on me' and I meant it."

"It's about your daughter," George blurted the words out, forgoing the smoother ways he had concocted in his mind.

"What about my Chloe?" Bill asked, then held up his hand again. "Whatever it is, I'd like to tell you a little about that girl of mine for a second. She loved sunsets like this one." He waved his hand through the air, pointing out the horizon. "She would call them 'cotton candy clouds,' and she'd get a whimsical smile on her face. She was always one who got down to business and didn't get too distracted by other things. This was different, though. This was nature, and this was her playground. It made her come alive in ways I don't know that I'll ever understand." He paused for a moment, taking a long sip of his beer. "I sit out here a lot and think about her. I watch the sunsets and I can almost feel like she's still here with me. That said, there haven't been too many things involving her lately that have been good news, so whatever you've got to say, I'm all ears."

"She was a wonderful person, Bill. I'm not here to say anything to the contrary." He cleared his throat, this time taking care to find the right words. "Fact is this is as much about my daughter as it is yours."

Bill nodded, pursing his lips. "Figured as much."

"You knew?" George shook his head.

Beside him, Bill shifted in his seat and shrugged. "I didn't know while it was happening. I put some puzzle pieces together after the fact and I asked. I got the truth, so I've known for a little while. But I was sworn to secrecy."

George felt like the breath had been knocked out of him. "Who told you?"

"Amelia did," he said, turning to face George. "After Chloe's death, Amelia showed up at the house with some muffins and things for the detectives and for our family—well, for me, since I'm most of the family Chloe had. She and I talked a bit that day, and she said some things that stuck with me. She was tryin' to be careful and cover her tracks. I sincerely doubt she wanted to tell me before she told you, but I poked and prodded my way to the bottom of it, mainly because I wanted to know if someone loved my Chloe in that way. If they did, I wanted to know what they knew of her, who she was. It was part of how I found comfort. She told me because I asked, George."

The muscles in George's neck tightened and he closed his eyes, warding off signs of weakness. Men didn't cry in front of one another, but all he wanted to do was break down into tears. "Okay," he managed, his voice thick with emotion. "That makes sense, I suppose. She told me this morning, and I'm not sure what to do about it."

Bill leaned back in his chair, tipping his beer up to take a long drink. "Thing is, I'm not sure you *can* do much about it. I always knew I couldn't change Chloe's mind, from the very beginning. As time went on, I realized it wasn't her mind. It was her heart. It was who she was, and there's no changing that about someone."

Having left his beer previously untouched, George downed a gulp. "That's kind of what I figured. I know her mama was talking this morning about not standing for it and wanting to help her change her mind, but I figured as much. I know my Amelia, and she's not going to be swayed on something she feels convicted of. She's too strong a woman for someone to tell her what to do, and I've never been the type of parent to tell her what to do. I want her to make her own decisions."

"That's the tricky part," Bill cut in. "At some point down the road, you might have to realize these aren't decisions per se. They're ingrained in who she is. At least that's what Chloe always told me and I never had a reason to doubt her word." Bill looked up to the sky, as if searching for answers. "Has Amelia ever lied to you?"

"No." He shook his head. "Well I mean she kept this pretty big truth, but it's not something I can imagine having to talk to anyone about. I wouldn't know how to have a conversation like that, one that I thought would change the way people who loved me looked at me. So I don't blame her for that. But nah, she's never lied to me. In fact she was the kid who would tell on herself before she ever got caught."

"Then you might want to listen to her on what she's telling you. I'm not sayin' it's going to be easy. Actually it might be the hardest thing you've had to do. Listen and try to understand. I'll be honest," Bill said, pausing to sip his beer, "it's damn hard. I still don't get it fully, other than I know Chloe fell in love with women. Always did. And I found ways to make sure our relationship never changed because of it."

George nodded and Bill leveled his gaze, making eye contact. "It didn't happen overnight," he continued. "I can tell you that much. It happened after a lot of soul searching on my part, but I think you're on the right road here. You sought help, so you're already leaps and bounds above where I was that first day. Chloe came home from high school her sophomore year…I think that's when it was. And, in true Chloe fashion, laid her soul bare at the dinner table. She was excited to have 'figured out who she was,' and I was devastated. I was supposed to be the hero of her life, the one who helped her find her way and figure out tough situations. Only she turned the tables on the life I thought we were supposed to have, and all of the sudden, I was in brand new territory. I didn't have answers or advice, until I realized I did."

"What do you mean?" George asked, throwing his hands up in the air in desperation. "That's what's been eating at me. I'm supposed to be able to guide my little girl in the right direction. I realize she's not a little girl, but I don't know how to help her or even attempt to be the one with the answers in this scenario."

"What I mean is she'll have the answers when it comes to who she is. You have the dad answers. You're still her father and can still be her rock. You take your time in deciding when you're ready to do that, but there are answers you do have."

George looked at him, his brow knitting together in confusion.

"You know women—well, at least as well as anyone can know women." Bill let out a small laugh. "And this is the part that takes time, but if you want to be there for her, you can be the one she turns to when she needs advice, when she's had her heart broken. You can find little ways to still be that hero. It just takes time."

George settled back in his seat, trying to process all he had heard today. It all felt so jumbled still, but he took comfort in Bill's words. It would be okay.

"Think on it for a bit, and have another beer," Bill said, handing another cold bottle to George.

George graciously accepted the other beer and popped the top, tipping the bottle up in the air and taking a long drink. "Thanks." He nodded in his friend's direction.

"I know it still seems weird, and it might not ever feel normal," Bill said. "But for me it did after a while. I learned to remember that my daughter was the same girl she'd always been. Granted, she gave me a lot of time to digest the information. I thought she was being a rebellious teenager, but I was wrong. She told me, and then she let it slip to some others. Soon everyone knew. She was just being honest. That's what Amelia is doing for you, too. And that honesty comes at a price for some." Bill closed his eyes and looked down at the ground. Kicking the dust, he sighed. "It comes at a hefty price."

"I'm so sorry," George said again, searching for words that might make it hurt less.

"It's done, George." He shook his head. "It's done, and I can't change that. I think maybe that's my best advice. Don't try to change things you can't. Instead, cherish the time you have with your daughter. I take comfort in the fact that she was there for Chloe, that they were happy."

"You might not think that if Amelia's fears come true," George said, letting out a deep breath.

Bill turned his body in his seat. "What are you talking about?"

"Amelia said something about her prints being found around the house, and I'm not sure what that even means for her."

"They don't think *she* did this?" Bill rose. His cheeks shone red and he balled his fists up. "She had no part in this. I know as much. And yeah, I knew her prints were in that house. Why wouldn't they be?"

George rose to his feet and placed a hand on Bill's shoulder. "I don't know what they think. I just know Amelia told us so we didn't find out in some other way."

Bill took a breath and shook his head. "They better not go after her. Then they're just making a bad situation worse."

George took his seat again, and Bill paced back and forth in front of him. Watching, George tried to understand why Bill was so protective of Amelia. He waited in silence, giving Bill time to chew on the information.

"My daughter already got killed for being who she was," Bill finally said, spitting the words up into the sky. "Your daughter doesn't deserve to be framed just because she was gay, too. We all know Amelia wouldn't hurt a fly, and this is bullshit." He kicked the ground again, and George wished he hadn't said anything.

"I just thought you deserved to know." George shrugged.

"No, I appreciate you telling me," Bill said in a much deeper voice. "I tell you what, like I'm instructing you to do, I'm going to sit on this for the evening. But if they come after her in the slightest, I'm marching myself into that police station and telling them what I think."

"Mind if we sit and think on it all together?" George asked, pointing back to the chair and untouched beer beside him.

"Okay." Bill took his seat again. "I need to drink this beer anyway."

"Helps you think, right?" George said, trying to add some good-natured humor back into the evening.

"Something like that." Bill nodded.

Sipping their beers in silence, they caught the last bits of the sunset in all its glory. When darkness fell, Bill reached behind him in the cooler and pulled out two more beers. "One more and then we'll all go home, just like the old days," he said, handing one to George.

George laughed. "Yeah, those were some good old days."

Bill nodded. "And there will be good days up ahead too. It's all a little cloudy right now, but it'll make sense again."

"You think so?" George asked, not for his sake but for Bill's. He knew he could do his best to maneuver the situation at hand for his family. Bill's was going to take more than just a little time, though.

Bill shrugged. "I have to think so. Otherwise I would have followed right after her. I couldn't be here if I didn't think there was something worth sticking around for. As it is, life is different. But hell, that's life. Life changes every single day, sometimes in big ways, sometimes in small ways. We roll with the punches, though. That's what we're made for."

"I think you're onto something there." George laughed, as it occurred to him they'd never had a conversation quite this deep. "Hard to believe we're those same old boys who never thought we'd get emotional or sit out here talking about feelings."

"Yeah, those good old boys from the good old days are gone, and they left two crazy old men in their place." Bill laughed. He turned to face George once more. "For what it's worth, that Amelia of yours is good as gold."

George raised his bottle in the air, clinking the glass against Bill's. "To our girls, both good as gold."

In the silence that followed, George contemplated his next steps. Whatever it took, he was going to heed Bill's advice and enjoy whatever time he might have with his daughter. Life was too short to live any other way.

# CHAPTER SEVENTEEN

Garth Brooks played out from the old jukebox in the corner, singing about having "friends in low places," and the lights of the bar gave a comforting glow to the afternoon. Louie wiped down the counters and set out the stools, the same daily routine he had practiced for over twenty years. Looking around the place, he smiled. Everything looked perfect and even the pool table edges seemed to gleam in the glow of the light. He looked to the bar, satisfied to see it fully stocked and ready for the evening.

Maybe it made him a bad bartender considering this was his favorite time of the day, when the bar was completely empty and he didn't have to worry about anything other than preparation. There was nothing around but good music and a man dedicated to making sure people had a good time.

It was the time when this place still held hopes. It seemed to be a realm of possibility. Maybe today someone would come in, looking for encouragement he could offer, or maybe someone would walk through those doors lonely and find a friend or perhaps the start of their love story.

He smiled and shook his head. At the core, he was still the same damn dreamer he had always been. But it had worked in his favor. If this place were his only legacy, he would still be pretty proud of that fact.

Through those front doors, he had watched as hopeless and depressed folks had come in looking for someone to talk to, someone to help them forget. More often than not, they'd left happier. He was no therapist, but he did seem to have a knack for helping people through the difficulties of crummy situations. He smiled as he reminisced over first kisses he'd witnessed and people deciding to go home for the night because talking through their problems was better than drinking them away. For the most part, he'd seen positive things come from his days here, although he'd seen his fair share of fights, angry drunks, and devastating alcoholism.

In the back room, he cleaned and readied the engraved mugs he'd had made for his most loyal customers, the ones he knew would most likely be coming through his doors after work tonight.

He lined them up one by one on the cabinet, laughing to himself about some of the antics pulled by his regulars. At the back on the top shelf, one mug caught his eye, and he winced.

"Chloe the Cowgirl," it read. He had engraved it himself. She had been so thrilled when he presented it to her brimming with her favorite stout from the tap last Christmas. Every time she came in, he'd fill the glass and present it anew, as though it was a surprise every time.

Between her dazzling, genuine smile and her contagious laughter, she alone had the power to light up an entire room, and more often than not, she had turned this old bar into a full-fledged party. She'd play wingman for the young cowboys coming in for a drink after work, convince people to get off their stools and dance, play deejay at the jukebox and dedicate songs to people in good-natured ribbing, and make sure everyone had the time of their lives each time she entered the bar.

Laughter bubbled up inside him as he remembered the time one of the guys had challenged her to an arm wrestling contest. When she beat him with ease and grace, he challenged her left-handed. Again, she slammed his arm to the table, this time teaching him a lesson and rising with a cocky grin. Still undeterred, he decided he could at least outdrink her. The poor old sap had been wrong. Louie shook his head. That woman had been a pistol.

He looked up at the ceiling, wishing he could hear her voice just one more time while she regaled him with her lively stories or pour her another drink and offer her a kind smile.

He pulled her mug down, wiping the single tear from the corner of his eye. Gently polishing off the dust the mug had collected over the past few months, he ran his fingers over the engraved area.

"We miss you around here," he whispered, hoping there was some way she could hear him. "We all do—especially me. And I'm sorry I didn't do better that night. I didn't have all the answers, but I damn sure thought I was protecting you the best I could. I see the error in that judgment now. I wish I could go back and figure out a way to make it right, but I want you to know we miss you. And I'll be damned if I'm ever going to let someone else get hurt the way you did."

He shook his head, anger seething through his veins at what had happened, as he put the glass back in its place on the top shelf. That's where it would remain. A top shelf gal deserved a top shelf space.

The sound of footsteps in the bar area caught him off guard. He opened the doors at two o'clock in the afternoon every day, but never had people in before three. With it being a quarter after two, he thought he still had time. He laid down the rag in his hand, placed his palms on the countertop for support, and took a deep breath, allowing himself just a moment to gain composure after the onslaught of memories.

Righting himself, he headed for the front. "Good afternoon," he called out before he could even see who had graced him with their early afternoon presence.

"Good afternoon," a young man said, tipping his hat in Louie's direction. He was wearing a black polo with the FBI logo emblazoned on the right breast pocket.

"What can I pour for ya?" Louie asked, noting the way the young man's face was contorted in concern. "That's a whiskey face if I've ever seen one," he added when the man didn't respond.

"Wish I could," the man said, stepping forward with a frown. "My name is Clayton Turner, and I'm here on business, so I guess that whiskey drink will have to wait until the end of the day."

"Bummer," Louie said, adding a laugh to keep the mood light. "Well, in that case, what else can I do for you, and would you like a water?"

Clayton smiled and let out a sigh, taking a seat on one of the center barstools. "A water would be great. Thank you."

Louie filled the glass with ice water and set it in front of Clayton. Pulling up the stool he kept behind the counter, he sat down, eye level with Clayton. "What's going on? What kind of work brings you to a bar?" he asked, even though he figured he already knew the answer.

"I'm sure you've probably got a hunch, judging from your tone," Clayton said, taking a drink of his water and letting out another sigh.

"That cop training did you some good, didn't it?" Louie laughed. "I guess I won't try to bullshit you on anything else. Yeah. I can guess why you're here."

Clayton nodded. He cast his eyes downward, looking defeated. "Same thing cops have been working on around here for the past few months. Same reason I'm in this town in the first place. Anyway, I need to talk to you about something a little different. I'm sure you've had your share of cops in and out of here, detectives asking you questions, and I've read your testimony. I already know where you stand on it, who you think did it, your evidence and more. I've read it all, and I've studied it. I'm not here to drag you back into that hell."

"I appreciate that," Louie said, shaking his head. "It is hell going back over all the details, wondering if it could have been prevented, remembering her in her last moments, and knowing the things that son of a bitch did." Even though Clayton had promised not to drudge it up, the memories came back full force. Bile crept up the back of Louie's throat and he swallowed hard.

"I understand that," Clayton said. He let out a deep breath and took a drink of his water. "It seems like everyone around here feels that way, even though few are willing to go all in and place blame."

"I've placed blame, and I'll do it again. I don't give a damn what position that boy thinks he holds in this town." His voice was rising, so he shut his mouth.

Clayton waved his hand through the air. "I know," he said. "But like I said, I'm here on another issue about the case today. You mentioned to the other detectives that Chloe was a regular here."

Louie nodded, wanting to keep his words minimal so he didn't have another outburst of passion.

"How regularly would you say she came in here?"

Scratching his head, he looked around the room, visualizing her here, walking around talking, joking, dancing and singing. He propped his elbows up on the counter. "I would say she was here a couple of times a week. Sometimes more, sometimes less. It all depended on what was going on with work and her personal life."

"What details can you give me on her personal life?" Clayton asked, reaching over and grabbing a napkin from the pile stacked on the bar next to the wooden support beam.

When Louie didn't immediately answer, Clayton fished a pen out of the breast pocket of his shirt and looked up to make eye contact with Louie. "People confide in bartenders all the time. What did she disclose about her personal connections?"

"What do you mean?" Louie wiped his sweaty palms on his pants' legs. He hated open-ended questions geared to make him betray the confidence of his customers. Even if it was a dead customer, she deserved some respect instead of having her life ripped apart by vultures in the name of the law, especially when they already had the guilty party in custody. "Why don't you ask what it is you want to know?" he added when Clayton didn't reply.

"I want to know if she talked to you about things." Clayton took a moment to scratch a few notes on the bar napkin. "I want to know if she was dating anyone."

"She didn't talk too much about those things," Louie said with a shrug. "She kept her love life to herself a lot. At the time she passed, I didn't know of anyone she might have been seeing."

"But she did talk to you about those types of things in the past?" Clayton tapped his fingers on the bar top. "Did she tell you about other women she dated? Was she open about those things, or did she just bottle it up? Seems to me a woman so confident and happy to be who she was wouldn't have been shy. And if I've heard anything about Chloe Stanton, it's that she wasn't a shy type of person."

"Don't presume to know Chloe just because you've heard stories." Louie shook his head. "In fact, I'd say no one, even those who knew her, had her all figured out." He wanted to pop this young punk in the jaw but thought better of it, clasping his hands together. "She had told me a thing or two from time to time." Louie eyed Clayton suspiciously. "Why does that matter?"

"It just does. Who had she dated? It doesn't matter if it was in the past, I just need to know."

Louie sighed. Looking down at the FBI patch, he figured he'd better stop being such a hard-ass and give in to the man's persistent questioning. "A while back she was dating a girl from up the road in Oklahoma. It was some girl who didn't live here, a pretty brunette she said, if memory serves me correctly. That was over two years ago, though. She told me about that girl because I pressed her for the information. I had told her I wanted her to be happy, regardless of what the other fools around here thought."

"Did you have these conversations about her love life when others were around?"

"Never." Louie shook his head. "She didn't like to open up too much about things. She always told me no one wanted to hear about it, so she'd be happy in her own world. And she was.

I don't imagine she told things like that to anyone around this place."

Clayton narrowed his eyes and then focused on the napkin in front of him. He moved it out of Louie's eyesight and wrote down something. Louie thought he could make out two words but shook his head. He didn't care what that man wrote down. This seemed irrelevant.

Clayton let out a sigh, and Louie hopped off his stool, pouring himself a glass of water and topping Clayton's glass off. This entire process was irritating.

"Who else might have known who she was seeing when she died?"

"Why do you think she was seeing someone at the time of her death?" Louie threw his hands up in the air. "And what does that have to do with anything? I don't know anything about it if she was in a relationship then. I know about the girl from Oklahoma and that's all. I've got nothing else to give you."

"It's important to the case," Clayton said, his words pointed and stern but quiet. "I need you to help me answer these questions as best as possible."

"Fine." Louie let out a sigh. "I'll help, but only because this is for her. The truth is I don't think anyone else knew. She might have told her father about that girl from Oklahoma, too. She seemed pretty happy about it and told me they had been together for a while. But I know they broke up or something didn't work. All I know is she lost that happy-go-lucky bit of herself for a while and seemed a little down in the dumps probably a month or two after she told me about the girl. I asked how things were going with her new flame, she told me it was a 'non-issue.'" Louie added air quotes for emphasis. "No one else was ever mentioned, even if I asked. She'd wink and tell me to be polite and not ask a lady about her personal matters. I don't know if that's because they wanted to keep it a secret or she did. All I know is that it was clearly unsafe for her to say anything. *This...*" he said, waving both hands through the air, "this whole thing happened because people couldn't tolerate it, so I think she knew the environment she was in and knew better than to rock the boat. I'm sure she had other partners from time to time. I'm sure some of them were even people who might have lived or worked in the community. But she damn sure didn't open her mouth about it."

Clayton nodded, but his scowl grew deeper. "So you're saying her father might have known, if anyone did? Did she have close friends?"

"She had a ton of friends," Louie said. "She was a salt-of-the-earth, life-of-the-party girl. Her friends and acquaintances were numerous, but confidantes? She didn't have those. She dealt with life on her own terms and in her own way. She actually told me one time that she didn't need to burden people with the daily details of her life. I think that's how she liked to live."

"Thanks for your time," Clayton said, standing. Louie overheard him mutter "Another dead end," as he walked out the door.

* * *

Three visits and all had turned up useless. Clayton slammed his fists against his steering wheel. The beloved bartender, Chloe's father, and the girl down at the salon who everyone said knew anything there was to know in Knell all knew nothing.

Chloe's father had admitted that he knew of Chloe's most recent partner, but even he was told only after her death. Clayton thought about the pain in Bill's eyes as he'd recounted again all that he knew. Clayton shook his head. He *had* to stop putting that man in the hot seat, or it was going to drive him over the edge of an already jagged cliff. He looked over in the passenger seat at his useless heap of notes and snatched them. One by one: the bar napkin, the piece of paper torn from a notebook that had been lying in his car, and the back of a receipt from the barbershop. He hadn't even been smart enough to remember his notebook today. He thought about tearing them up, but opted for crumpling them in his hands and throwing the ball into the floorboard. Stomping his feet, he let out a string of curses.

"Fuck this town!" he shouted, not caring that no one was around to listen. "Fuck this case. Fuck it all."

Seething, he started the ignition to drive to his hotel. Another wasted day with nothing to report. He rolled down his windows and put his left arm outside, letting the breeze calm and ground him. He was supposed to be better than this—better than empty reports and certainly better than temper tantrums.

Taking a deep breath, he let everything from the day play back. A trained detective, he couldn't give up this easily. There had to be something—*anything*. Louie didn't know a thing. Although Chloe confided in him once, she hadn't told him about Amelia. And although her father admitted he knew of her important past relationships, he hadn't known at the time of her death.

*She didn't have confidantes.*

Louie's words replayed in Clayton's head. When he'd questioned Amelia, she'd been caught off guard, confused, and then bewildered. No one was supposed to know. But Trent did. Trent had known. *How had he known?* Whether he'd seen something or heard something, he had known.

As if a light bulb had turned on, Clayton pulled the car over on the shoulder. Putting the pieces of the puzzle together, he turned the wheel sharply, performed a U-turn and headed for the station. It was a long shot and he'd have hell proving it, but this dead-end of a day might just hold the answer he'd needed.

Fumbling to pull his phone out of his pocket, he swerved into the other lane. Correcting the car quickly, he punched in numbers. "Gloria, it's Clayton," he said when the station receptionist picked up the phone. "I need to talk to Westwick when I get back. Go ahead and have his lawyer called. I think he's going to want him there. Or give him the option. I don't really care. Just let him know he's being taken back into questioning and I'll be there as soon as I can."

He floored the accelerator. Even if it was only a thirty-minute drive out to the county facility, he didn't want to waste time—not when he thought he was finally onto something that mattered in this godforsaken case.

Flipping through the stations, he settled for classic rock and turned it up. Mentally preparing himself to ask the right questions and make sure he didn't miss his mark, he ticked off his to-do list.

Be smart, ask the right questions, be persistent, show no fear, show no emotion. Adrenaline coursed through his body. No longer feeling like a rookie, he was determined to make this one count. Maybe the dead ends weren't a place to stop, but a place to find a new, undiscovered route.

As the guitar solo from a Guns N' Roses classic kicked on, he was so lost in his jam session that he almost didn't hear his phone ring. Rushing to turn down the volume, he caught the call on its last ring before voice mail.

"Detective Turner," he answered.

"Hey Clayton. It's Gloria." Her voice was flat, defeated.

"What's going on?"

He heard her sigh. "Seems like today isn't going to work out."

"Why not? This needs to happen."

"I know," she sighed again. He could see her shaking her head the way she always did when she tried to remind the officers she didn't run the world. "He refuses to speak without his lawyer, and his lawyer is preoccupied."

"With what? Shouldn't this be his most pressing issue?" Clayton knew he was being dramatic, but the Westwicks had spared no expense in getting their son the best lawyer, and he knew they were paying him hand over fist to defend Trent. "What's he doing?"

"Turn on your television when you get home, or turn on your radio in about ten minutes. Mayor is holding a press conference, if office gossip is right."

He slammed his palm into the steering wheel, but reminded himself to be polite. Thanking Gloria, he hung up the phone before spewing off a string of curses.

Gritting his teeth, he flipped through the local radio stations to the local all-day news station, where he heard an overly excited announcer commentating on waiting for the mayor's speech.

"As you know, the mayor's family has been wrapped up in a bit of a scandal," the man's voice boomed through Clayton's speakers. "For the first time, the mayor is planning to publicly address his son's case today."

Chatter in the background made him want to scream. These people who had gathered were fools. Clayton grimaced as the announcer continued his overview of the case at hand.

"He's on the stage," the announcer said, and Clayton listened as the station's clearly cheap equipment clicked over to the microphone on the podium.

"Good afternoon," the mayor's voice came across the speakers, pristine and pretentious. "I'm thankful to all who have gathered here to let me clear the air on a few issues. I know in a town this size there can be gossip and chatter. I've heard concerns from some of you that I'm failing you all as mayor because my family is involved in something of this magnitude." He cleared his throat and his voice went up in pitch, as though he was smiling. "I want to assure you that's not the case. I am a father and husband first and foremost. That is true. However, I am dedicated to running this incredible town and to ensuring each and every one of you has a safe place to live, work, and play."

Clayton reached for the dial but stopped himself. It was political bullshit, straight from a canned response, but he needed to listen, if for nothing else to know what they were facing.

"I've had letters and phone calls. I know many of you, myself included, have been shaken to the core to remember that violence can strike anywhere, *even* here in our hometown. You all want to know that your families are safe, and that's what I want for each of us. As far as my son is concerned," he paused and cleared his throat, "I believe he is innocent. I know many of you grew up with Trent or watched him grow up into the fine young man he is. I have not addressed this issue publicly to date, as we know this is a conflict of interest. I just wanted to put rumors to rest and say that we are all working hard to ensure the safety and wellbeing of everyone in Knell."

Clayton could hear the shuffling of people and their whispers and for a brief moment, he wished he were there. Was the crowd disappointed with his shitty response? Did they believe a word he was saying, or did they see it at face value for what it was?

"We all deserve a safe place to live, and I'm sure you've noticed the influx of law enforcement in town. They'll get to the bottom of this case, make sure the right person is eventually placed behind bars, and most importantly, make sure nothing like this happens here again. I have been advocating for them to follow every possible lead, and I can assure you they are doing just that. There are several possibilities, and I want to make sure they're not just focusing on the wrong person. We're committed to providing safety, well-being, and a thorough investigation to sort this out together. We are a community. We've always been strong, more like family than neighbors. And I am working every day, as I know you all are, to make sure that legacy continues. In the meantime, my family and I will be sorting out our matters privately to help law enforcement and to help get our son out from behind bars and back in the community where he belongs. It is important to remember who we are. We stand behind our own, we help pick each other up, we offer each other a safe haven, a cup of sugar, a helping hand. We are neighbors, we are family, and we will rebuild."

Someone in the crowd shouted a question, but it was too muffled for Clayton to understand.

"Have a good evening," the mayor said in closing.

Disgusted, Clayton reached up and turned off the radio. That prick was abusing his position to sway public opinion on an ongoing investigation. It was bad enough that he'd been putting so much pressure on the officers and detectives that they were wasting manpower on stupid witch hunts to disqualify any other suspects when the facts of the case were pretty damn obvious. But this was too much. And worse yet, Clayton knew that no one would hold him accountable for his egregious misuse of power. His stomach turned.

The Westwicks, mayor included, would get what was coming to them when he was done with them.

# CHAPTER EIGHTEEN

As Katy Perry's "Rise" played loudly over her speakers, freshly baked goods and coffee filled the air with a pleasant aroma. It seemed as though the world was working to create an aura of peace and empowerment, but Amelia was more intrigued and pleased by the smell of the newspaper in her hands.

"Hot off the presses," she said, smiling to herself as she unwound the rubber band holding the rolled paper together. As she slid it off the roll, she took note of her hands, thankful and a bit proud at the way they didn't shake. As she had been doing, she sat back on the couch, reflecting on her journey and what she felt. For the first time, she didn't feel afraid.

Perhaps it had something to do with growing up and coming into her own, or perhaps it had to do with the utter bliss in which she had been immersed. Her thoughts lingered for a second on the sweet way she had been woken up this morning, with Dominique nuzzling her neck and trailing kisses down her shoulders.

She shook her head, snapping out of her daydream. There would be time for that later. A giggle bubbled up inside her and sprang forth with such intensity, she figured if anyone could have been watching, they'd have deemed her crazy. But she didn't care.

With excitement bubbling through every nerve, she pulled open the paper and saw her picture on the front page. Her heartbeat accelerated. She hadn't expected to be the feature story. Regardless, her eyes tore through the article.

There in the middle of the page, she saw her quote pulled out to the side and italicized. She read it twice, making sure they had followed her instructions. Relieved, her smile grew. No more hiding. As she had asked, the quote was printed in full. No partial quote would do it justice. She let out a deep breath, exhaling gratitude for living in a small town where one could make such requests of the media. Even so, she found it comical that her quote—probably the most unimportant part of the story—had been a featured segment.

*As more details come forward in the ongoing murder case, it will inevitably be said that I was Chloe Stanton's lover, girlfriend, or whatever term deemed appropriate by the one telling the story. For this reason and for the sake of authenticity in a town I have always called my home, I am breaking the silence. What you will hear is true. I am a lesbian, and I am proud of this part of my identity. I was dating Chloe Stanton, and facts will likely emerge that I was often at her house. I have chosen to speak out prior to these facts becoming common knowledge, as I would like to make our town a more open place, where we accept people for who they are. May what happened here in the name of hatred never occur again.*

She read through the rest of the story and shook her head. Laughing, she set the paper down. Some reporting. But what could be expected in a town that hired kids fresh out of high school for news staff? Nothing was even mentioned about the knife. She scratched her head, wondering why something so important to the story would be redacted. The only pertinent revelations unearthed in the article were that she was gay, that her fingerprints were found around Chloe's house, and that the police had ruled out finding suspects by the prints that were found. They were moving onto other avenues of evidence to proceed with Trent Westwick's trial.

*Ongoing case.* The words flashed in her head like a neon sign. This was all too new to her, but either way, she was excited for what was to come. More than anything, she was excited to move forward with her life out in the open and to see Trent face justice.

Would he face any type of suitable justice? And for that matter, was there any suitable type of justice? She shook her head, knowing if she wallowed in the thoughts, she'd lose half of her morning trying to solve the world's problems, when she really should be getting to work.

Glancing around the coffee shop, she relished the peace and quiet. Even if it might stay this way for an entire day or even two, she figured they'd come back sooner or later. After all, when you had a monopoly on coffee and pastries to-go in a town of this size, full of busy people on the go, you had something worth stopping for.

As she set to work cleaning, she heard the door chime and scurried to the front.

"Congratulations," Dominique said, smiling and holding out a bouquet of roses.

Amelia threw caution to the wind and her cleaning rag to the ground and ran around the counter to throw her arms around Dominique's neck.

"I like this kind of welcome," Dominique said, before Amelia covered her mouth with a kiss.

Dominique smiled, mid-kiss, breaking the contact. "What's gotten into you?"

"I'm just invigorated, I think," she said, her own smile growing. "It's nice to know that I can just be me. I don't have to put on a mask anymore. I don't have to hide out or pretend to be someone I'm not." She looked around and twirled, holding her arms outstretched and letting the moment of pure ecstasy take its course. "This place will be busy again sometime. Not today, but I'm confident it will. And it will do so with my customers knowing exactly who I am. That is reason enough to celebrate."

"That's why I brought you 'coming out' flowers." Dominique winked and set the flowers on the counter.

"Thank you for that," Amelia said, leaning as casually as she could on the counter. She bit her bottom lip, her senses tingling. "I want you," she added, dropping her voice an octave.

Dominique raised an eyebrow and put her hands on her hips. "I just came here for a cup of coffee," she said, laughter bursting out as soon as she got the statement out of her mouth. "But I guess I could go for a couple of other things." She walked slowly in Amelia's direction, her eyes twinkling with each step.

"Yeah?" Amelia asked, offering a sideways grin. "What kinds of things did you have in mind?"

Dominique let out a sultry laugh, tracing her fingertips up and down Amelia's body. "I think you can figure it out, but here's a little hint." She leaned in close enough so her breathing tickled Amelia's ears. "I want you, too. I want to fuck you," she whispered. Amelia let out a ragged breath, her heart beating faster.

The door dinged, signaling she had a customer. Amelia let out a deep breath and decided to go for it. She leaned in and gave Dominique a quick kiss before sliding back behind the counter to make eye contact with her customer.

One of her favorite older customers, Mrs. Day, stood in front of the counter, eyes wide. She opened her mouth but shut it again, quickly switching her focus to her purse. Fumbling through the contents, she pulled out an old leather wallet. "I'd like a cup of decaf, Miss Amelia," she said, handing money over without looking Amelia in the eye.

"Coming right up, Mrs. Day," Amelia said, careful to keep a smile on her face. "How are you today?" she added, while she poured the cup.

"Doing okay," Mrs. Day said. After a moment of silence, she cleared her throat. Grabbing the counter, Amelia braced herself for a slew of angry words. "Can I also get one of those turnovers?" she asked, the tone in her voice rising. Amelia smiled to herself, knowing the sweet old woman was smiling, too.

"Absolutely." Amelia turned back to face her. "Do you want apple or cherry?"

Mrs. Day pursed her lips and looked upward, her smile turning mischievous. "I'll take one of each. But don't tell Carl," she laughed when she mentioned her husband

"It's our little secret," Amelia said with a wink.

"He doesn't need to know that it's cheat day," she smirked. "At least, that's what our granddaughter calls it. I just call it Tuesday, and it's a Tuesday when I want two turnovers."

"I like that logic," Amelia said, breathing a sigh of relief at the normal direction the conversation had taken.

She counted out Mrs. Day's change and bid her a good day.

Mrs. Day took the change and leaned in, dropping her voice to a whisper. "She's really pretty," she said. She winked and gathered her things.

Stunned, Amelia watched Mrs. Day walk out the door. She closed her eyes and gulped, seeing Chloe's face in her memories. No doubt Chloe had paved the way for her here, but she was going to take it one step further and ensure that hatred and bigotry didn't stand in this town.

"That went well." Dominique beamed as she stepped up to the counter.

Amelia leaned on the counter, letting out a deep breath. "I didn't realize how much I was holding my breath while she was in here," she said, shaking her head. "I wasn't sure how it was going to go. In fact, I'm not sure how any of this is going to go."

"You can never be sure," Dominique said, running her fingers across Amelia's palm before clasping her hand tightly. "None of us can be sure how any interaction will go, whether we'll face judgment, get a sideways look as we walk down the street, or even have someone make off-color comments. That's the thing none of them understand. Until they've walked in my shoes or yours, they'll never know what it's like to have so much unsolicited advice thrown your way, so many unwelcome advances, or to be treated differently so often. They don't understand that, but we can try to understand them a little bit. She was kind, and she seemed like the best type of interaction you'll likely get—at least for a little while. The others will vary. But they're also trying to take in something new about you, and it's something they can't see as just a part of you that's always been there. Like I was when I first got here, you're now an outsider. You're not one of them, and it's like you're an entirely different person. They're going to take some time to get used to that."

"It's going to hurt, but it'll be worth it in the end." Amelia glanced down at the floor, as reality came crashing down on her. "It will, won't it?"

"Hey," Dominique said, leaning down to make eye contact. "It's going to be okay." She brought Amelia's hand up to her lips and placed a gentle kiss on it. "I'm going to be here every step of the way, and this is a time to celebrate. They're all going to come around. Hell, Mrs. Day already did. In fact, she bought twice what she came in here for. The rest of them are sorting things out. They'll be back. And in the meantime, I'll be right here with you."

Amelia planted a soft kiss on Dominique's forehead and nodded. She gave a sad smile. "You're right. It'll take time. Minds don't change overnight."

"Never have. Never will, unfortunately. But you're not going at this alone."

Amelia closed her eyes, refocusing on positives. She took a seat on the couch and patted the cushion next to her. Dominique nodded, agreeing to her silent plea, and took the seat next to her. Dominique moved in and wrapped her arms around Amelia, pulling her over to rest on Dominique's shoulders.

A tear slipped from the corner of Amelia's eye as she lay in Dominique's toned arms, feeling the warmth and support of the embrace. She looked up to the ceiling, watching the fan whirring overhead, trying to decipher whether they were tears of loss or tears of joy. She used her free hand to wipe them away, deciding it didn't matter. There would be things to feel—some genuinely unpleasant things, she was sure—but she was willing to go through the fires.

She straightened her shoulders and looked Dominique in the eye, wiping the last remaining tears from her cheeks. "Are you busy today?"

Dominique raised an eyebrow in questioning and shook her head. "Not really until this afternoon. I have a couple of meetings later. Why?"

"I want to get out of here," she said, standing and wiping her hands on her jeans. "Let's go somewhere, even if just for a few hours. Let's get out of here, go for a drive and get lost in each other. This will all still be here." She paused, watching as Dominique's face set into an expression of concern. "I promise I'm not running from my problems," she said, planting a kiss on Dominique's head. "I know better than that. I have to feel all the things inside me, and I will. I promise. The thing is, I don't know what to feel now, and I want the chance to think that through and evaluate what's going on. I want the chance to spend the day with you. All this will be here for me to deal with this afternoon when we come back."

Dominique bit her lip, considering the proposal, and eventually nodded. "Let's do it," she said, standing and taking Amelia's hand.

Amelia put together a bag of muffins and two to-go coffees and together they shut off the coffeepots, switched off the lights, and flipped the "Open" sign to "Closed."

As Amelia locked up, she smiled, her plan for the morning taking shape. "Hop in my car," she said, winking at Dominique.

"Where are we going?" Dominique asked, climbing into the passenger seat.

"Trust me."

"I do," Dominique's voice was soft and tender. Amelia's smile grew as she brought her hand to intertwine with Dominique's.

Knowing she needed a bit of space to think, even if she wanted to do so by Dominique's side, Amelia turned up the radio and rolled down the windows, letting the country station on the radio fill the car with peaceful sounds.

She maneuvered through several turns down back roads, watching out of the corner of her eye as Dominique took it all in. The rolling hills and fields that had turned yellow were quite the sight to see. Throw in the bronze, scarlet, and rust-colored leaves of fall, and it was picture-worthy.

She smiled, massaging Dominique's hand as she made her final turn and ended up down by an old abandoned barn.

"What is this place?" Dominique's voice was breathy and awestruck.

"It's my grandpa's old place," Amelia said, spreading her hands out before her to showcase the entire view. "It's all in really great condition still, but it hasn't been kept up. That's a fault of our family, I suppose. We've been too busy running our lives to really think too much about continuing on this legacy."

"Think there's anyone in there?" Dominique eyed the place.

"No." Amelia laughed. "It's so hidden back here. I think if there were the chance of squatters finding it, my father would be a little more careful about making sure we came around. As it is, it's pretty much long forgotten, except by me. I come out here every now and then to think, to remember, to find my happy place."

Amelia grabbed the bag containing their breakfast and motioned for Dominique to follow her.

As she threw open the big barn doors, she closed her eyes, allowing the long faded scents to return in her memory. She stood still, memories washing over her and taking her back to carefree days of laughter, eating homemade cookies, and soaking up her grandparents' love.

"It's beautiful," Dominique said, coming up behind her and wrapping her arms around Amelia's waist.

"It is. It feels like home to me when nowhere else does. Let's go inside." She climbed up onto the hayloft, taking a deep breath and laying out the breakfast items on the plaid blanket she had left up there.

"You have this all set up?"

"I keep it up here, because sometimes when I'm out driving, I end up here, and I want a comfortable place to sit while I'm here."

"Thank you for sharing this with me." Dominique smiled broadly and Amelia's heart skipped a beat.

"How did I get so lucky to be sharing things like this with someone so beautiful and kind?" Amelia asked, shaking her head. "If you hadn't been here, I'd still be sorting things out in a chaotic mess. I'm sure I'd be dealing with them in my own way—probably the wrong way—but I'm so grateful for the way you make me want to be a better person, the gentle way you help me open up. So thank *you*."

Nestled together on the blanket, they enjoyed their breakfast. In the moments of silence, Amelia took the time to sort through her thoughts. Mostly she decided she was grateful for the fact that she could exist like this with Dominique, in comfortable, non-pressured silence. She opened her mouth, about to express her gratitude, but shoved a bite of muffin inside instead. It seemed such an odd thing to say out loud. Content, she leaned her head against Dominique's chest and stared up into her big, brown eyes.

Dominique stroked her hair and popped the last bit of muffin into her mouth. After she swallowed, she turned her head to the side and brought her lips to Amelia's for a single, sweet kiss.

"This was only stop number one," Amelia said when the kiss ended. "I have something else up my sleeve for you, if you're willing."

Dominique's eyes sparkled and her nose scrunched up as she smiled. "I'm willing and ready for whatever you have planned."

Amelia giggled and hurriedly climbed down from the hayloft, her mind spinning with the possibilities as she led the way.

# CHAPTER NINETEEN

The fall air was as calming as it was crisp, and the birds singing their songs outside the rolled down window seemed to set the perfect ambiance for a carefree, autumn day. Dominique smiled, looking over at Amy as she drove. She admired this woman and her tenacity. Amy had been correct. She wasn't running from her problems, but she was working much more effectively to solve them than she would have been sitting in an empty shop, wondering if it would ever be full again.

Amy sang along with the tune that was softly playing from the radio. It wasn't one Dominique recognized, but she decided it was one of her favorites. Amy's voice rose and fell, showing off her vocal range. Dominique wanted to hear more of that sound, more singing and more uninhibited joy.

"I love this song," Amy said, smiling.

"I've never heard it, but I enjoyed it as well," Dominique said, her voice coming across lower, huskier than she had intended. But Amy didn't seem upset by it. Her eyes twinkled in the sunlight and she winked.

"I love that rasp you get in your voice." She laughed and raised an eyebrow. "It turns me on."

"It does?"

Amy nodded, biting her lip and letting out a low moan. "It *really* does."

"Your singing had the same effect on me, just so you know," Dominique said, running her fingers up Amy's arm. The softness of her skin and the electricity that seemed to flow between them tightened every muscle in Dominique's body.

"What do you think we should do about that?" Amy asked, already turning the steering wheel to head down another dirt road. Dominique started to answer but looked around outside. None of this looked familiar. It wasn't the path they had taken earlier.

Chuckling, she shook her head. "It looks like you've already got that part figured out."

"I might have an idea or two."

Dominique watched in amusement as Amy maneuvered through the winding roads until they were parked in a secluded area of the riverbank, hidden by the hills nearby.

"I think I like your idea," Dominique said, looking Amy up and down.

Amy unbuckled her seatbelt and moved closer, drawing Dominique into a passionate kiss. Every bit of stress she had felt throughout the past several days escaped her body. The kiss consumed her. Amy trailed her kisses down, letting her lips softly caress Dominique's neck and shoulders.

Amy tugged at the base of Dominique's shirt and pulled it up over her head. Dominique looked out the windows and considered protesting, but Amy's mouth covered one of her nipples, causing a low moan to escape her lips. There was no going back. Dominique embraced her adventurous side. As Amy's tongue licked over the tip of her already hardened nipple, lust grew inside of her. Entranced, she moved to pull Amy's shirt off as well, using her hands to explore every inch of Amy's beautiful body. As she slipped inside Amy's jeans with her fingers, a pleasured sigh escaped Amy's lips.

She massaged Amy's hardening clit, eliciting a string of moans. Feeling the tension rise as Amy's breathing quickened, Dominique slid into her. Amy moaned as Dominique drove herself in and out with quickening pace.

"I need more," Dominique said, her breath ragged with passion. "I need more of you."

Amy pulled her head up, breathless and wide-eyed. "What more can I give you?"

"This," Dominique said, sliding into the backseat and pulling Amy along with her. Deftly she laid Amy beneath her, pulled her jeans off, and discarded them on the floor. Admiring Amy's black lace panties for a second, Dominique didn't want to waste the treat in front of her. It was a tight fit, but with her knees on the floorboard, she leaned down between Amy's legs, smiling at her as she licked the lace, teasing her for a minute and enjoying the feeling of the slick material against her tongue. As Amy moaned and arched her back, Dominique knew she was ready for more, but she wanted it to last. Kissing around Amy's inner thighs, she delighted in every tremble.

"I need you," Amy said through ragged breaths. "I need you now."

Dominique stopped her kisses for a moment, just long enough to make eye contact. Amy's green eyes were bright with desire, her lips parted and panting. "Please," she begged. Dominique winked and pulled Amy's panties to the side, intoxicated by the taste of her nectar. Slipping her tongue inside, she lapped up Amy's juices and brought her tongue back up to massage Amy's hardness.

Her desire to make it last wasn't going to be an achievable goal. Amy bucked her hips and her body trembled. Driving her fingers inside, Dominique filled Amy to the hilt, thrusting in rhythm as her tongue worked its magic.

"Oh. My. God!" Amy screamed as she convulsed, her orgasm rocking her body as much as it rocked the car.

Dominique slowly drew her fingers out and brought them up to her mouth. Smiling at Amy and winking, she licked them clean. Amy's eyes fluttered and she let out a labored breath.

"God," she said, breathlessly. "You're sexy."

Dominique looked her up and down before kissing her way back up Amy's body until their lips met. "You are," she said, pulling back from the kiss and laying her head on Amy's chest.

"How is it possible to want more right after something that earth-shattering?" Amy asked after a moment. "I'm insatiable with you."

"Rest up for a few minutes, and then whenever you're ready, we'll go for round two."

"I want all the rounds," Amy said with a laugh.

"We'll go as many rounds as you'd like."

"Mmm," Amy moaned. "I want all the rounds you'll give me."

"In that case, I think you have an infinite number of rounds waiting for you, as well as an infinite number of breakfasts, dates, and whatever else you'd like." With her head on Amy's chest, Dominique heard Amy's breath catch in her throat. "Unless that's not what you want," she added quietly.

"It's exactly what I want," Amy said, kissing Dominique's cheek softly. "I just want you."

"And I just want you."

"It's settled then." Amy playfully ran her fingers through Dominique's hair. "And that makes me really happy."

"Me, too." Dominique gazed up into those bright green eyes, basking in the gratitude and warmth of their connection.

Amy cleared her throat and looked longingly into Dominique's eyes. "I don't really know how this is supposed to work," she said, shaking her head. "But do you want to see *just* me?" She let out a deep breath. "Do you want to…" she trailed off and shrugged.

"Do you want to be my girlfriend?" Dominique asked, smiling broadly. "Is that what you're asking? Do we want to be exclusive and committed to one another?"

Amy bit her lip and nodded rapidly.

"Yes. That's what I'd very much like."

"Me, too," Amy said, her devilish grin returning. "In that case, let's celebrate with round two."

"I like the way you think." Dominique squealed as Amy shifted her weight and pulled Dominique up onto the seat only to straddle her.

"Round two of many," Amy said, her eyes twinkling as though she was securing her prize.

# CHAPTER TWENTY

Fiddling with the cuff buttons on his button-down shirt, Clayton looked in the mirror and nodded. His decision to dress up today made him feel more confident. He pushed out his chest and straightened his shoulders. Steeling his eyes, he put on his no-nonsense face and exited the station bathroom.

"Morning, Stark," he called out down the hall as he saw Joe Stark heading toward his office. He picked up his pace, trying to run the old man down before he got settled at his desk. It was of no use. He sighed, following Stark into his office. "Morning," he said again, poking his head inside Stark's office.

"Good morning, Clayton," Stark said, gruffly nodding his head.

"Did you get my email, sir?" He looked down at the floor realizing he probably should have used another method of communication.

"I haven't turned on my computer yet. What's going on?"

Clayton forced a smile and silently reminded himself to be more patient. His generation was prone to checking email after hours. It wasn't Stark's fault that he preferred to be called. He cleared his throat. "I need your help this morning, if you have some time."

"You've got it. What can I do for you?"

Glancing around the hallway and smiling to himself, Clayton took a step closer, shutting the door behind him. There was too much hustle and bustle outside for him to explain exactly what he needed, and he wasn't ready to let the cat out of the bag until it was a done deal.

Stark narrowed his eyes but kept his expression as neutral as possible. "You're not quitting, are you?" he asked, while Clayton took a seat.

Clayton let out a laugh. "No, sir. I'm not planning on going anywhere. But I do need some help."

"You mentioned that," Stark prodded, cocking his head in Clayton's direction.

"I wanted to be the hero, and I think I'm onto something big." Clayton shrugged and smiled sheepishly. Stark was his superior, and he hated having to ask for help. But it would be worth it. "But I'm also not stupid enough to think I can do it alone."

"Admirable," Stark noted.

Clayton let out a sigh of relief. "Thank you." He nodded, and launched into his plan. He laid out the details as he knew them—or rather, the lack of details. Talking in hushed tones, he outlined all he had unearthed in his most recent round of questioning. No one else had known about Amelia, and in that lack of knowledge, there might just be an answer if they played their cards correctly.

As he finished, Stark smiled. "You're right, kid. You might just be onto something. So you needing a little 'good cop, bad cop' scenario staged? If we do, he hasn't seen me yet. I've been doing the behind-the-scenes stuff and haven't yet had the pleasure of meeting the kid face-to-face, so we have the element of surprise on our side."

Clayton moved his head from side to side, considering the approach. "If we do that, I'll have to be the bad cop. He already hates me."

"You're doing your job then," Stark said, shaking his head. "If I had a nickel for every criminal who's hated me over the years, I could have retired years ago."

Clayton pursed his lips, taking another deep breath. "Do you think he is a criminal? I mean, I've heard enough to form my own opinions."

"What are those opinions?"

"My gut says he's a spoiled, rich brat who thinks he can get away with anything, and he probably wasn't thinking too clearly that night. We have it on good authority he was drunk as a skunk, and shouldn't have been driving in the first place. That's a side point, though. The point is that he was drunk. He felt invincible. His daddy has always found a way to get him out of his scrapes before, just like he's trying to do now. This case is a little too heavy for the mayor to work his charm, though, and I think he knows he's in trouble. I think he did it. My gut tells me there's too much guilt behind that smug smile." Clayton laid his hands out palm up on the desk and shrugged. "Everything else has come up empty. We've chased lead after lead, and we've found nothing other than evidence pointing to what we already know has to be the truth. That has to mean something, right?"

"Hit the nail on the head, Clayton," Stark said, reaching across the desk to give Clayton a fatherly pat on the shoulder. "Like I've said from the beginning, we've had enough to keep him behind bars. But he's got the best lawyer money can buy, and there's no doubt they'll bring a tough case. If we want this damn thing solved, we've got to cover our asses, and we've got to tighten down our case. That said, I want justice—not just some guy behind bars. So no matter what our guts say, we can't let that interfere with the truth if, for some reason, the truth is that he's innocent."

"Right." Clayton nodded, not letting Stark's reminder take the wind out of his sails. "The truth will come out."

Stark nodded. "Good. We're on the same page. Now, let's set out a game plan. We can't go in there without his lawyer. We need this airtight. We don't want to be one of those cases that gets tossed because we screwed up our questioning process. If we're going to do this right, we're going to have to employ a little strategy." He glanced at his watch. Holding up one finger, he signaled for Clayton to be patient. Picking up the phone and hitting a couple of buttons, he cleared his throat. "Gloria, it's Stark," he said into the receiver. "I need you to rally up Westwick's lawyer. Have him meet us this afternoon. We'll go down to the County Jail, so we can talk to Trent." He paused and scribbled some notes on the notepad by his phone. "That works. We can be flexible. You let me know the time, and we'll get going when they're ready."

He hung up the phone and smiled across the desk. Clayton wanted to do it sooner but bit his tongue. With his jaw set, he nodded at his superior.

"Don't worry." Stark shrugged. "It'll come in time. We just have to be patient and hold our horses for a bit. It's best to do this the right way so it counts."

Clayton sighed, remembering he had chosen to ask for help. He leaned forward, setting his own notebook on Stark's desk. There were details that still had to be presented in order for this to be effective.

As the morning pressed on, Clayton's head throbbed. There was too much at stake for this to be a long shot. This *had* to work. Stark had lunch ordered in, and Clayton had only managed to escape the small office for a single bathroom break.

He was ready and restless. He wanted less talk and a great deal more action.

He glanced at the clock. There were still twenty minutes to go until they had to leave for their scheduled meeting. He tapped his foot anxiously.

"You're like a dog waiting to be let out of his cage," Stark said, shaking his head. "I'm going to need you to rein it in just a bit. You can't go in there all eager beaver and expect results. Be patient."

"I've been patient," Clayton snapped. "But this process is getting old."

"It's tried and true," Stark said, slapping his desk. "I know how this goes. You youngsters on the force come in heavy-handed, thinking you know best. But I'm going to tell you that I've seen men like you come in and blow up a case completely.

We can't have that. Not when all of this is at stake." He stood, his voice rising as he did. "I am just as sick of working on this as you and every other detective here. It's exhausting, and the bullshit being handed down by the mayor doesn't help at all. We're under strict orders to investigate every possible lead. That means I'm stuck here, just like you are, questioning every single person in this godforsaken town, even pulling in innocent women like that Brandt girl for relentless questioning. I'm stuck, just like you are. But getting in a hurry won't help anyone. In fact, if we blow even a portion of this, we go back to square one. Is that what you want?" Stunned, Clayton sat in silence. "Is it?" Stark's voice boomed as he slapped his desk again. "Do you want to be stuck on this for the rest of the year? Or do you want to take a little advice, do it the right way, and possibly walk away from this day a step ahead?"

"Sorry," Clayton said quietly, looking down at the floor. Stark had a point. "You're right," he added after a moment of silence.

"I know I am," Stark said, pacing a few steps before taking a seat again. "We have to be on the same damn page or this isn't going to work. Got it?"

Clayton kept his mouth shut and nodded. He listened as intently as his stubborn mind would allow while Stark, for the millionth time, outlined the so-called "game plan" in his notebook.

After a few minutes, Stark stood and nodded. "I think we're ready, so I'm going to go take a few minutes to myself to grab some coffee. I suggest you do the same, or go get some fresh air. We'll leave in ten minutes, but we need to be crisp when we do."

Clayton nodded but waited until Stark had vacated the office before he stood. He hated the waiting game. He let out a sigh and strode out of the building. He might only have ten minutes, but he was going to take Stark's advice and clear his head.

Gloria stood beside the building, one leg propped up on the wall behind her, her fingers curled around a lit cigarette. She took a long drag and looked in his direction. "You want one of these?" she drawled, exhaling a cloud of smoke.

"I don't usually smoke." He watched as she drew in smoke again, and smiled lazily at him.

"I don't usually either, but every once in a while, it calms my nerves."

"What are you nervous about?" he asked, taking a step closer.

"Everything." She laughed and then shrugged. "It seems like this place is a ticking time bomb, and I'm just waiting for the next shoe to drop before it explodes. This case is a joke, and it shouldn't be. There was a life lost and this town should care more about that than anything, but it just feels so far from the town I once knew."

"That's right," he said, nodding. "I forgot you're from here. You're one of them."

"No, I *was* one of them. Who they are now, I don't want any part of that."

She held out the box. Nodding, he gave into whatever offer of comfort—no matter how fleeting—she had to give. Lighting the cigarette, he took a slow drag. As the smoke filled his lungs, he coughed. Gloria laughed, shaking her head.

"You were right," she said. "You don't smoke."

"I did once or twice as a misguided teen," he said, exhaling the smoke. "It was never a lasting thing." His senses tingled as the nicotine swirled in his blood. "But you were right as well. This does have a calming effect."

"I saw you in there with Stark all day." She let her arms drop to her sides. "Seems like every day lately needs a little infusion of calming. Do you feel like you're making progress?"

"Hard to say," he answered, exhaling another puff of smoke. "It's always hard to say lately, but I think we're onto something that could help close this damn train wreck of a case."

"Good." She put out her cigarette on the bottom of her shoe, tossed the butt into a nearby trashcan and checked her watch. "I have to get back in there, but you'll be fine. Go do what you know how to do. The rest will come with time, and maybe you're right." She looked up at the sky and the slightest signs of a smile played on the corner of her lips. "Maybe you've got something that will close this thing up. Then the mayor and the rest of the powers that be in this hellhole will finally shut up and let us do our jobs. And maybe, eventually, everything can go back to the way it once was."

He nodded and waited until she was inside to put out his cigarette as well. He didn't have the heart to tell her that nothing would ever be the same in this town. Whatever came from all of this, Knell was forever changed. There was no "normal" anymore.

Once he was back inside, he headed to the bathroom to wash the smell of smoke off his hands and then headed for Stark's office.

Stark was already waiting, pacing back and forth. Clayton sighed, glancing at his watch. They still had five minutes, but Stark liked to be early.

"Let's go." Stark grabbed his keys and walked out the door. Pressing his lips together to stifle a sigh, Clayton followed like a dutiful child. On the drive over, he stayed silent, determined to take the last few minutes of his solitude.

Once they arrived, his head had cleared. He followed Stark down the long hallway, but kept silent. As was their agreed-upon approach, he would go first. Walking up to the room, he stopped and stared. The one-way glass gave him a moment to watch Trent's interaction with his lawyer. He wasn't sure whether or not to be relieved by the fact that Trent appeared to treat his lawyer with the same insolent disregard that he did everyone else. Either way, he was relieved to see the polished lawyer look at his watch, give a nod, and signal that it was time to come in, even though he couldn't see Clayton waiting.

Clayton stood still a moment longer. He had already interacted with William Clarke on this case. But today, he needed to know more about the man he was up against. Bought and paid-for came to mind as he looked inside the window. The pinstripe suit Clarke wore likely cost more than Clayton's annual salary, and no doubt those polished shoes were worth hundreds. His slicked back black hair seemed to shine, even in the worst lighting, and his striking features echoed what Clayton already knew about this town. Somehow the pretty people all seemed to have money, and they all looked just as fake as could be. He sighed and shook his head. This would do him no good.

Rounding the corner, he opened the door and cleared his throat. It was time to be all business.

# CHAPTER TWENTY-ONE

*This guy again.* Disgust bubbled up inside Trent. He looked at Clayton with a scowl. "Can't you all ever find someone new to send in here?" He spat the words in Clayton's direction and ignored William shaking his head beside him. He turned his scowl on William. "I know what I'm supposed to say and not supposed to say. I'm innocent, so I can at least say with certainty I hate this guy, okay? Stop treating me like a child, or I'll find someone else to sit in on these pointless little chats."

William narrowed his eyes, but Trent didn't care. He was sick of this bullshit. He had told his father as much, and he'd been promised that this would stop. It hadn't, and he was beyond angry. He slammed his fists on the table. The cuffs on his wrists cut into his skin, but he didn't care. When he finally got out of here, he was going to get his revenge.

"What is it today?" he asked. William nudged him under the table, and he took a deep breath, trying to stifle his anger for a moment. "Come in here to ask me more about stuff I don't know?"

Clayton cleared his throat again, and Trent wanted to scream. He bit his tongue and set his jaw. He didn't have to like it, but he had to stay quiet long enough to get out of this shit hole.

"Actually I came in here to talk to you about information you knew that you shouldn't have been privy to," Clayton said, stretching his legs before casually crossing them and setting out his notepad in front of him.

If Trent weren't hand cuffed to the table, he would have wiped that smug grin right off Clayton's face. That would do him no good, though. A growl rumbled deep inside of him before escaping his lips as a heavy sigh. "And what is that?" he asked, making sure he sounded every bit as condescending as he hoped he did.

"Why don't you tell me? It seems like you had information about Chloe's life that didn't quite match up with the lack of close relationship the two of you had."

"I didn't have any relationship with that woman." Trent pounded his fist into the table again. "I didn't want anything to do with her. I am a good man. I didn't associate with her kind."

"Why do you hate homosexuals so much?" Clayton's words were calm and even, his eyes piercing.

Trent's heart hammered, and he closed his eyes, warding off the horrific memories. "They're disgusting," he said, swallowing hard after a moment of silence. Exhaling, he narrowed his eyes. "I believe there's right and there's wrong. She..." Trent was careful not to use her name. "...And everyone like her—they're all screwed up in the head."

"Was it growing up in this town that made you think that way? Or maybe your father's teachings? Church? Personal experiences with homosexual individuals?"

Trent jerked his wrists against the cuffs and looked off into the corner of the room. Gritting his teeth, he shot a death stare at Clayton. "This stupid shit has no business on the case. I'm a God-fearing man. Why don't you go ahead and ask how I feel about politics, religion and everything else that makes no difference here?"

"It makes quite the difference, actually." Clayton casually leaned forward, lowering his gaze and looking straight into Trent's eyes. Trent gulped, but tried to hide the movement. With a stare that intense, it seemed like Clayton could read into Trent's mind.

Trent cleared his throat. "Can we stop talking about gayness and all that indecency for a minute and get to the bottom of why you called me out here?"

"I ask the questions," Clayton snapped and slapped the table. "You're in no position to weasel out of this or to think you run the show. In here, I'm boss."

Trent stiffened, taking the challenge. "Fuck you," he muttered under his breath. He saw Clayton's smirk, and he wished again he could hit him. He looked over Clayton's head to the back wall. "Fine," he finally managed, slumping back into his chair.

"What was it about Chloe—about lesbians and gays in general—that you didn't like?"

"What's to like?" Trent hurled the question. "What is there to like?" When Clayton didn't answer, he straightened in his chair. "You tell me, Mr. Detective. Do you like the fucking queers?"

Beside him, William nudged him and cleared his throat. He mouthed the word, "Enough."

"No," Trent said, directing his attention at William this time. "I'm sick and tired of being told what I can and can't say. You can get the hell out of this room."

Though he tried to stop the train, he couldn't. His hands were shaking as he fought with all his might to keep memories—painful memories—at bay. He forced a deep breath, and narrowed his eyes, silently demanding William listen to his order.

"That's not advisable," William said, keeping his tone low but firm. "You and I both know you need someone in your corner right now."

No one had ever been in his corner, not really, aside from his dad. He shook his head, every ounce of resentment rising within him. "I said *get out!*"

When William still refused to move, Trent lunged his chair in William's direction, using the only free part of his body, his feet, to kick it. "Go. I don't want your help. I don't want you on my case. I want you to get the hell out. You're fired. I don't want a lawyer if you're only going to sit in here and tell me I can't distance myself from someone who was so blatantly sick in the head. It wouldn't help my case at all if people thought I was someone who would hang around with Chloe fucking Stanton and her wild, god-awful lifestyle."

William pressed his lips together and stood, straightening his suit jacket and shaking his head. "Your mistake, kid," he muttered as he strode out the door.

"No it's *your* mistake, and it's a big one. I'll make sure it costs you every penny you have." Trent hit the table again as the door slammed shut and focused back on Clayton.

"Are you sure you don't want a lawyer?" Clayton asked, adjusting the tape recorder and sliding it closer to Trent.

"I don't give a damn if that thing is recording all of this. I don't need a lawyer. That guy is just a dumb country bumpkin in a suit. My father fucked up in sending him in here to defend me. I don't need defending anyway. I'm innocent." He settled his voice back into a calmer tone, trying to choose his words. "So ask me your questions, and I'll give you my answers without a lawyer in here."

Trent saw Clayton smirk as he took notes in his notepad. For a second, he wondered if he *had* made a mistake. But his anger was too strong to ignore. He focused on breathing, slowly and intently, calming his nerves and his anger. When Clayton didn't fill the silence, his hands shook again, and he fought to keep composure. "Go ahead. Ask your fucking questions." He kept his words a whisper, but made sure they sizzled off the tongue.

"Okay," Clayton said with a shrug. "I'm going on record to restate that you have requested to be questioned without a lawyer."

"Get on with it."

"How do you know details about Chloe's personal life?"

"I just know them," Trent said, straightening his shoulders. "It's a small town. People talk."

"Which people?"

"People," he said, glaring at the tape recorder. "Everyone talks."

"Okay," Clayton said, writing on his pad again.

Trent wished he could slap it out of his hands and watch it fall to the floor. He eyed Clayton. The minute he was out of cuffs, he'd beat that prick to a bloody pulp.

"If you didn't associate with 'Chloe's kind of people,' as you've dubbed the gay community in previous interviews, which types of people knew the details of her personal life? It seems to me Chloe didn't have too many close friends in whom she confided. Did you have another friend who might have been a lesbian who told you this information?"

Clayton was smirking, as if he was enjoying pouring salt into one of Trent's wounds. And Trent felt the sting, fresh despite the years that had passed. He shuddered. "I already told you. I don't hang out with, associate with, or even talk with *those people.*"

Clayton raised an eyebrow and cleared his throat, jotting a few things down on the notepad again. Trent wanted to crane his neck to see what was being written down, but he didn't want to let on that he was curious.

"Aside from the night of your encounter at McCool's, when was the last time you remember talking to Chloe Stanton?"

"I already told you. I didn't make a habit of talking to her. Hell, I didn't even make a habit of being in the same place as she was. It's not my fault that whore happened to be in the same damn bar where I was getting drinks that night. She's a lush from what I've heard, so she frequents the place. Me and my buddies usually go elsewhere. We go to classier places, places outside of town. But we wound up there, and she was there too. It is what it is." He shook his head and spat in the corner of the room, grinning at the disgust in Clayton's face.

"So you can't remember the last conversation you had with her prior to that night?"

"Can't say that I do."

"And how well would you say you knew Amelia Brandt?"

Trent narrowed his eyes. "Where is this going?"

"You need to answer the question," Clayton said, leaning back in his chair, casually tapping his pen against the notepad.

Trent let out a sigh and shook his head. "She serves shitty coffee, and I'd been in her shop a time or two. We're not friends by any stretch. I don't spend my time with a lot of the people around here."

Clayton's eyebrow shot up and Trent wanted to strangle him. "Why then did you throw out her name as someone who would know something?"

"What? Did she know something?" He scowled. "Maybe she did this."

"Maybe." Clayton shrugged, never diverting eye contact. Trent didn't look away or show weakness. "Maybe you shouldn't go around throwing out accusations, though. And maybe, you can shed some insight onto how you knew details about who Chloe hung around with. But you've also stated you don't associate with lesbians."

*Lesbians.* The word hung in the air and threatened to slice through every shred of self-control Trent had left.

"Why do you hate lesbians?" Clayton asked, his expression amused.

Trent slapped the table and delighted when he saw Clayton flinch. "I'm done talking to you, you son of a bitch!" He frowned and shook his head. "I'm done with you."

"Okay," Clayton shrugged and stood. "Have it your way." He walked out without another word, and Trent sat dumfounded. He stared at the doorway. It had never been that easy.

"We're done in here!" He called out, hoping the dumb kid who escorted him to and from his cell would come in and let him go back. He looked around at the gray walls and spat again in the corner. This place was a dump, and from the looks of the leak-stained ceiling tiles, it was about to fall down. Closing his eyes, he wished for that moment—a glorious moment when this place collapsed and everyone around here went to hell right along with it.

He tried to take deep breaths, but his anger made his heart race more quickly. The sound of the door opening jolted him from his thoughts. He jerked his head upright and glared at the entrance.

In the entryway stood a tall, broad-shouldered man with gray hair and a soft face. He looked like someone's grandpa, Trent thought, trying to wrap his mind around the sudden shift.

"Who are you?" Trent said, keeping his voice flat. If he'd learned anything during his stint here, it was that you didn't discount someone right away. You needed friends in this place, and there were surely enough enemies.

"My name is Joe," he said, taking the seat that Clayton had occupied only moments before.

"What do you want, Joe?" Trent narrowed his eyes, watching the guy's every movement.

Joe shrugged his shoulders and set his hands on the table. Trent examined the man. There was no sign of that irritating pen and pad that Clayton always carried, tapped, and scribbled on. It was just this guy and the same damn tape recorder in the middle of the table.

"I just want to talk to you," Joe said quietly. "For starters, they told me tomorrow is your birthday. So happy birthday. Other than that, I just want to talk. I know you've had a rough day, what with losing your lawyer and having Clayton in here ruffling your feathers. I just want to see how you're doing."

Trent leaned back in his chair. "So this is a house call? Checking to see if the sheets are too scratchy and the food is too bland?" He scoffed. "That's bullshit. Why are you really here?"

"The sheets are scratchy?" Joe nodded and let out a sigh. "I'm sure they are, and I'm sorry to hear that. Unfortunately we deal with what we have according to the budget. But aside from your accommodations here, I'd like to focus a little bit more on how you feel the questioning process has been."

"It's been fucked up," Trent said. He laid his palms out on the table. "The people they have around here..." He looked and didn't see a badge on Joe's shirt. He knew he was taking a chance, but he didn't care. Even if this guy was one of them, he could hear the truth. "These people they have around here—hell you might be one of them—they suck. They run around like fucking buffoons. They don't know anything, and they're barking up the wrong tree looking for answers. Sitting me in here every week or so to ask me the same damn questions, hoping for different answers, won't do anyone good. And I'll be damned if I'm going to be stuck in this hellhole while they're letting whoever actually did this run free. I want out of here, and I want out of here *now*." His words came out like an angry hiss, and he sat breathing heavily through a set jaw, making intense eye contact to drive his point home.

"Trent," Joe spoke slowly, "you don't have to get upset right now. I'm just here to help. I want to get it on the record that you don't want to talk with Clayton anymore. Is that the case?"

"Like I have any choices in here," Trent shook his head and hit the table again. "I'm chained to this damn chair and forced to listen to that bastard recount things I said that he thinks have meaning but they don't. They have no meaning and neither does any of this."

Joe sighed and leaned forward. "I understand your frustrations."

Trent scooted his chair back as far as the cuffs would allow. "Is this some kind of 'good cop, bad cop' thing y'all are doing? Do y'all really do that? Are you a fucking cop too?"

Joe smiled. "I'm one of the good guys," he said, leaning forward. "I want to help get to the bottom of this case. You're innocent until proven guilty, so you do need to speak to someone. It doesn't have to be Clayton."

"I don't want to talk to anyone right now," Trent hissed, recoiling as he considered talking to yet another cop. "I want my space."

Joe shrugged. "I can give you that. I have a couple of questions first."

"Do I have a choice?" Trent spat into the corner of the room again. Joe didn't even flinch. He cocked his head to the side. "What is it?" he asked.

"We do need to know some things," Joe said, shrugging. "Murder cases are multi-faceted, and there are little details that don't always add up. It's usually in the details. So I need to talk to you a little about Chloe Stanton."

"I don't know anything about her." He tensed up, leaning as far back as his cuffs would allow.

Joe propped his elbows up on the table and smiled. "You don't have to know everything. I'm just asking. Why don't you start with what you did know about her?"

Trent looked side to side. As much as his heart was racing, he made sure to keep a calm expression. No matter what happened or what he said, they twisted it. "She worked on a ranch," he said flatly.

"Very astute observation, Mr. Westwick," Joe said with a laugh. "Sorry. Have to find humor where you can some days, am I right?" Trent narrowed his eyes and watched as Joe leaned back and crossed his left ankle over his right knee. "Do you like laughing, Trent?"

"There's not much to laugh about these days, in *this* place."

"Sure there is. Tell me a joke."

"It's a joke that I'm in here. A l—" He bit his tongue and frowned. "Lesbian," he forced the word out finally. "A lesbian was murdered, and for some reason, they think I did it, all because I believe in God."

"Why is that word so hard to say for you?" Joe asked.

Trent glared. "I'm done. I'm done talking to all of you. Get out!"

"I'm going to give you some space," Joe agreed too quickly. "I'm also going to get you some water. I'll be back in just a few minutes."

As he walked out the door, Trent tried to steel his emotions. The door was already shut, but he wanted to be left alone.

"I don't want you to come back. Stay the fuck away. Stay the fuck out. Leave me alone!" He was shouting to himself in a room the size of a fucking shoebox, and he knew he needed to get his shit together. But he wasn't sure what to think. No one in this place really wanted what was best for him. Even his own father had been too much of a coward to truly take a stand. He was there for him, sure, verbally at least. And monetarily. But that wasn't enough. He needed "someone in his corner," as Joe had said. But it wasn't Joe. Hell, it wasn't anyone in here. Just like he always did, he'd wait for that someone, and more than likely never find them. Gritting his teeth, he let out a low growl of frustration.

*Why do you hate lesbians?*

Clayton's question bounced around in his head, clattering and making him feel crazier than he already did. They'd been through this multiple times, and he'd held the memories at bay while sitting in these interrogation rooms. Today, though, they wouldn't stop. Playing through his mind, as it had hundreds of times since that night, he heard the screams, saw the scuffle, felt his rage. But this time, it wasn't Chloe's face in his mind. It was his mother's. His memories faded back to childhood.

*"Go to bed baby," her voice cooed through his near sleep daze. "When you wake up, we'll celebrate your birthday. Eight years is a big deal."*

*He smiled, reaching for her hand. But before he could connect, the sound of breaking glass from the kitchen rang through the air.*

*"I have to go," she said, leaning down to give him a kiss on the head.*

*Throughout the night, sounds rang through the air. Angry shouts, obscenities, more breaking glass, his mother's pleas for his father to be quiet.*

*The word "lesbian" thrown about like a curse. Her pleas for his father to stop, the sound of blows being thrown, her cries in the night.*

*He covered his head with pillows and tried to think about his birthday, but it was of no use. He wanted to ask what a lesbian was, but figured it wasn't safe. He closed his eyes tight, thinking maybe it would make more sense tomorrow. When he heard the front door slam, his mother's words echoed in his mind. "I have to go."*

Trent shook his head violently. If it hadn't been for her stepping out, things would have been better. That's what his father had always said. Same with Chloe. If she hadn't been a deviant, things would have been better. They both deserved whatever happened to them. Only problem was, he had no idea what had happened to his mother. Nineteen years to the day she'd walked out. That was a long damn time not to know where she was, or if she gave a single fuck about how he was. A hot tear slid down his cheek and he grit his teeth harder, until they hurt.

He heard the door open again and saw Clayton standing in the doorway.

"I said I was done with you." Trent let out a low growl. "I said I was done with that other guy, too. I'm fucking done with this entire thing."

Clayton held his hands up. "Look, I was just informed by Joe that I was a little hard on you," he said. He shrugged and took his seat again. "Personally, I think you're a punk, and you deserve it. You string us along, we push harder. But I was told to loosen up."

"Oh, so you're just a puppet? Someone has their hands shoved up your ass, and you do what they say?"

"Watch it," Clayton shot back, his tone a clear attempt to remind Trent of his place. But this wasn't his place, and Clayton needed to be reminded of *his* place.

"I will not." Trent glared at him. "I will not be told what to do any longer. You don't know what life is like here. You don't know me, and you don't know who you're messing with."

"I know damn well," Clayton said, placing his palms on the table. "But we're not in here to talk about me. In fact, I'm in here to apologize. I asked you *why* you hated lesbians. I never asked *if* you hated them. Do you?"

Trent pounded the table. "Fucking stop!" he shouted, no longer able to blur the image of his mother's face from his memory.

"I can't stop." Clayton's tone was even, too even and too calm. Trent's heart pounded, drowning out any other sound. He could tell Clayton was still talking, but he couldn't hear any more of what he had to say.

*I have to go.*
*Hate lesbians.*

*I have to go.*

Bits and pieces of the phrases he had heard reverberated in his thoughts. Closing his eyes, he slammed his fists down on the table again. "Go," he said, his voice thicker than it had been. "Just go."

He leaned back and tried to take a deep breath when he heard the door click again. He blinked. Clayton was gone, but the door opened and Joe stepped back inside.

"Trent." Joe's voice was smooth and calm. Trent wanted to scream. How could they be so calm? And why did they care so much about scum being destroyed? He was talking still, and Trent tried to listen. "My buddy Clayton is a little trigger-happy. I'm going to try to talk to you like the upstanding guy you are. You're a gentleman, and so am I. Can we talk like gentlemen?"

Trent shook his head. There was no time for niceties. There was no time for anything right now.

"I'm going to ask you the same question he did, though," Joe said, standing at the edge of the table. "We came in here wanting to know how you knew about some of the more personal details of Chloe's life, about the company she kept. But now, we have new questions. We get that you don't like gay people..." He let out a long, slow breath. "Why is that?"

Trent saw the piercing blue of his mother's eyes flash in his mind. Closing his eyes, he whispered, "I have to go." Anger and resentment rising within him, he felt his heart rate increase. His hands shook and his voice trembled. "Get out," he said again, although he knew this was their show. They'd do whatever the fuck they pleased. They always did.

"Why?" Joe pressured.

"Go!" Trent screamed.

When the door shut behind Joe, Trent grasped for breath. It wouldn't come. Over and over, he heard his mother's words, saw her face as she bid him goodnight—the last time he'd ever see it.

"I have to go," he repeated. "I have to go!" He screamed the words, tears falling from his cheeks. Westwick men didn't cry. Stifling his emotions, he pounded his fists against the table.

Leaning back as far as he could, he brought his forehead crashing down against the metal of the table. "Fuck!" he shouted and leaned back to do it again. It felt good to feel something other than rejection. Slamming his head into the table for the third time, he looked down at the blood pooling on the table and frowned. If only it could be Clayton's blood or the blood of the officers who felt the need to keep him behind bars instead of his own.

He closed his eyes, and smashed his head into the cool metal one more time. On the way back up, he thought back to his own stupidity that had landed him here. He should have never mentioned Amelia's name.

"You're so fucking stupid," he whispered. "Say her fucking name and now everyone knows you were there. You heard it. You saw it. You did it."

He looked over to the wall and watched as the gray paint swirled. At the sound of the open door, he looked to find his father. "Dad," he whispered, shaking his head. "Why can't you get me out of here?"

From the doorway, his father shook his head. Trent smashed his head into the table one more time and looked up, only to find the doorway empty. He scanned the room, but his head was spinning too much to make sense of it.

From somewhere in the background he heard the words, "I'm not your father," but he couldn't place where they came from. Frantically he looked from side to side, but it only made his dizziness increase. The ringing in his ears made it impossible to hear anything other than his heart pounding.

"Yes, you are," he said. "You don't get to leave me, too. I'd understand if you wanted to. Everyone else has. This is my fuck up," he dropped his voice lower. "It's not yours. I was the one who ran my big mouth. You were right. If I kept myself quiet, I could have skated through this, but I told them something. I knew who she was sleeping with, just like you knew who Mom was sleeping with." The thoughts came back violently and he slammed his head against the table again.

"Fucking lesbians." His voice gurgled. He felt himself slipping in and out of consciousness, but fought to stay awake. He needed to tell his father, so he'd understand. Maybe if he understood, he would actually help him in the fight. Maybe he wouldn't leave. Forcing his eyes open, he stared at the ceiling and watched the dots of paint circle each other. "She said the name that night, and all I could think about was how sick she was to bring Amelia down into that pit of sin with her, so I drove the knife right into her. She deserved it." He was drooling and tears mixed with blood ran down his face, but he couldn't stop. His father shouldn't have to see him like this. No one should. Words his dad had spoken to him from the time he was young repeated in his mind. *Be strong. Put on a good face. You're mine, and people will judge us by what they see. Don't let anyone see you weak.*

He covered his head, putting it on the table. "She deserved it, and if I had the chance, I'd do this to all of those damn gays. They ruin lives. They ruin people. They deserve this."

His eyelids were heavy and his head felt like it weighed a ton. Blood ran into his eye, but try as he might, he couldn't lift his cuffed hand enough to wipe it away. Giving into the urge to sleep, he closed his eyes.

A sharp smell hit his nostrils. Trent's eyes fluttered open and he jerked his head upright. He looked down at the table covered in blood, and his heart raced, hammering inside his chest. As his breathing accelerated, he looked around the room. Joe was sitting in the chair again, and nodded at Trent's wide-eyed stare.

"Glad to see you're okay," he said. The smile he had worn during questioning was now a look of concern. Joe shook his head, scowling. "You gave yourself quite the beating there. We're going to get you stitched up in the infirmary, and they'll take you to your cell."

"What happened?" Trent's words were labored. "My dad was here."

"No." Joe shook his head. His stare was almost sad. "I told you several times I wasn't your dad. You thought he was here."

As the dots connected in his head, Trent's eyes widened. He turned his attention back to Joe and then to the center of the table. The red blinking dot on the recorder sent alarms through his body. His stomach lurched and, without warning, he vomited on the table.

Casting his eyes downward, his mind raced. What had he done? "I need a lawyer," he croaked.

"Yes. You do," Joe said.

# CHAPTER TWENTY-TWO

Dominique's distant humming, accompanied by the sound and scent of bacon sizzling in the kitchen, made Amelia smile. She wanted to join the breakfast-making party, but she couldn't pull herself from the comfort of Dominique's exquisite bed. She nestled deeper into the luxurious pillows, wondering why they even bothered to ever stay at her house.

Images of her family and her business popped into her head, but she shook her head, clearing her thoughts. None of that mattered right now. Nothing mattered aside from doing exactly what Dominique had asked her to do this weekend. Unplug. Disconnect. Relax. *And fuck*, she mentally added to the list. Her smile grew and she let out a quiet moan, thinking of how incredible it was every single time. She moved her body against the soft sheets, longing for Dominique to come back in and join her.

Closing her eyes, she silenced everything but Dominique's sweet hums. As she listened, her smile grew. She began to make out the notes of "Sunday Kind of Love."

Quietly she sang along to the beat, letting the words resonate within her. Dominique's brown eyes, her sweet smile, her gentle reassuring touches and encouragement. She tossed the concept of a "Sunday kind of love" into the mix and mulled it around. She had never been certain of much when it came to love, and she wasn't sure enough in her judgment to call this "love." But it definitely was something. What she had, she would fight for, and there was no pleasure in the world she had ever unearthed greater than sharing just a moment in Dominique's presence. Maybe this *was* love. She shook her head and opened her eyes, staring up at the ceiling and then looking around the room with a smile.

Everything was so intricately decorated, and somehow both urban and rustic at the same time. She stared at the bookshelves Dominique said she built from scratch, the wood-burned, intricate art piece that hung on the wall, and the stylish furniture. Amelia breathed in deeply, taking in Dominique's scent that still lingered on the pillows. She wanted to know everything there was to know about this woman, and she was pretty sure she understood exactly the feeling Etta James sang of.

"Rise and shine," Dominique cooed from the entryway, breaking into Amelia's thoughts.

Amelia looked and her breath hung in her throat. She dropped her jaw. Dressed in nothing but black lace stockings, black underwear and a black, lacy bra, Dominique held out a tray of bacon, pancakes, and orange juice. Amelia opened her mouth to speak, but words failed her. Nodding, she smiled wider and brought her hand up to motion Dominique over to the bed.

"Are you hungry?" Dominique winked. No doubt she knew exactly which buttons she was pushing and was delighting in watching Amelia come undone.

Amelia nodded. "For so many things," she said, finally finding her voice. "You're like a walking fantasy right now."

Dominique laughed and set the tray on the bedside table.

"And you brought pancakes?" Amelia asked, shaking her head. "You're almost too good to be true."

"What do you mean *almost*?" Dominique laughed. "There's a mimosa there, too."

"That does actually put you over the top to the too good to be true category." They shared a laugh while Dominique raised her own mimosa glass in the air.

"To you, the joy you bring into my life, and to us as we start this journey together," she said, gently clinking her glass against Amelia's.

"To all of that, and to the way you keep me on my toes with so many good surprises," Amelia added, taking a sip. Dominique set her glass down and leaned over to kiss Amelia. The kiss was far more decadent than any she had ever tasted, completely disarming her. Blissfully entranced, she set her glass on the bedside table, and pulled Dominique on top of her.

"For the past two months, I've been saying I could get used to this," she said between kisses. "And the thing is, I don't think I'll ever get used to how you make me feel."

"Yeah?" Dominique leaned back and raised an eyebrow.

"Yeah," Amelia bit her lip. "Don't get me wrong, I'm definitely getting spoiled with every breathtaking aspect of this." She waved her hand to incorporate the bed, the breakfast and Dominique in front of her.

Dominique raised an eyebrow. "You mean waking up next to me and having breakfast?"

"That. And being here in your home, in Austin. I think I like it here."

Dominique straightened her shoulders before sliding off and sitting on the bed beside Amelia. "I thought you said Knell was always going to be your home." The creases in her forehead intensified and her eyes darkened with concern.

Amelia laughed, holding her hands up in the air. "I'm not talking about running away. I'm just saying I wouldn't mind spending some of my weekends here. We could go back and forth, you know?"

"We could make something like that work," Dominique whispered. She gently ran her fingers across Amelia's forehead, sweeping the hair out of her eyes. "It's a journey, and I'm excited to take it with you, wherever we decide to spend our time."

Propping herself up on one elbow, Amelia reached for her mimosa, took a sip, and then set it back on the table. She let out a sigh, half in contentment, half knowing she was about to break the bubble of bliss that had covered the morning.

"I want to wait to see what happens before I decide anything concrete," she said after a moment. Dominique cocked her head to the side. "Not about us," she added quickly. "I already made up my mind about us a while back. I don't say things I don't mean, so you can rest assured I've already decided about us. But there are factors that will play into where I want to go or what I want to do." She looked up to the ceiling and forced a deep breath. "I need to see what remains of my home once this horror story comes to a close." Dominique squeezed her hand, giving her the confidence she needed to continue. "After the trial is over, I feel like I'll have some closure and I'll know more of what remains of the place I've always called home. It was a safe haven. It was quaint. It was full of good people. And I don't know how much of that still exists."

Quietly, Dominique moved over to the other side of the bed, laying close to Amelia and wrapping her arms around her. With the tender touch and the reassurance that Dominique was by her side, Amelia's heartbeat settled back into a normal rhythm. "I just want to figure out what's left of the good people I once knew." She kissed Dominique on the top of the head and moved closer into the embrace, needing to be held. "With Trent's confession last month, it seems like it should be an open and shut case. He should be sentenced with the maximum punishment. It should be tried as a hate crime, but it's all still so up in the air, and I'm scared. They've gone completely silent. The police station won't give updates, the news stories just relive the rest of the bullshit we already know, and the mayor's office keeps issuing vague non-statements. I am terrified that the evil that was exposed will prevail, he'll be given a slap on the wrist, and nothing will ever change. The fact of the matter is that, as awful a situation as this is, our town has the opportunity to rebuild. But I'm scared that's not going to happen."

"I know," Dominique said quietly. "There is still the hope for justice. I know it doesn't change what happened and nothing will ever make that better. The home you knew is forever changed. I know that's a difficult concept to grasp and I know you've struggled with it. I'm here with you while you figure it out, and I'll be there by your side every step of the way to make sure they remember us, they know why this should be a hate crime. They may think they can intimidate us, but they won't."

"Thank you," Amelia said. "Thank you for everything." She turned and let Dominique be her big spoon. Dominique tightened her hold and kissed Amelia's neck softly.

"It's all going to happen," Dominique said between kisses. "That's all I can promise. It'll happen. Good or bad, we don't know yet. We have no way of seeing how this will go, so I can't tell you it'll all be okay. I can only tell you that we have been anything but passive. We have worked hard to open up the minds of everyone in that community. I have been in the community almost non-stop, just to make sure we have a voice. You have taken a bold stand and demanded justice at every turn. We've made sure they know the weight of this trial. But we can't be sure what they will do with what they've been given. All I will promise—all I *can* promise is that we will be okay, we will keep fighting, and we will be together while it happens. Once it does, we'll figure out how to make it good. Because we will make it good again."

Amelia nodded and took a deep breath. Rolling over to face Dominique, she shook her head. "I'm the worst," she said, letting out a sad laugh. "I'm sorry I ruined your sweet breakfast surprise with my moody morning thoughts."

"Don't worry about it," Dominique shook her head. "Your breakfast is still here, and so am I. I never want you to feel like you can't talk to me."

"I know." She smiled and ran her fingers up and down Dominique's soft skin. "I think I'm done talking for a while. You're right. At the end of it all, what will happen is going to happen. We can only do our part and encourage others to do the same. For now, I want to get back to why you had me visit in the first place."

"And why was that?" Dominique winked and the corners of her mouth turned up into a sexy smile.

"To get closer to you, to get away from it all, to have breakfast in bed." She shimmied her body seductively and moved in for a deep kiss. "And for sex," she added, biting Dominique's bottom lip.

"Yes to all of that," Dominique said with a giggle. "And so you can meet my friends after we take our time this morning just for us."

Amelia nodded, her heartbeat increasing again. "Do you think they'll like me?" she asked.

"I think they'll love you," Dominique said, "just like I do."

Amelia's breath caught in her throat and her eyes widened. She replayed Dominique's words in her mind. She opened her mouth to speak but words didn't come out. She saw the intensity in Dominique's soft brown eyes. She smiled, thinking about everything they'd been through, the ways she had seen Dominique fight for what she believed in, the tender way she broke through the walls of Amelia's fear and doubt, the ways she inspired Amelia to be the best person, and the simplicity with which they were able to share joy, laughter, and passion. Amelia swallowed hard. "You do?"

Dominique nodded and kissed Amelia's forehead. "I do. You don't have to say it back, but I wanted you to know. I've tried to keep it to myself and I can't anymore. I'm bad at lying and about keeping things to myself, and you should know that I love you."

"It's not that I don't feel it, too," Amelia said, carefully choosing her words as her heart jackhammered. "I'm just in shock. I love so many things about you, and I love being with you."

With a wink, Dominique slid closer, pulling Amelia into a sensual kiss. "Let's get dressed and ready, so you can meet my friends. We have a fun day planned to show you how the other side lives."

"Other side?" Amelia wrinkled her nose.

"Yeah," Dominique laughed. "The other side, those of us who have places to go that don't care if we're gay, places I can hold your hand in public. We'll show you the ropes."

Dominique kissed her once more and hopped out of bed, grabbing a piece of bacon to pop in her mouth, before turning on the speaker in her bathroom. Bubbly music filled the air, and Dominique sang along. Amelia listened to Dominique's melodious voice and contemplated what she had said. Hugging the pillow tightly to her chest, Amelia knew she too had fallen.

With a smile, she rose from the bed, feeling like a new, free woman.

\* \* \*

The morning had been a blur of happiness and now the streets buzzed with excitement. There was nothing extraordinary happening in Austin, but it was a lively place—especially on a Saturday evening. Street performers played guitars and drunken partiers bar-hopped. Dominique glanced to her side. Amy seemed to come to life here, with her green eyes blazing and her soft smile never wavering. When Amy reached for her hand, Dominique's heart leapt with joy. She wanted Amy to feel happy and safe here.

"Did you enjoy lunch?" Dominique asked, finally breaking the silence.

"That was hours ago," Amy's laugh spilled off her lips with ease. "But yes, I did. And I'm looking forward to what's next."

"Good." Dominique gave her a quick kiss on the cheek and led them around the corner, away from the Sixth Street partiers.

"I thought we were going out?" Amy stopped walking for a second to turn around and point back to where the party crowd had clearly already gathered.

Dominique winked. "We are. We're going out to our spot. You'll see. It's just up ahead."

When they reached their destination, Dominique held out her hands as if she was presenting a prize. "Ta-da," she added for dramatic effect. Amy eyed her quizzically, leaning back as she looked the place up and down. She turned to her right, watching two women with spiked hair walk arm-in-arm into the bar.

The lines in Amy's brow deepened and she shook her head. "What is this place?" She asked, gulping.

"It's a gay bar," Dominique said. "What's wrong?"

"I know it's a gay bar, okay?" Amy said. She shook her head and shoved her hands into her pockets. "Why are we here though? I thought we were meeting some of your friends."

"We are." Dominique walked over to where Amy stood with her feet planted several feet away. "They're already inside." Amy tapped her foot against the pavement, and Dominique watched as her eyes flitted from side to side. "What's going on? I thought you'd enjoy it. We can go somewhere else if you'd like." Dominique looked again to the front of the building. Nothing about the red brick and velvet rope should be so off-putting, but she wanted to get to the bottom of this.

"I've just..." Amy started but then looked at the ground. "I've just never been inside one of these, and I don't know what to expect. I don't know how to act in front of your friends anyway. I've never really gone through any of this. I know I don't *look* like a lesbian. I don't know how I'm supposed to look or act or be in there."

Her babbling-when-nervous habit gave her away, and Dominique put a reassuring hand on her shoulder. "It's okay to be nervous, but there's nothing to be nervous about. You don't have to act a certain way in there. In fact, it's quite the opposite. That place," Dominique pointed for dramatic effect, "that's our sanctuary. We can go in there and be whoever we truly are without judgment, without fear. Those women you saw walking in may be gay, and they may not be. You know as well as I do that looks don't mean anything. We can't judge books by their cover, and everyone in there will know not to judge you for how you look. You'll see. There are butches, femmes, gay men of all varieties, and everything in between. Straight people come here, too. But behind those doors, you don't have to look gay or straight. You don't have to act any certain way. It's a place for all and a place that celebrates people like you and me."

Amy's frown was still intact but she nodded. "Okay. I'll give it a try, because I trust you."

"Okay," Dominique said. She smiled and grabbed Amy's hand. "If you hate it, we'll leave. But I think you might just find it a bit freeing. I know I did the first time I walked through these doors."

"When was that?"

Dominique glanced to the side, careful to keep her voice low. "When I was nineteen. I got a fake ID just so I could sneak in and be with other gay people. I needed somewhere to fit in, and this was the place that saved my life when I was at my lowest and most hopeless point."

"Saved your life," Amy repeated.

Dominique nodded. "Yeah."

"I didn't know. I'm sorry."

"Don't worry about it." Dominique shrugged it off. "Let's just get inside and get you a drink."

Once inside, Dominique let her eyes adjust to the darkened room. With a punk band playing on the main stage and neon lights scattered about, she breathed in deeply. Even though this place smelled of old booze and cigarette smoke, it felt like home. She watched Amy out of the corner of her eye. Her shoulders had relaxed, but she still seemed bewildered. Certain it was unlike anything Amy had ever seen before, Dominique gently took her hand and led her to a tall top in the back, where she had spotted Cheyenne.

"Chey!" she called out as they approached the table.

Cheyenne turned around and smiled, jumping off her barstool to greet Dominique with a hug.

"Long time, no see, stranger," she said, her broad smile growing as she turned her attention to Amy. "And it's so nice to meet you. I'm Cheyenne," she said, going in for a hug. "I've heard so much about you and how happy you make my girl."

"It's nice to meet you, too," Amy said, her face softening into a genuine smile. She took the seat offered, and Dominique climbed atop the barstool next to her, grateful to have her two worlds collide.

Over small talk, she watched Amy relax, and after two screwdrivers, Amy and Cheyenne were laughing and telling jokes. Dominique sipped her drink, chiming in to the conversation when appropriate.

When Cheyenne disappeared off to the dance floor, Dominique turned to face Amy. She took a long sip of her drink and leveled her gaze, wrapping her fingers through Amy's. "There's something I want to talk to you about," she said, mulling over her approach as she bought time by taking another drink.

"Go for it," Amy said. "By the way, I really like this place." Her smile lit up the darkened room.

Dominique bit her lip, looking off into the distance. "There's really no gentle way to do this, I guess. And I've always been a bit of a bull in a china shop." She took a deep breath and decided to bite the bullet. "I want you to be sure it's me you want," she said with a shrug. She had gone over this a hundred times in her head to make sure it didn't feel like she was setting a trap. She knew it would hurt if Amy agreed but she needed to know, and either way, she would take the answer. With a sigh, she put her drink back on the table and gestured to the crowd. "I know Knell is small, but the world isn't. I love you, and I know that with certainty. I know that it's a genuine connection I have with you, but I also don't want you to feel pressured just because I was the only one available."

Amy's smile fell. Dominique hung her head. "The last thing I wanted was to make that smile go away. I just wanted you to know that you're really not alone. Neither am I. There are so many more people like us, and I don't have to be your only choice. I want to be, but I also want you to know your options."

With an eyebrow raised, Amy eyed the crowd. When she smiled, Dominique's heart caught in her chest. She should have kept her damn mouth shut. "The brunette in the corner *is* pretty cute," Amy said, turning her attention back to Dominique. Amy toyed with the straw of her drink. "But not nearly as cute as you," she added, her smile widening. "I know there are other women out there. I also know that what I feel for you isn't based on the fact that you were the only other lesbian in town. You're not a convenience to me. In fact, you're somewhat of an inconvenience to the quiet little life I used to live." Dominique stiffened until Amy reached over and put her hand on her leg. "And I wouldn't have it any other way. You disrupted my life in a way that changed it for the better." Amy took a deep breath and squeezed Dominique's leg. "You said something earlier, and I want you to know that I feel it too. I love you." She smiled and a single tear slid down her cheek. "I've never actually said that to someone in this way, but it's true. I love you for who you are. No one here can hold a candle to you, to your tenacity, to your kind heart, to your sense of humor, to the fire that lights up your eyes when you're so stubbornly set on making a change. No one here has that, because no one is you. You're who I want."

In an instant, whatever remained of Amy's shyness faded. She leaned forward, wrapped her fingers in Dominique's hair and tilted back her head, kissing Dominique's neck, earlobes and finally her lips. When she pulled back, she smiled. "And I don't care who knows that I'm in love with the most incredible person I've ever met."

Behind them, the band continued playing and dancers continued moving about the floor, but the only thing that mattered was getting lost in Amy's fierce love.

# CHAPTER TWENTY-THREE

Saturdays were typically filled with yard work, running errands for his wife, or relaxing and watching the Longhorns play ball on television. But today, that wouldn't do. George Brandt looked at his reflection in the mirror. He'd never been big on appearances but he wanted to look nice today.

He trimmed his beard and put on a polo shirt and a nicer pair of blue jeans. No need to be super fancy, but it might help to show he put in some effort. After all, he had some making up to do.

"I'll be back after while," he called out to Carol, who was gardening in the corner of the yard.

Perking up, she rose from her spot. "Where are you going?"

"Out to take care of some things." He motioned back to her garden. "I'll be back by the time you're done with that."

She raised an eyebrow and put her hands on her hips. "George Brandt." She paused, letting the effect of her angry tone sink in. "You expect me to just let you waltz out of here on a day you were supposed to help me move those pallets in the back into the garage and make me a shelf?"

"Carol, I'll be back. This is important."

Her eyes bore into his soul, but he shook his head. Throughout their marriage, she won most of these battles. Today was his to win.

"Fine," she said, throwing down her gardening sheers. "You go out and do whatever you think it is that's so important, and I'll be waiting for you when you get home."

He nodded, keeping his mouth shut. She might have been his wife of thirty-six years, but that didn't mean she had to approve of where he went today. And he wasn't about to tell her where he was headed until he tested the waters. He waved and called out, "Love you," before he headed for his truck. He didn't give her a chance to say it back, knowing her stubborn streak would keep her from reciprocating any type of affection, at least until she cooled down.

In the truck, he took a deep breath and rubbed his temples. Carol's anger at current situations had manifested into a huge, ugly, volatile monster of a temper. She was prone to shoot off at anything, for any reason—or no reason—whatsoever.

He pulled out of the driveway, needing time and space to think as much as he needed to make a trip up the road.

*When she's ready to be an adult and admit she has the choice to make on how she wants to live her life, she can come to us, George.* He could hear Carol's clipped words in his memory, her inability to budge on the issue, no matter how hard he had tried to convince her they might need to extend an olive branch to their daughter.

He pulled into the coffee shop and saw Amelia's car, but let his truck idle when he saw four other customers inside.

Business was good at least, he noted, smiling with pride for his daughter's hard work. But he wasn't about to interrupt her day when she had people to take care of. He'd wait. Turning up Reba on the cassette player, he leaned back in his seat and watched her work.

She had her mother's smile, and it lit up every time she greeted someone. He waited while she poured coffee and served pastries to everyone in line. When the last one came up to the counter, the teenaged girl took her coffee, gave Amelia the money, and left.

Fortunately for him, everyone had taken their orders to go. Taking a deep breath, he got out of the truck.

He checked his reflection in the driver's side window and straightened his shirt. Walking to the door, he reminded himself he didn't have to be a superhero. He just needed to be her father.

"Good morning," he heard Amelia's chipper voice call out from the back room where she must have gone to gather things from the kitchen.

"Morning, sweetheart," he called back.

He heard something drop to the ground in the back, a muffled curse, and footsteps. In the silence while he waited, he tried to figure out what to say to make this situation easier, to make up for the fact that more than a month had passed. Still blank when she walked around the corner, he smiled.

"Dad?" The lines in her forehead deepened as she stared at him. "What are you doing here?"

"I came to see you and to tell you I love you."

Her face tightened, and she looked as if she might cry. Instead she closed her eyes and took three deep breaths. "I love you, too," she said quietly. "Can I get you some coffee?"

"I'll take a cup. And grab one for yourself, if you have time to sit and chat for a minute or two."

She looked around the empty store and ticked off items on her fingers. "I should be free for a while," she said after a minute's pause. "I'll grab us both a cup and come meet you over on the couch."

He saw her hands trembling as she grabbed their Styrofoam cups and his heart broke. He never wanted her to feel uncomfortable in his presence. As he took his seat on the couch, he didn't take his eyes off her. She walked with a façade of confidence. She was guarded.

She set down a cup in front of him and clutched hers close to her chest, as if it were a shield. "What did you want to talk about?"

He cleared his throat and moved one of the couch pillows so he could settle in. "I wanted to see how you were and make sure you knew you had me in your corner."

She raised her eyebrow at him and cocked her head, unspoken questions looming between them.

"I know you didn't see that much of my support when you talked to us a while back," he said, setting his cup on the table and leaning closer to her. "I was in shock, and I didn't deal with my response the way I should have. For that, I'm sorry. But I've done a lot of soul searching, and what you said is right. You're still my baby girl. I don't understand this and I may never. But it doesn't change the love I have for you."

Amelia nodded, her lips tightly pressed together.

"Your mom isn't quite in the same boat yet. She loves you, but she's stubborn. So it'll be a while before she reaches out. Regardless, I needed you to know where I stand."

"Where's that?" Her voice was barely a whisper, as she pulled her legs up to her chest and took a slow sip of coffee.

"On your side of life, willing to help you in any way I can and willing to try to understand even when I don't have the answers."

"Thank you." The tear that had been hanging on by a thread finally made its way down her cheek. "Mom isn't going to try to *fix* me, is she?"

"She talked about some therapy options and church counseling, but I told her you're an adult and need to make your own choices."

"This isn't a choice." She shook her head vehemently and closed her eyes. "If it was a choice, I might have picked something a little easier."

"I'm trying to understand that, too," he said removing his hat and putting it in his lap. He shifted his weight forward and reached out to lay a protective hand on her knee. "I have no reason to doubt you, honey. You've never lied to me before. You've never done anything to make me question you, so I trust you. These are waters I've never had to navigate, but I am damn sure going to try."

She reached down and wrapped her hand around his, giving it a squeeze. She let out a deep breath. "That means a lot. It really does."

He looked off and stared at a painting on the wall, beautiful flowers spiraling up an old gate. It would be easier to focus his attention there, but he owed his daughter more. Leveling his gaze with her, he cleared his throat. "I'm sorry."

"Why are you apologizing?" She leaned back against the pillow on her side of the couch.

"I'm sorry you lost someone close to you and none of us knew enough to make sure you were okay during that time." A lump formed in his throat as he thought about his little girl hurting in silence. "And I'm sorry you've had to face a struggle this big, not feeling like you could come talk to me. You're a trooper, Amelia. You always have been. You come out swinging even when the odds are stacked against you, and you've always been a lone wolf. But I want you to know that I admire your strength and I can't imagine having to deal with something like this—especially all alone."

She pulled the pillow from behind her back and clutched it to her chest, trying to steady her breathing as tears streaked down her face. "I'm sorry I couldn't tell you sooner," she said, her voice broken by quiet sobs.

"You don't have to apologize, and I'm going to do the best I can from here on out to make sure you're not alone anymore."

She nodded and let out a sigh, reaching for the box of tissues on the table. Wiping her tears away, she smiled at him. "Thank you," she said again. "This is kind of surprising to me and I don't really know how to take it, but thank you."

"I read your statement in the paper the day after you stopped by," he said, clearing his throat. "It was an eye-opener for me, I think. And I wanted you to know I'm proud of the way you handled yourself."

"Did Mom read it?" Her lip quivered and he wanted to comfort her.

"She did." He kept emotion out of his voice, but her eyes darkened, knowing he was holding back. She motioned for him to continue, stiffening before he delivered the blow. "She crumpled the newspaper into a ball and threw it across the living room."

"Bad enough I ruin her life, even worse I run the family name through the mud, if I was guessing?" she asked.

"Something like that." He shook his head. "She will come around, though. I know she will. She's struggling right now, and I've actually asked her to keep her distance for a while. Nothing said or done now needs to put a strain on your relationship with your mother in the future. She's not reacting well. Hell, I didn't react well at first, and I've never been one to sugarcoat things. This isn't easy for me, and I know it's going to take some time. It's not the way we were raised to view the world. But I'm trying, and I know in her own way, she is, too. But I don't want you to see that right now and think you're alone."

Amelia set down the pillow and reached over to wrap her arms around his neck. "Thank you, Dad." When she pulled back, she was smiling through the tears. "You really are incredible."

"You are too, and we'll face whatever life throws at us together," he said. Taking her hand again, he looked deep into her eyes, thankful she hadn't seen him cry over this, struggle with everything he had always believed, and break down. He was thankful she could see his love and hoped one day she would see it from her mother too.

He took a drink of his coffee and cleared his throat. "Anything else you need to talk about?"

She looked at him curiously, cocking her head to the side.

"Is there anything else? I know you've been through hell and back, and through a ton of heartache on your own, so if you need to talk it out, I'm here."

"I'm getting better," she said. Confidence shone in her eyes. "I had some hard days and nights. It's been a struggle, but I've found productive outlets, and I have made a really close friend who's helped me through a lot of the issues I've had."

"I'm glad you have a good friend to talk to. Anyone I know?"

"She's not from around here, but she's been in town helping out after all of this." She opened her mouth to speak, but bit her lip instead and shook her head. "She's a great person," she added with a curt nod.

"Friend?" George asked, the wheels turning in his mind.

"Something like that," Amelia said with a shrug. Her face reddened and her foot tapped nervously on the floor.

George stroked his beard, trying to make sense of it all. "So there's someone new?" he asked, breaking the silence.

"There is. "Amelia smiled as the words left her lips. "She's pretty special. We love each other. She's there for me, I'm there for her, we laugh together, and she makes me want to be a better person." She wrung her hands together, looking to the side.

"Okay," he said slowly. "This is new territory for both of us, having a conversation like this. But that doesn't mean it's a bad thing. What's her name?"

"Dominique," Amelia's words were less than a whisper.

"Pretty name. Does she treat you right?"

Amelia's smile grew. She nodded. "She really does. In fact sometimes I think she treats me better than I deserve. There's nothing but respect and trust. It's great."

That twinkle in her eye was something he hadn't seen there since she was a kid. He cleared his throat, straightening in his chair. "Okay, so you're happy?"

Amelia pursed her lips and shifted her eyes to the side. She shrugged. "Happy with her? Yes. I'm happy with her. Am I happy in general? I'm not sure how to answer that. It's hard to skip gleefully in a field of wildflowers, when the field is on fire. But I have hope that together we'll be able to go through that fire and come out stronger for it. She makes me happy in so many ways, and I want her by my side as I figure out this mess called life."

He smiled and patted her on the knee. "Well, I think you've got a good grasp on life, sweetheart, like you've always had. The field catches fire from time to time. We just have to make sure we've got the right person beside us to help us enjoy the beauty of the blaze."

"Pretty poetic," Amelia said with a laugh. "It's a weird time in my life. Everything is changing. Chloe is gone. I've stepped out of hiding into a brand new, scary world. I thought I lost you all. But through it all, I've found myself. And I'm not going back into hiding. I'm not fighting who I am or who I fall in love with. I think it's going to be really good, but..." she trailed off, looking at the ceiling.

"What is it?"

"I'm scared," she said, turning her gaze back to him. "I'm really scared, but I'm thankful I don't have to face it alone. I have her, and I have you in my corner. And that will be more than enough to help me stand back up, stronger than I was before."

"I wouldn't have it any other way," he said, bringing her in for a hug. "I'm always going to be here." He stood, tossing his coffee cup into the trash. "I'm going to let you get back to your work day, but you can always call me. In the meantime, I hope you get to see your girl tonight. When you do, tell her I said 'thank you' for being there for you."

"I will," she said, her smile lighting up. "I love you."

"I love you, too," he said, heading for the door. He always had, and he always would.

# CHAPTER TWENTY-FOUR

Pacing back and forth in the bakery kitchen, Amelia wrung her hands around the towel she was holding, darting her eyes back and forth from the small television she kept in the back to the floor. Dominique was there, in that courtroom, surrounded by a huge crowd advocating to preserve their golden boy—advocating for injustice. Amelia's stomach lurched, and she stopped pacing long enough to take a deep breath.

"The jury has reached its verdict," she heard one of the men say. Snapping her head back to the live feed, she bit her lip. Clamping down, she didn't even wince when blood trickled into her mouth. He was still talking, but she couldn't make sense of it. Her head swirled as she recounted the month-long trial. Never before had she watched the live feed, opting instead to get feedback from Dominique and occasionally read a newspaper article. It hurt too much to watch them relive the gritty details. All she had needed to know was that he had been charged with murder and the trial had been gruesome.

The sharp pain in her lip brought her out of her stupor. Releasing her bite, she filled the place with her fingernails, biting as she waited.

"Guilty of murder," he said finally.

She let out a sigh and slid down the back wall, until she was sitting in a heap. Taking a series of steadying breaths, she watched as they panned the camera around the courtroom, showing the shocked faces of the crowd.

If she had the strength, she would have stood and turned it off. But she couldn't. Her legs were wobbly so she shut her eyes. Bringing her hands up to cover her face, she shook her head. It was far from over.

As if putting together a puzzle, she fit the pieces together. The prosecution had asked for life in prison, but she had done enough Google searches to know that, under Texas law, sentencing for murder could range greatly.

Gritting her teeth, she forced herself to think of anything optimistic. Dominique's face popped into her mind, and she smiled. If nothing else, this would soon be over, and she would get to carry on with her life, with Dominique by her side.

Bracing herself on the counter, she pulled her body upright. They might not be able to change this town, but together, they'd do their best to make life beautiful. She looked upward, straightening her shoulders and taking a deep breath before shutting off the television.

"Enough for one day," she muttered, throwing the towel on the counter and shutting off the lights.

As she headed out the door, she knew there was only one place she wanted to be, and that was snuggled in Dominique's arms. Even so, she couldn't shake the feeling that doomsday was approaching. But if it was, she was going to prepare them a decent last supper.

\* \* \*

When the first hints of sunlight streamed through her curtains, Amelia let out a sigh of relief. Even though she had been lulled to comfort by the rhythmic sounds of Dominique's breathing throughout the night, she hadn't been able to fall asleep. Her unruffled pillow and her racing mind seemed to mock her in the early morning light. Even so, it felt good to be surrounded by the love radiating from Dominique's body. Unable to figure out which emotion was winning, she rolled over to face the wall. Stilling her breathing so she wouldn't disturb Dominique, she closed her eyes and tried to focus on something else—anything else. But, as if a neon sign were flashing, all she could think was *today is the day*.

She stood and walked to the kitchen. Coffee was a must. Aside from that, she wasn't sure what she needed. She put the coffee on and paced back and forth in front of it while it brewed. Instinctively, she brought her right hand up to her mouth and chewed off one of her fingernails.

"Are you okay?" Dominique asked from the doorway. Amelia jumped.

"Sorry," Amelia said, turning around. "I didn't hear you there. I guess I was a little lost in thought."

"I figured that might be the case today," Dominique said, walking up with a cautious look. "Is there anything I can do to help?"

When Dominique opened her arms, Amelia sank into the embrace. Leaning on her, she took a deep breath. "I don't know," she answered. "I've thought about it all, and I've been avoiding the trial for the last month. I thought I might want to be there in person to hear the sentencing, but now I don't think I want to be in that courtroom. I don't think I want to see his face or listen to whatever they conjure up to try to make this better. The defense's claims that he was unstable or momentarily insane, that his childhood was tarnished, have all been painful enough to read about in the paper. I know none of that will be brought up today, but I also know that it may factor into decisions. I know you've been there and you've seen it, and just like I asked, you haven't brought it up at home unless I asked for a recap. But I don't think I can do it. I don't want to see his face and hear it if they make this seem like it wasn't horrific. I wasn't there, and it's been months, but I still get chills and have nightmares whenever I think about it." She patted Dominique on the shoulder, a silent "thank you" for being there, and continued pacing around the kitchen while the coffee finished brewing. When it was done, she busied herself pouring two cups, as Dominique took a seat at the breakfast bar.

"I already told you I'm not opening the shop today, right?" Amelia asked, even though she already knew the answer. Dominique nodded and Amelia set down a cup of coffee in front of her. "I was thinking maybe we could go somewhere, maybe to the lake and just spend the day outside. What do you think?"

"Whatever you want, we can do it. I just have to be somewhere with cell service, so I can issue our statements once the sentencing is read."

"Okay." Amelia braced herself on the counter. "Thank you. I'll make sure we're within range, so we can both be updated and you can get your work done." She paused, the weight of her selfishness hitting her like a ton of bricks. "Do you *need* to be in that courtroom? If you do, I will pull myself together and sit through it." She tried to smile, but instead let out a forced, ragged breath.

Dominique's expression faded into a soft, grateful smile, and she rose from her spot, walking over to place her hands on Amelia's shoulder. "I don't have to be there. That was never something that was agreed upon. I just have to be ready to comment and figure out the next steps. Other than that, I don't have anywhere I have to be, other than where I *want* to be. And that's with you. I want to be by your side, and I'll go wherever you go."

Amelia bit her tongue and closed her eyes, silently willing her tears to hold off. But when Dominique pulled her into an embrace, her composure cracked. Muffling the soft sobs against Dominique's shoulder, her body shook as every ounce of pent-up emotion spilled forth.

"It's okay. I'm right here, and I'm not going anywhere."

After several minutes, Amelia took a deep breath. Even with her puffy eyes and her face now a mess, she felt somewhat better.

Dominique was right. Whatever happened, they would figure out a way to make things okay again. She kissed Dominique on the cheek and pulled back from the embrace. Straightening her white T-shirt, she nodded. "Let's get ready then. I'll pack a lunch, and we'll take a hike." She went through the possibilities of things they could do that would occupy her mind and her energy, all while keeping them in range of cell service. She tapped her foot, finding none of the options good enough. She grabbed her coffee cup and downed it as if she were taking a shot. "No," she said, after a moment of deliberation. "That's not good enough. I'm strong enough to do this, and we both should be there. You need to be there, and so do I." She set her cup down and gripped the counter. "We'll be there, in that courtroom, and we will make sure they know the faces and names of people this affects."

Dominique nodded slowly and raised an eyebrow, her unspoken questions looming between them.

"I'm sure," Amelia said, holding her head high. "I want to be able to look future generations in the eye and tell them to fight as hard—if not harder—than I did. Now isn't the time to cower in the corner. Now is the time to take a stand. Through this whole thing, I've been reminded that silence, hiding, and taking the easy route aren't options. I've had you by my side for that journey." She walked over and took Dominique by the hand. "And that's what I'm going to continue to do, whatever the outcome may be."

Dominique's smile grew, and she nodded. "That's my girl," she said quietly, leading the way back to Amelia's bedroom. "Let's get dressed and ready for whatever is to come."

As if her veins had filled with steel, Amelia tightened her grip on Dominique's hand and marched ahead, making no mistake that they were going to enter a war zone.

Dressed in her favorite black slacks and blazer, with a conservative maroon camisole underneath to add a pop of color, Amelia looked in the mirror. Smiling at her reflection, she noted the way her green eyes blazed with intensity. Gone was the carefree, happy-go-lucky look she had worn so often in earlier days. In its place was the face of a battle-ready warrior.

No longer was she content just to sit on the sidelines and watch as her future was decided. She set her jaw, reminding herself this was *her* future, as much as it was anyone's. She took a deep breath, running her fingers through her hair one more time. Turning on a heel, she glanced to the corner of the room, where Dominique had put the finishing touches on her own outfit.

"I'll drive," Amelia said, keeping her voice steadier than she felt.

"You sure?"

Amelia nodded, needing to take control of something, *anything*, at this point. On the drive over, she contemplated making small talk, but opted to let music serve as the only background noise. There was too much to say and none of it helpful.

Once in the courtroom, she looked around wide-eyed. This place was a zoo. Secretaries to lawyers scurried about the room, handing over notes and documents. The media shuffled around the room, circling like vultures. She shook her head, trying to make sense of it all, but her head only seemed to cloud more. Familiar hints of dizziness danced at the corners of her vision, and she blinked, pushing them aside. After what felt like an eternity, Dominique selected seats for them close to the aisle in the back row. Thankful to blend into the crowd, Amelia placed her hands in her lap.

Her palms were sweaty, but when she finally felt the dizziness dissipate, she looked up to see the judge. A mainstay in the community, his presence filled her mind with memories from early childhood. She assessed his grandfatherly look, his long, gray beard and the deepened lines around his face. In her mind, she could hear his drawl, the same one that had livened up parties and had read stories to children at annual Christmas gatherings. Gripping the seat beneath her, she reminded herself that many memories could be tarnished today. She shook her head, vowing to exert only positive vibes. He also stood the chance to echo justice in the room today.

The courtroom came to life with the tap of the gavel. She sat still and stoic, listening to what sounded like a slew of incoherence. One glance to her left caused her to jerk her head away in disgust. The mayor sat in the front row with his head held high. Her stomach churned at his defiance and arrogance. She bit her lip, attempting to jolt herself out of her stupor. Turning her attention on the judge, she watched him with intensity, feeling every bit like a child who couldn't focus during a church sermon.

Sitting up straighter in her seat, Amelia's body stiffened. As the words were read, Amelia's throat constricted. Her heart raced and she grabbed Dominique's hand for support. Beside her, Dominique gripped Amelia's hand harder.

"Having been found guilty of murder," the judge spoke, and Amelia momentarily let out a breath of relief even though he said what she already knew. With her mind reeling, dizziness crept in and she closed her eyes. Taking a deep breath, she jerked her head back and stared into the judge's eyes while he talked. He cleared his throat and she stiffened. "Six years…" Her ears rang, and the words echoed in her mind, shutting down anything else that might come from the judge's lips.

Closing her eyes, she no longer wanted to see the faces of anyone around her. Her heart pounded so loudly, it shook her internally. Dominique's grip loosened, and she felt the tap on her arm. Looking up, her head swam with confusion. Dominique's lips were tight and she nodded, motioning toward the door. She stood, straightened her jacket and took Dominique by the hand. Even though her thoughts were jumbled, she walked out as proudly as she could manage, ignoring the way her stomach lurched.

"I need just a second," Dominique said, once they were outside the building. On the front steps, she pulled out her phone, punched in something, and leveled her gaze at Amelia. "That set society back at least twenty years," she muttered, before taking Amelia's hand again and making a beeline for the car.

"What do you want to do now?" Dominique asked, when they were back at the car. Amelia turned to face her. Dominique's face was somber and drained of color. Her expressionless eyes stared ahead, haunted by questions that she wasn't yet willing to speak. Amelia took a deep breath, unlocking the car and getting in. Wordlessly, Dominique climbed in beside her.

"I want to do a million things. I want to cry. I want to scream. I want to get drunk and yell obscenities. I want to blaze through town with banners fighting back and making them see their error. I also want to hole up in my house in fear. I want to move, but at the same time, I want to stay. I want someone to explain that lenient sentence to me in some other terms than because Trent had a fucked-up childhood or because he acted in a moment of passion. I'm unsure if I ever want to hear anything about the case ever again. I want to punch the mayor and his son in the face. I want someone to feel the weight of this heartache." She paused, allowing herself the chance to breathe. She reached over and placed her hand on top of Dominique's, giving it a reassuring squeeze. "The problem is that I want too many things—too many conflicting things at that. So I think the real question we have to answer is what we *need*."

Dominique turned, looking at Amelia from the corner of her eyes. "And what's that?" she asked, her voice breathy and quiet.

Amelia closed her eyes, remembering every time they'd had this conversation in reverse, with Dominique encouraging her and giving her strength. This was her turn, despite the loss that she too had suffered. She swallowed and gripped the steering wheel with her free hand. "Today, we mourn," she said, reaching up to tilt Dominique's face toward hers. "We grab some wine and head back to the house. We pour a glass or five and cry. We feel the weight of the sorrow for what has happened to one of our own and for the injustices of this small town. We mourn for ourselves, for Chloe, for Knell, for the precedence this sets for increased hatred."

"And after that?" Dominique looked to the floorboard and shook her head. "I'm sorry. I'm not supposed to be so weak. I'm just stunned."

"You're not being weak," Amelia said, kissing her on top of the head. "You're being human, and we all deserve the chance to feel this—you especially, given your months of hard work and dedication." She weaved her fingers around Dominique's. "After today..." She paused and shook her head. "After we've mourned," she corrected. "You can't put a timeline on mourning. After we've mourned, we stand back up, and we fight. We use our voices and we work to make this place—and all places—better. And we don't stop fighting. That's really all I know. This is devastating, but it *cannot* stop us from working toward what's right."

"You're right." A single tear slid down Dominique's face and she exhaled, closing her eyes.

"The best thing I can add is that we'll do it all together." She used the words Dominique had spoken to her time and again in moments of reassurance. They would do this together.

Despite her tears, the corners of Dominique's mouth lifted into a smile. "Yes we will," she said, quietly but with confidence.

"Regardless of what has happened, I have found you, and I love you," Amelia said, running her hands up and down Dominique's arms tenderly. "I will be forever grateful that I met you, despite the hopelessness I feel now and the confusion of what's to come. I am grateful to know we are in this together, and this love is something that cannot be squelched by small minds."

Amelia opened her arms, and Dominique took the cue, settling into the warm embrace. She lifted her head and mouthed, "Thank you." Amelia leaned down and sealed her lips with a kiss. Out of the corner of her eye, she saw people stopping in the parking lot, looking into her car, but she didn't care.

Closing her eyes, she deepened the kiss, determined to live, fight, and love out loud.

Bella Books, Inc.

*Women. Books. Even Better Together.*

P.O. Box 10543
Tallahassee, FL 32302

Phone: 800-729-4992
**www.bellabooks.com**